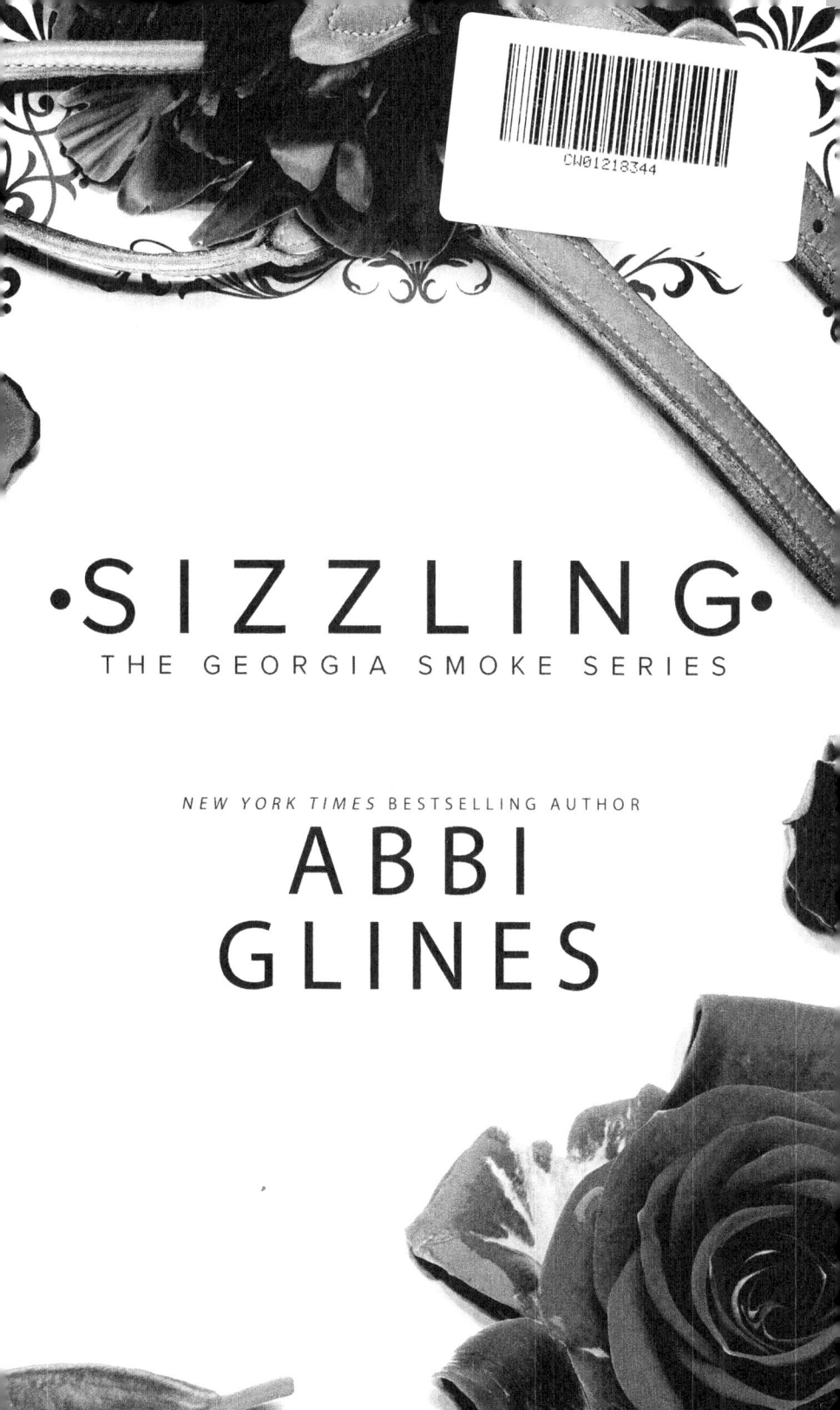

·SIZZLING·
THE GEORGIA SMOKE SERIES

NEW YORK TIMES BESTSELLING AUTHOR
ABBI GLINES

Sizzling
The Georgia Smoke Series
Copyright © 2024 by Abbi Glines
All rights reserved.
Visit my website at https://abbiglinesbooks.com

Cover Designer: Sarah Sentz, Enchanting Romance Designs
Editor: Jovana Shirley, Unforeseen Editing
www.unforeseenediting.com
Formatting: Melissa Stevens, The Illustrated Author
www.theillustratedauthor.com

No part of this book may be reproduced or transmitted in any form or by any means, electronic or mechanical, including photocopying, recording, or by any information storage and retrieval system without the written permission of the author, except for the use of brief quotations in a book review.

This book is a work of fiction. Names, characters, places, and incidents either are products of the author's imagination or are used fictitiously. Any resemblance to actual persons, living or dead, events, or locales is entirely coincidental.

• THE FAMILY •

started by Jediah Hughes. It began with horse racing, moonshine, and illegal arms in the early 1900s

Jediah Hughes

Eustis

Elmer
(died from Typhoid at ten years old)

Feldman

Tipper

Garrett

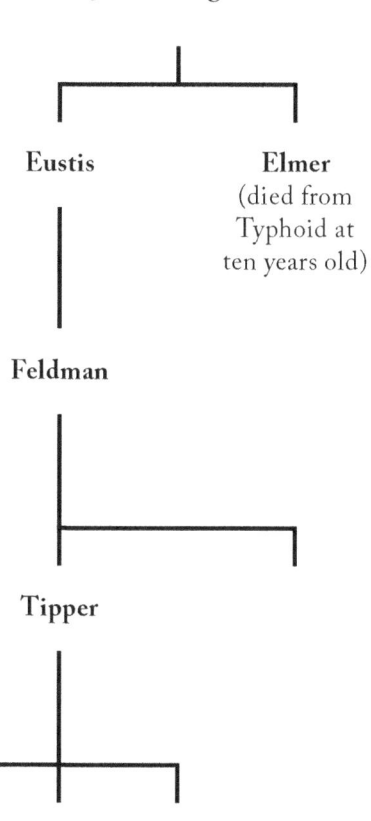

Gregory
(died at three years old in a house fire)

· THE HUGHES ·
Hughes Farm

Garrett Hughes (BOSS in books 1-9)
Wife: **Fawn Parker Hughes** → *SCORCH*

Blaise Hughes (Current BOSS/oldest son)
Wife: **Madeline Walsh Hughes** (parents Etta Marks/dead and Liam Walsh/President of Judgment MC)

Cree Elias Hughes → *SMOKESHOW* and *FIREBALL*

Trev Hughes
Fiancée: **Gypsi Parker** (also stepsister) → *FIRECRACKER*

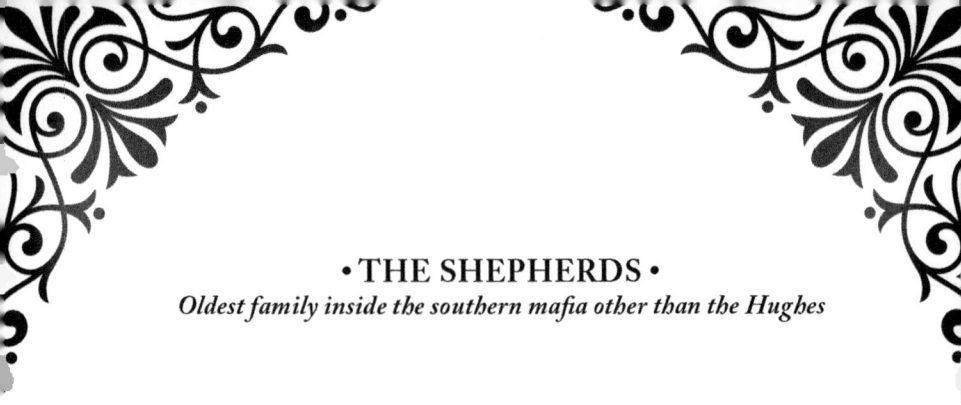

· THE SHEPHERDS ·
Oldest family inside the southern mafia other than the Hughes

Charles Livingston Shepherd
Best friend of Jediah Hughes

- **Gerald**
- **Joseph**
  (became a priest)
- **Jeffrey**
  (died from Spanish influenza at fifteen years old)

Children of Gerald:
- **Charles II**
- **Darwin** (died from gunshot at twenty-four)

Children of Charles II:
- **Charles III** (drowned in childhood)
- **Joshua** (became a missionary)
- **Lincoln**

Children of Lincoln:
- **Lincoln II (Linc)**
- **Stellan**

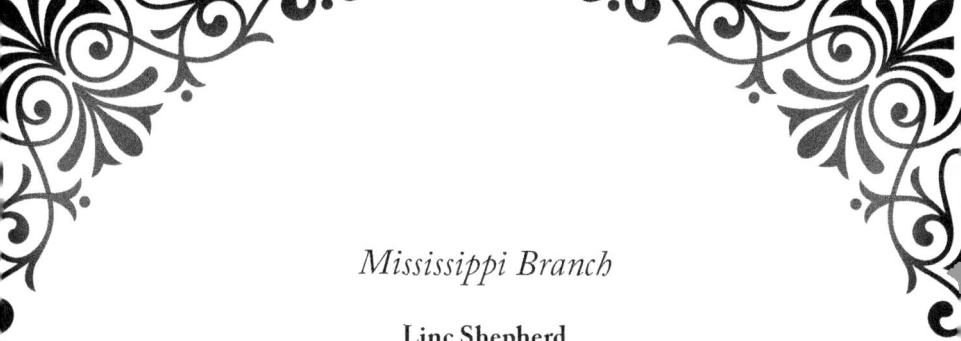

Mississippi Branch

Linc Shepherd
(left Florida to run Mississippi Branch when **Levi** was twenty-two)

Florida Branch

Levi Shepherd
Wife: **Aspen Chance Shepherd** → *WHISKEY SMOKE*

Georgia Branch
Shepherd Ranch

Stellan Shepherd
Wife: **Mandilyn Shepherd**

Thatcher
→ *DEMONS July 2024* and
THATCHER'S DEMONS
August 2024

Sebastian
2 books coming
Fall 2024

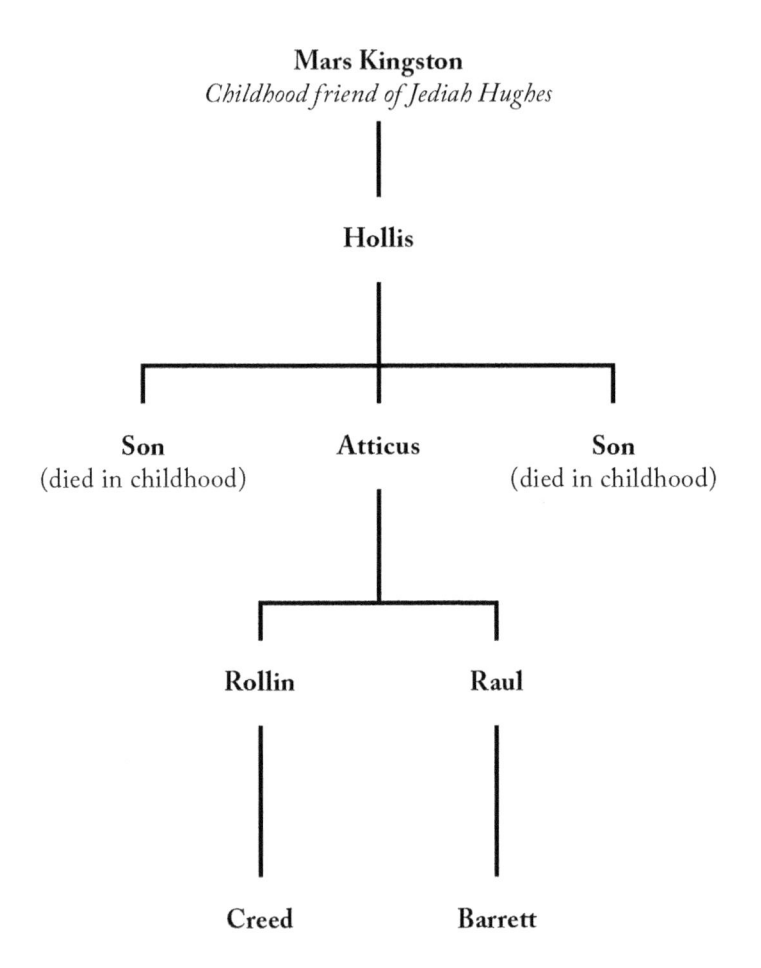

• THE KINGSTONS •
Mars Kingston joined the family in 1921

Mars Kingston
Childhood friend of Jediah Hughes

Hollis

- **Son** (died in childhood)
- **Atticus**
- **Son** (died in childhood)

Rollin — **Raul**

Creed — **Barrett**

Florida Branch

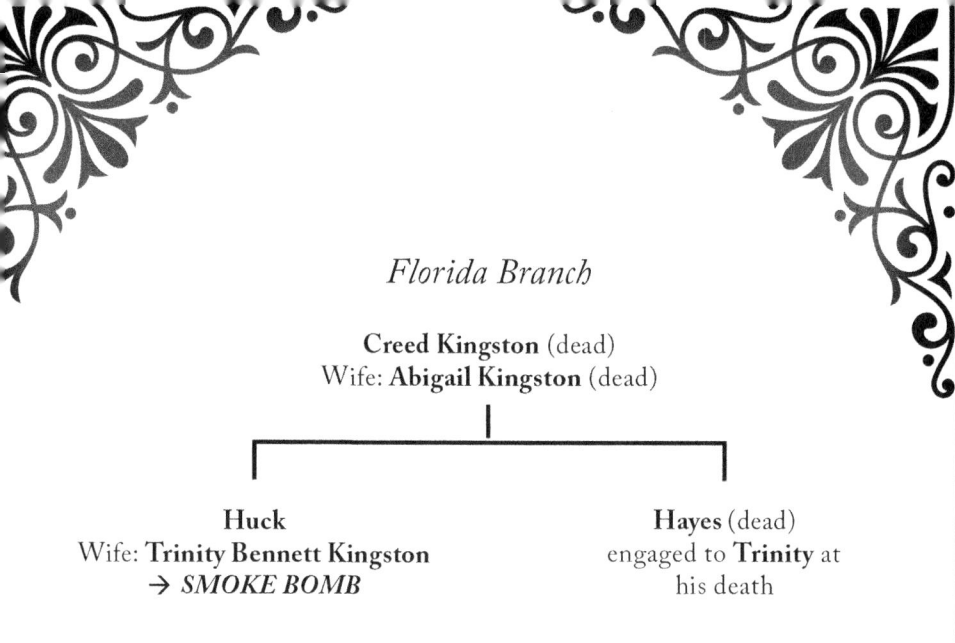

Creed Kingston (dead)
Wife: **Abigail Kingston** (dead)

Huck
Wife: **Trinity Bennett Kingston**
→ *SMOKE BOMB*

Hayes (dead)
engaged to **Trinity** at his death

Georgia Branch

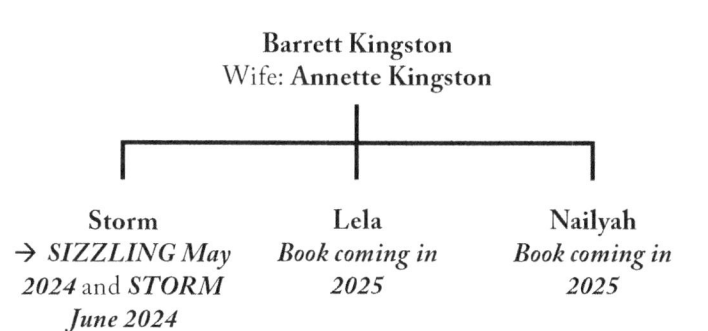

Barrett Kingston
Wife: **Annette Kingston**

Storm
→ *SIZZLING May 2024* and *STORM June 2024*

Lela
Book coming in 2025

Nailyah
Book coming in 2025

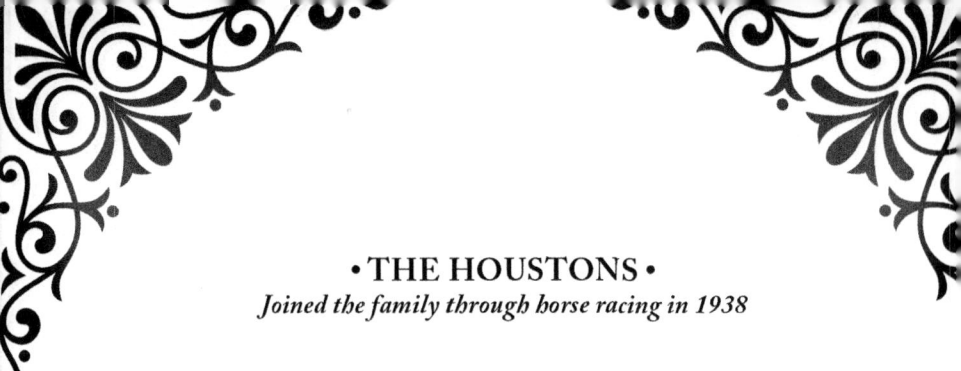

• THE HOUSTONS •
Joined the family through horse racing in 1938

Kenneth Houston Wife: **Melanie Houston**
Moses Mile Ranch

Saxon Houston
Wife: **Haisley Slate Houston** →
SMOKIN' HOT

Winter Noel Houston

• THE LEVINES •
Joined the family in 1977

Alister Levine

Mississippi Branch

Luther Levine
Ex-Wife: **Chloe Wall**
(Moved from Florida when **Kye** was nineteen)

Florida Branch

Kye Levine
Wife: **Genesis Stoll Levine** → *BURN*

Jagger Henley Levine

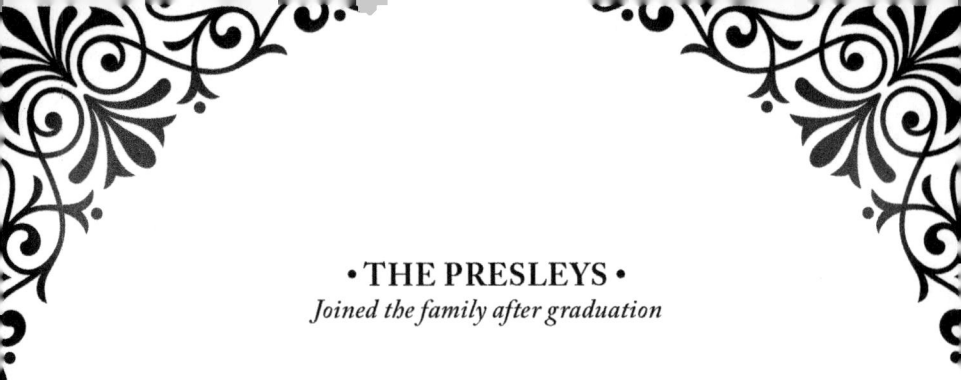

• THE PRESLEYS •
Joined the family after graduation

Gage Presley
Best friend of Blaise Hughes in high school
Wife: **Shiloh Carmichael Presley** → *STRAIGHT FIRE*

· THE SALAZARS ·
Joined the family through horse racing in 1958

Georgia Branch only

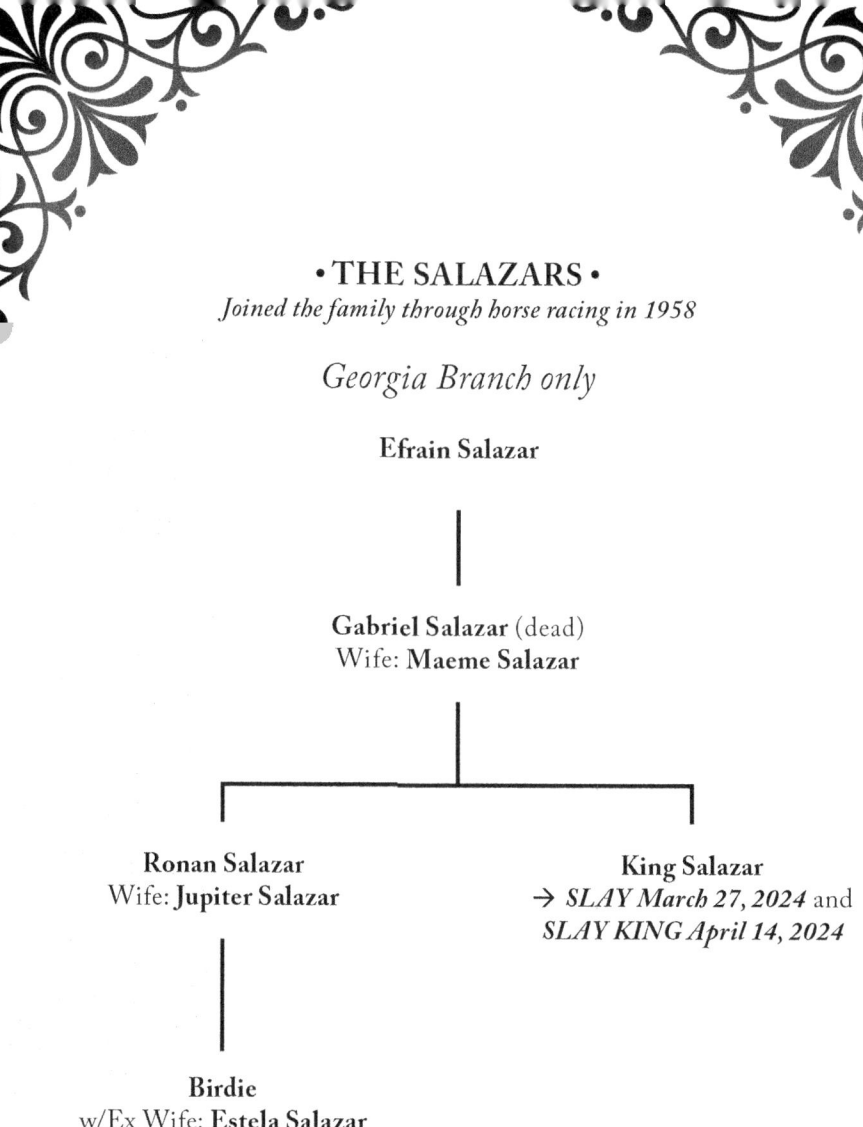

Efrain Salazar

Gabriel Salazar (dead)
Wife: **Maeme Salazar**

Ronan Salazar
Wife: **Jupiter Salazar**

King Salazar
→ *SLAY March 27, 2024* and
SLAY KING April 14, 2024

Birdie
w/Ex Wife: **Estela Salazar**

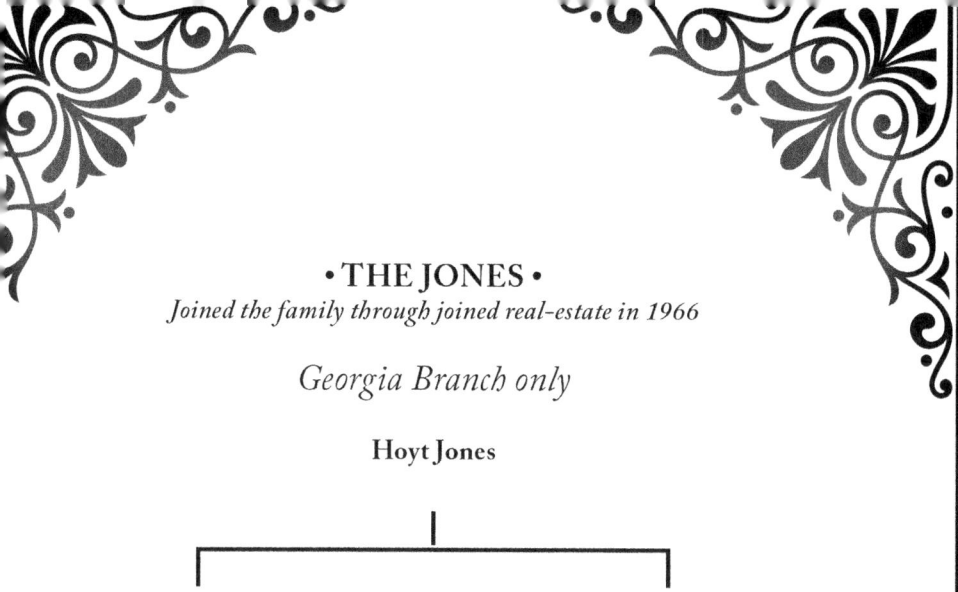

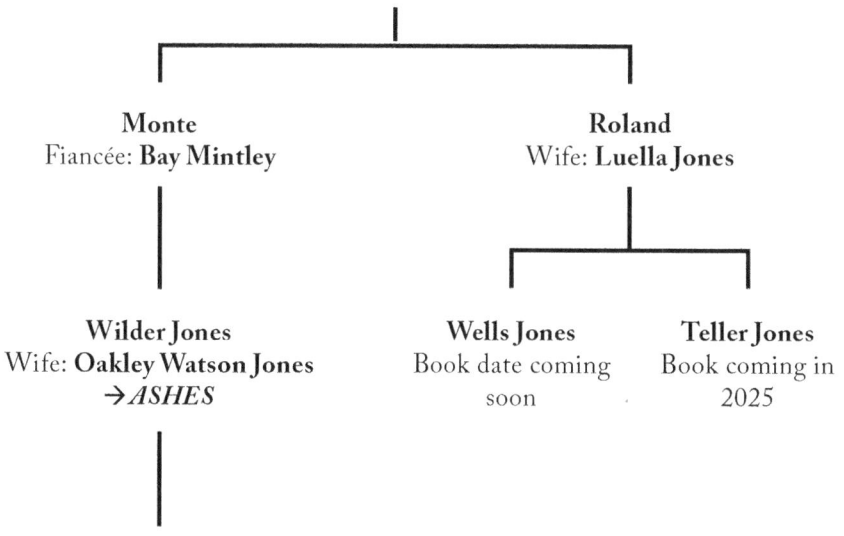

· THE JONES ·
Joined the family through joined real-estate in 1966

Georgia Branch only

Hoyt Jones

- **Monte**
  Fiancée: **Bay Mintley**

  - **Wilder Jones**
    Wife: **Oakley Watson Jones**
    →*ASHES*

    - **Sarah Jones**

- **Roland**
  Wife: **Luella Jones**

  - **Wells Jones**
    Book date coming soon

  - **Teller Jones**
    Book coming in 2025

• PLAYLIST •

Keep Up
RaeLynn

Gold Digger
Kanye West

Put the Gun Down
ZZ Ward

Honky Tonk Women
The Rolling Stones

Come Through
Regrettes

Gangsters
LOLO, featuring Giggs

Playing with Fire
Thomas Rhett

Toxic
Britney Spears

I hate it
again&again

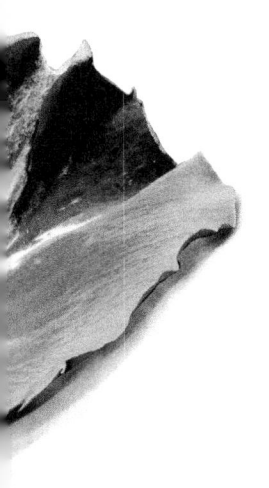

Peaches
Justin Bieber, featuring Daniel Caesar and Giveon

Bad Things
Machine Gun Kelly and Camila Cabello

Anti-Hero
Taylor Swift

Vulnerable
Selena Gomez

Wrecking Ball
Two Worlds, Nick Voelker, and Adiel Mitchell

• ACKNOWLEDGMENTS •

When I prepared to write Storm's story, I already knew exactly who Briar would be. I had her personality in my head talking to me. But Storm was one I had to think about awhile. Decide just where he stood in the morally gray area. Come to find out he's *really* close to the dark side. Darker than I even expected. I can't wait for you to read STORM. It gets darker and even more twisted, but it is all in the name of love...

To the people I couldn't do this without-
Britt is always the first I mention because without him, I wouldn't get any sleep, and I doubt I could finish a book.
Emerson, for dealing with the fact that I must write some days and she can't have my full attention. I'll admit, there were several times she did not understand, and I might have told my seven-year-old "You're not making it in my acknowledgments this time!" to which she did not care. Although she does believe she is famous after attending some signings with me. But that is not my fault. I blame the readers ;)
My older children, who live in other states, were great about me not being able to answer their calls most of the time and waiting until I could get back to them. They still love me and understand this part of Mom's world. I will admit, I answer Austin's calls more now because he happens to have my first grandbaby on FaceTime when he calls.
My editor, Jovana Shirley at Unforeseen Editing, for always working with my crazy schedules and making my stories the best

they can be. This summer she has gone above and beyond with this crazy schedule of mine and this fall it doesn't slow down. She's a rock star.

My formatter, Melissa Stevens at The Illustrated Author. She makes my books beautiful inside. Her work is hands down the best formatting I've ever had in my books. I am always excited to see what she does with each one. Each book seems to be better than the last! It's amazing.

Autumn Gantz, at Wordsmith Publicity, for saving me from losing my mind and taking over all the things that I can't keep up with anymore. Her help allows me to write more. Send her cookies.

Beta readers, who come through every time: Jerilyn Martinez, and Vicci Kaighan. I love y'all!

Sarah Sentz, Enchanting Romance Designs, for my book cover. I am in love with the way it looks.

Abbi's Army, for being my support and cheering me on. I love y'all!

My readers, for allowing me to write books. Without you, this wouldn't be possible.

*To every girl who found that they had a thing for toxic men
when they chose Spike over Angel.
You are my people.*

• ONE •

"You boys must be lost."

STORM

Well, damn. This little mission that we'd come on was turning out to be more interesting than I'd expected. When King had asked us to come with him to seek revenge on a man who had hurt his fiancée when she was a child, I hadn't expected we'd end up here. Glancing over at Thatcher, I knew he hadn't either. He was as intrigued as I was, and getting a reaction from him was hard to do. We'd hunted down and killed many hits in our life, but this was definitely a twist.

"Who's the singer?" King asked the bartender, although he already knew the answer to the question.

She was why we were here. The only lead we'd been given when the man King wanted to torture wasn't where he was supposed to be.

"Briar," the man replied, smirking before setting a glass of whiskey in front of King. "And she's taken."

We'd already known she was using the alias Briar Landry, but she'd been born Melissa Ball. That much we had traced down easily enough.

She had gone off the radar from the age of fifteen until she turned twenty, where she reemerged as Briar Landry. She moved around a lot the first three years and had over fifteen different jobs, and from what King had dug up on her, she dated some high-profile men—or rather had affairs with them. Large sums of money were deposited into an account with her name just before she moved out of town. That account had since been drained and closed.

Watching her, I could see how she'd managed to reel in the men she had. A couple of politicians, a minister at mega church, and a CEO. They were always married men with a lot to lose if they were caught cheating. I imagined her tied up, naked, on my bed. Wasn't like I could go there. Not when King was hell-bent on finding her father and killing him slowly.

Long, dark ginger hair hung in loose curls at the ends, and her blue eyes twinkled with mischief as she held my gaze. The smooth drawl in her voice as she sang while her fingers expertly played the guitar in her hands made a lethal combination. She had every man in here ready to worship at her feet, and she knew it. She expected it. Bastards had no idea they didn't have a chance.

When the third song we'd listened to came to an end, King drank down his glass in one gulp and set it on the bar. "Let's go," he said, standing up.

I already knew we weren't actually leaving. We were going to find the back entrance and meet Briar Landry backstage. If King tried to talk to her in here, she'd have a roomful of men ready to protect her, and we'd end up causing more damage than was necessary.

"Keep it quiet and tidy," was all Blaise Hughes, our boss, had told King when he asked if we could do this.

I'd known King all my life, and if this had been pre Rumor, his fiancée, I would have been able to guess how he was going to get the information out of Briar. But seeing as he was now a fucking psycho whenever Rumor was concerned, I wasn't so sure what to expect. Thatcher didn't seem too worried about it as we followed King to the exit. But then I wasn't sure Thatcher's brain worked like the rest of ours. He was emotionally detached from things. I wasn't going to be able to let King hurt the woman. Not just because she was a fucking stunner, but also because she was a female. This wasn't her fault. She hadn't hurt Rumor.

Sure, I'd pulled a gun on her stepmother earlier, but the crazy bitch had grabbed a knife and thrown it at King. He easily dodged it, but still, that had been unnecessary. Thatcher had taken her knife with ease and held it at her throat, forcing the whereabouts of her husband from her while trickles of blood from where he'd pierced the skin ran down her chest.

When the door to the bar closed behind us, King turned right, which was like I'd expected. We weren't headed to the SUV. We were going to find another entrance.

"I volunteer to fuck the info out of her," Thatcher said as we walked around the building.

"Shut up," King snarled, not looking back at him.

"It's better than you putting a bullet in her," he replied.

I wasn't so sure about that. Thatcher had some twisted shit in his head when it came to sex. But then I didn't want to see King hurt her either. This was about her father. Not her. As for her profession as a gold digger, that wasn't our business. If men allowed their dicks to control them, then that was their issue. Not ours. I felt the need to remind King of that.

"You're gonna let her talk first," I said, "before you threaten her."

Thatcher glanced back at me, looking amused. "You offering to fuck her too?"

"I'll do what I need to in order to get the info," King replied as we reached a single metal door at the back of the bar.

Two cars were parked back here, and there was one surveillance camera, but it wasn't working. I could tell just by looking at it. The *twenty-four-hour surveillance* warning that was posted beside the door was a joke.

King tried the knob, and it was locked, so he stepped back so that Thatcher could work his magic. He pulled out a tiny screwdriver from his back pocket. I'd seen him use it countless times over the years. It took him less than five seconds, and the door was open wide. King stepped in front of him and stalked inside with a determined look on his face.

Hopefully, the woman gave him the location of her father. I didn't want her to end up like the stepmother. Sure, we had left Netta Ball alive, but she'd been tied up in the small, filthy apartment we'd found her in with a sock shoved in her mouth. King had told her if she was lying, he'd be back to finish the job. Although I knew when someone was lying, and the woman had told us the truth. Which was why we were here.

King opened doors as we passed them until he finally entered one. When I stepped inside the room, I didn't see anyone else, but it was clearly a dressing room for a female. The light scent of perfume that lingered in the air, the full-length mirror and vanity table that sat beside it, and the pair of heels placed neatly on the floor beside a brown leather duffel bag made that obvious. However, it was the guitar case that stood in the corner that was the clue King was looking for.

"Search her things," he said, going over to the duffel bag and picking it up.

Thatcher went to the vanity, and I headed for the guitar case. These were the obvious places to look first. I doubted we were going to find information on her father here, but best to be sure. She'd be back here soon enough.

"You boys must be lost."

The feminine Southern drawl stopped me from picking up the case, and I turned to see Briar stepping inside the room. There was a flirty smile on her full lips, which either meant she wasn't very smart to walk into a room where three men were going through her things or she relied too much on her looks in life and thought they were gonna save her. In this case, they just might. Because up close, she was even better, and I hadn't thought that was possible.

King dropped her duffel and glared at her, which was unnecessary. "You can take us to Roger Ball."

I watched her as she continued to smile as if she were charming a roomful of her fans. "Excuse me?"

Don't do that, darling. This will go bad real damn fast.

King took a step toward her, and I had to force myself not to move. Not yet. I was here for King. Not some female I didn't know who used her pussy as a weapon.

"Not gonna play games," King warned her.

She let out a soft laugh. "Well, I didn't accuse you of such, now did I?"

Dammit, she was going to piss him off. I glanced at Thatcher to see if he was going to step in, but he just looked like he was enjoying the show.

"We just need to know where to find him," I told her. "We know he's your father, and Netta said he was last seen with you."

She blinked, and for a moment, a small glimpse of panic flashed so quickly in her eyes that I would have missed it if I hadn't been so damn focused on her. King would have seen it too. She was going to have to talk—and fast. When she took a step back, I thought she was about to run, but instead, she closed the door behind her. Was she stupid? At least if someone heard her or walked by, it would keep King from making things messy. Dammit, she wasn't helping me at all here.

"I do pity you that you were forced to breathe Netta's air," she said sweetly as she bent down. "She's a nasty bitch."

Perhaps if I hadn't gotten distracted with the view of her ass in the jeans she was wearing, I'd have seen the warning sign or question why she was bending down. But even then, I had to give it to her. She was fast, and the pistol she pulled from her right boot was pointed in King's direction before she was even standing straight up again.

Gone was the flirtatious smile. The hard line on her lips now reassured me this wasn't her first time pulling a gun on someone.

"Fuck me," Thatcher said with a touch of awe in his tone.

King's gun was out of his holster and pointed at her as he took another step in her direction. "Put the gun away," he told her.

"Thank you for the suggestion, but if you don't mind, I think I'll keep it out," she replied, her tone dripping with sarcasm.

"Disarming you would take seconds. Don't test me. Just take me to the fucker, and you can leave. Free. You aren't who I want," King said.

She smirked. "You made that clear, but seeing as how y'all aren't known for your goodwill and all, I think I'll take my chances."

Wait ... what?

"You know who we are?" I asked her, not sure I understood that right.

A real smile briefly tugged at the corners of her lips as she kept her eyes on King. "I've not made it this long, living on my own, without knowing who to stay clear of."

Thatcher chuckled. "You're just full of surprises."

"Then, you know this isn't a casual threat," King sneered, clearly not amused by this.

She held her shoulders straight as she looked him in the eyes, not backing down an inch. "I'm well aware. But I can't give you want you're asking of me."

King took another step in her direction, his finger too damn close to the fucking trigger. "I can make you disappear. No one will find a trace."

She let out a heavy breath, finally showing some concern for her life. "Roger is dead. Unless you want me to take you out on a boat in the gulf to the general vicinity his body was dumped in. Seeing as it's been three weeks now, I'd gamble the sharks have eaten his body, so it would be a pointless activity."

Damn.

"Is that so?" King asked, clearly not believing her.

"She's not lying," I told him. I could see the truth in her expression.

She barely flickered a glance in my direction before going back to King and the gun he had pointed at her.

"How do we know she's not telling us what was told to her?" he shot back at me. "I want to know who told you that and where I can find them," he demanded.

Her eyebrows arched as she lifted them. "No one told me," she replied.

"Listen, I'm done with your bullshit. You're wasting my time," he growled, taking another step toward her.

"Well, I'm done with you being in my room, demanding things from me," she snapped at him, then took a step back.

"Listen, as entertaining as all this is, you're real close to setting him off," Thatcher told her.

She swallowed and let out a sigh as she lowered her gun to her side. "I know because I killed him and dropped his body in the gulf. I don't know what he did or why you want him, but you're late."

Truth.

"Storm?" King asked, not lowering his gun.

"She's telling the truth." Or she was the best goddamn liar in the world.

"I just got hard," Thatcher muttered.

"What? The hot one is a human lie detector?" she asked, her eyes shifting to me.

"Close enough," I replied, unable to keep from smiling at the fact that she'd called me the hot one.

The interest in her eyes made it hard not to act on. It was always King's face that drew the females in. When he was in the room, they always noticed him first.

"Why would you kill your own father?" King asked, still not convinced.

Her eyes swung back to him. "Is that a demand or just a nosy question?"

"Does it matter? There are three of us, armed. If you shoot, one of us will return the favor."

She narrowed her eyes at him. "Because he molested me from the time I was nine years old until I escaped that hellhole. Is that enough for you? Or are you going to demand details?"

King lowered his gun and slid it back into its holster. A sick knot twisted in my gut. I'd had a feeling that Roger Ball had done

• 7 •

the same to Rumor, although King never said more than he'd hurt her.

"I have a question for you," she said pointedly. "What did you want with him?"

King didn't say anything at first. I watched his jaw clench as he stared at her.

"He did the same to the woman who owns me." He never said love. Claimed it wasn't strong enough of a description.

Briar swallowed hard. "A former foster kid, I assume."

King nodded.

A pained expression crossed her face. "Maybe you do have a reason to shoot me after all. That would be my fault. After I left, he hooked up with a woman because she was a foster parent. He needed another little girl to take my place. He must have moved on to Netta after that. But I made sure that cycle ended. And I'm sorry I didn't kill him sooner."

King's hands fisted at his sides, and I knew he didn't blame her, but hearing about what Rumor had been through was hard on him.

"It's no one's fault," I said, wanting her to stop talking about it. For all our sakes.

She looked back at me then. "I poisoned him and watched him suffer as he foamed at the mouth and convulsed. He didn't go quickly. He didn't deserve an easy death. And if I'd known the Mafia wanted to kill him, I'd have gladly handed him over." Then, she reached for the doorknob. "If that is all I can do for you, then I need to get back onstage. My break is up."

King nodded. "But if we find out you lied, we'll find you."

"No one wanted that bastard dead more than me," she replied, then opened the door and walked out.

• TWO •

I had to be at the beck and call of a man.

BRIAR
Seven Months Later

Sliding the slab of hardwood back over the floor under my bed, I reached for the area rug and pulled it back into place. Fifteen thousand five hundred forty dollars in cash wasn't bad, but it also wasn't enough. The pay and tips at Highwater, the bar I was currently working at, were good. The best I'd ever done at a bar, but Jameson Chester's payoff not to tell his fiancée about our fling would be worth it, and he hated me working there. Funny how that always happened. The jealous, controlling ones were always the cheaters. I was going to have to quit Highwater. This wouldn't be the first time I had to give up doing the one thing I loved because of a man.

That wasn't what was important though. I had my priorities. Cash flow wasn't an option. It was mandatory.

Standing up, I walked over to the floor-length mirror and stared at my reflection. This was all I truly had in power. How I looked. That and my ability to lie.

Shaking my head, disgusted with myself, but unable to change the way my life had played out, I turned to look out the window of the apartment I'd moved us into six months ago. Always on the go. Never getting to stay long and set up roots.

Getting attached to any one place was a luxury we couldn't allow. Netta wouldn't spend her money on looking for Roger. She'd assume he skipped town on her. But it was Dovie, her daughter, I worried about. If Netta ever put it together, which would be a stretch since the woman was an idiot, then she could take Dovie away from me. I wasn't even her real sister, and Dovie was only fifteen. She'd have to find us first and then get past me, but she wouldn't make it out alive. She'd already proven she couldn't be trusted to protect her own child.

Roger had moved from one foster mother to the next until he met Netta. A waitress at a bar who had a ten-year-old daughter. When I went to find him and make him pay for what he'd done to me, I found Dovie instead. Alone, dirty, terrified in a run-down trailer. I didn't get my revenge like I'd planned. But I took Dovie. That had been four years ago.

They hadn't even searched for her. No missing person report. Nothing. It was the only way I had kept her with me under the radar. She couldn't attend school and stay hidden. I was doing the best I could to teach her. The day she turned eighteen, I would have the money to get her the help she needed. Until then, it was on me to help her with what little education I had. Thankfully she read. I figured there was a lot to be learned from books. It didn't matter the genre.

Which was why Jameson was picking me up in three hours and taking me to some private party for the evening. It was the last thing I wanted to do, but we needed the money. I'd said I was done with this kind of thing two years ago, but unfortunately, money was growing short again after our last move, and I refused to touch the savings I kept put back for Dovie's future. Using men was the fastest way to get money.

So far, Jameson had given me a pair of diamond earrings and a bracelet that was appraised for over twenty-five thousand dollars. A Louis Vuitton purse would sell for over five thousand, but letting it go was going to be painful. The dresses and shoes that he had bought for me would make a pretty penny too. But I had to wait to sell them off until this thing with him was over.

My phone buzzed in my pocket, snapping me out of my thoughts. Slipping my hand inside, I pulled it out to see Jameson's name on the screen. He was already texting me his orders. His issue with controlling me wasn't new. I'd dealt with it before. Wealthy men craved power, and all seemed to require my submission. It wasn't always easy to do with my personality, but for the money I'd get in the end, I could deal with it.

Wear the silver Gigi gown with the tall Jimmy Choos I sent you last week. Style your hair up, and I'll have your jewelry when I pick you up.

Gritting my teeth, I glared at the phone. I had planned on wearing exactly that. But having him tell me was annoying.

Anything for you, Papi.

I added a kissy face emoji, then hit Send, and rolled my eyes before walking back up the stairs. Being a gold digger was exhausting. In truth, the whole thing disgusted me, but I would do whatever I had to in order to make sure Dovie was taken care of. I couldn't look any deeper into what I was doing. When I did, I got into a dark place that was hard to get out of mentally.

I headed across the hall into Dovie's room to find her lying on her bed with a book in her hands. She lifted her gaze to mine and smiled. I had bought a book on sign language and downloaded an app that helped teach you sign language shortly after I brought her home with me. We had learned it together so she had a way of communicating instead of writing things down all the time. She could hear just fine but she couldn't speak, at least not anymore.

"How does pizza sound for dinner?" I asked her, sitting down on the edge of the bed.

She took her dominant hand and made two circular motions over her stomach.

"Yummy, huh?" I replied with a grin. "Okay then, I'll order pizza and make sure it gets here before I leave. Hopefully, I won't be out too late, but you know how he is. Make sure the alarm is set and the door is bolted."

She pointed at her chest, then the side of her forehead.

"I'm aware you know, but I am just reminding you," I said, leaning over and looking at the book open in her lap. "Fantasy? That's new. I thought you were into romance."

She shrugged, then signed, "Curious about the hype."

I laughed and stood back up. "Let me know if it's good. I'll try it next."

She raised her eyebrows, then signed, "Since when do you read?"

"All right, smart-ass. I read sometimes."

She rolled her eyes and shook her head.

I reached for the throw pillow in her round powder-blue lounge chair and threw it at her. "Don't judge me, missy."

Grinning, she grabbed the pillow and hurled it back at me. I liked seeing her this way. It had taken her almost a year before she actually smiled. Now, I got to see her smile all the time. Sure, there were shadows in her eyes sometimes. They would always be there, lurking, just like the horrors she'd endured, but she would overcome it. I would do everything I could to make sure of it.

"Okay, go back to your reading. I've got to go make myself pretty."

"That's not hard to do. You wake up pretty," she signed.

"Aww. Are you trying to bribe me for more book money? Because it's working," I replied, then winked at her before leaving the room.

The apartment complex was safe. I'd made sure to get one in the nice part of town with security and an alarm system. Having to leave Dovie alone in a big city wasn't my favorite, but she was smart, and I paid a lot in rent to make sure no one could get to her.

    I missed our movie nights. We'd gotten into a pattern of doing them every Friday night until I had to pack up and move us to Atlanta. The rent was outrageous, but the city was big and easy to blend into. We stood out less here. Small towns made me nervous. People were too nosy. The drawback to this life was the cost of living. Which was why there were no movie nights for us right now. I had to be at the beck and call of a man. One I really couldn't stand.

THREE

"Just keep talking, kitty."

STORM

"Why the fuck are we here again?" Thatcher asked in a bored tone.

"Because Jameson Chester owes us money," I replied, although he knew the answer already.

He grunted as he slid his sunglasses on and walked over toward the bar. I didn't want to be here either, but we had to send our warning to the dipshit who owed us over half a million dollars. He'd made the mistake of ignoring Stellan's call. So, we were here to collect. Surrounded by rich, uppity assholes that we were expected to mingle with for the sake of appearances. King was getting out of all kinds of shit with a new baby at home. Since he was the first one to have a kid, I wasn't sure how long that would last and when he was going to have to get fully invested in family stuff again.

Stellan turned to look at me, and the slight nod of his head meant I had to start talking to folks and stop standing off alone, looking like I was here to kill someone. Which wasn't the plan. We were going to hurt him first.

Jameson Chester was an asshole. He'd been born into this life and not done a damn thing to deserve the successful business he was given. His father had been the one to build the whiskey empire that he was now running into the ground with his inability to handle funds. Taking him out of this world wouldn't be something to mourn. But that wasn't my call.

I saw Joel Highland, the state's chief justice, headed my way. It was too late to join Thatcher at the bar. I had to pretend to care what he had to say. The man was powerful, but he too was indebted to us. He'd had to ask for more than one favor over the years. In return, he was ours to control. Even if he liked to pretend otherwise.

"Storm Kingston," he said with a smile breaking across his round face. "How's your father? I didn't see him with Stellan."

"He's good. It's his and Mom's anniversary. They're off celebrating," I explained.

He chuckled. "Well, now, you gotta keep the wife happy. I hear Stellan has a horse in the Derby this year that's already being predicted to win. That's normally Garrett's good fortune. He's not racing one this year though, it seems."

I shook my head. "Not this year. Blaise is sitting this year out for the main race. Next year though, he's already preparing for."

He nodded. "Ah, yes. Blaise is now handling the horses too, I see."

I wasn't answering that. Not his business. What the boss did or did not handle within the family was something only we knew. Blaise Hughes had taken over his father, Garrett's, position as boss more than a year ago now. Stellan, along with my dad and the other older members, hadn't been sure about that move at first. Blaise was known for his brutality. However, he'd managed to gain more influence and power in a short time, proving everyone wrong and justifying Garrett's decision.

Joel shifted his gaze to the left and smirked. "He's got balls, that one," he muttered, then shook his head. "Sol Mercer will demand her daddy get his head on a plate if she finds out he's already cheating. But then you have to commend him on taste. His new one looks like a supermodel. Even makes Sol seem plain."

Sol Mercer was the youngest daughter of Dorian Mercer, owner and CEO of the Mercer restaurant chains. I had met her once, and hopefully, I never had to suffer the experience again. I turned my head to see what female Jameson Chester had arrived with while I straightened, preparing to alert Thatcher that he was finally here. I froze when my eyes locked on the woman Jameson had on his arm.

Fucking hell. This had to be a joke. I'd thought she was stunning in a pair of jeans, cowboy boots, and a halter top. I blinked, slightly stunned. Jesus, that woman was lethal.

"Beauty, isn't she? How did Chester manage that?" Joel asked.

I was pissed at my own reaction to her. I knew what she was, and I hated it. She was as shallow and manipulative as she was gorgeous. Sure, I respected the fact that she'd overcome a shit past, but there were other ways to do it. She'd chosen one that I couldn't overlook. Well, this time around, she'd latched on to the wrong guy. He didn't have the money to pay her off. He was in so much debt; he was barely keeping his head above water. I hadn't known he was engaged to Sol, but it made sense. He needed the money, and she had access to millions.

I saw Jameson tense the moment he spotted Stellan. His eyes swung right, and when he saw Thatcher leaning against the bar, watching him, I could see the sweat beads pop out on his forehead. I waited as his eyes scanned the room until he found me. I simply nodded my head once.

Yeah, fucker. You asked for it. Now, here we are.

I refused to allow myself to look at Briar again. She wasn't my concern. I was here to deal with her date. She probably needed to get an Uber home; Jameson wouldn't be in any shape to drive. Thatcher moved first, and Jameson smiled brightly as he headed in the opposite direction.

I turned my attention back to Joel. "If you'll excuse me, we have some business to handle."

Joel paled slightly, as if suddenly understanding, and stepped back, giving me a wide berth. "Of course. Be sure to tell your father he was missed."

I didn't respond as I walked over to Thatcher, who was moving in behind Jameson. He'd more than likely try and get himself surrounded by people, but it was a waste of time. There wasn't a soul here who would stand in our way.

Thatcher took a drink from his glass as a wicked grin curled his lips. "Did you see his date?"

As if anyone could miss her.

"Yeah."

He licked his bottom lip. "I forgot how fucking hot she was."

I hadn't. She'd appeared in more than one of my fantasies over the past seven months. I wasn't telling him that though. Knowing her scheme and seeing it in action were two different things. Didn't mean I wouldn't fuck her if I had the chance, but it did leave me with a certain disgust that took some of her appeal away. She could never be truly trusted. I'd know her lies, and it would make me dislike her more- even when they fell from her ridiculously plump pink lips.

"She's gonna need a ride home. Think I'll offer," he said as his eyes stayed locked on Jameson.

"Stay focused," I replied irritably.

Jesus, the woman even had Thatcher distracted.

Stellan stepped in front of Jameson, causing them to stop. We stood back and waited in case he was stupid enough to run. I knew other guests were watching. They all knew what was happening, and it was likely the crowd would clear out. None of them wanted to be an innocent bystander, not that we'd handle this in the open. Stellan would take him somewhere away from witnesses.

"He's trembling," Thatcher said with amusement in his voice.

Briar turned slightly and glanced back over her shoulder. When her eyes met mine, she tensed. I smirked, unable to help myself. She was putting the pieces together. Whatever Stellan was saying right now, I had no doubt she understood the real meaning behind his words.

Her hand slid away from Jameson's arm, and she said something with that bright showstopping smile of hers, then stepped back away from him. When she started in our direction, I was surprised. I had expected her to get away. Leave. Get the hell out of here. Not walk directly to the danger. I wondered where she had that gun of hers stowed. Probably the little purse she had tucked under her arm.

"Here, kitty, kitty," Thatcher muttered under his breath.

I didn't have time to tell him to shut up before she was in front of us.

Her eyes swung from Thatcher to me. "What's he done?" she asked point-blank.

"Hiss," Thatcher replied.

"Can't tell you that. But you should leave," I told her, wishing like fuck she didn't interest me.

She took a deep breath and studied me for a moment. "I see," she finally replied.

The disappointment in her eyes only managed to piss me off. Could she not even pretend like she cared about someone other than herself?

"Waste of time," she muttered, glancing back at him.

Damn, this woman was bold with her intensions. She didn't give a shit about hiding them. It was all about her gain. She could do so much more with that face and that voice. Yet she chose to be a manipulative, lying bitch. At least she wasn't using a nice guy. If anyone deserved to be fucked over by a woman, it was Jameson.

"Just keep talking, kitty," Thatcher said to her. "I'm getting harder by the second."

Rolling my eyes, I jerked my gaze off her. He wasn't wrong. The hard, ruthless shit, coming from someone who looked like every sin I ever wanted to commit, was hot. Even if it was twisted.

"Get an Uber," I snapped. "He won't be driving tonight."

"Or you can wait on me," Thatcher offered, which was so unlike him that I had to stare at him to see if he was serious.

He winked at her. *He fucking winked.* "I don't pay to fuck, but for you, I'd make an exception."

I winced, cutting my eyes back to Briar.

Her gaze narrowed, and the anger that lit up those ocean-blue eyes didn't surprise me. She might use wealthy men for what they could give her, but flat-out being labeled a prostitute wasn't something she was gonna be okay with. Why was it that gold diggers didn't realize it was the same fucking thing?

"I'll have to pass on that offer, sugar," she replied with a thick Southern accent, making that last word sound as sarcastic as she meant it to be. "I prefer my men on the right side of the law and mentally stable."

He chuckled as if enjoying this entire conversation. "Sweetheart, the law is always on our side, and mentally stable is overrated."

She cocked one eyebrow at him. "Perhaps, but the dark, twisted shit in your eyes isn't something I'm drawn to. I prefer the"—she paused, her eyes shifting to me—"sexy ones with a smile you can trust. I've had my fill of darkness."

Was that a proposition?

"Don't let his face fool you. I've seen him slice off a man's dick and shove it in his mouth until he suffocated on it," Thatcher said with a sadistic laugh.

She didn't flinch as she continued looking at me. A small lift of her shoulders, and she glanced back at Thatcher. "And I'd bet my life that the man deserved it."

Ah fuck. Don't do that. Don't make me like you.

Tearing my eyes off her, I looked toward Stellan just as he reached for the Glock hidden beneath the tux jacket he was wearing. Shit! I moved past Briar, taking out my own gun as I quickly assessed Stellan's reason for making this public.

Thatcher was opposite me, walking with his normal unaffected swagger as he grinned that unhinged, amused one he always had when things were about to go south. He lived for this shit. If he got to kill someone, he'd be happy. Especially if he got to use the knife in his left boot instead of his M220 that he favored if he had to use a gun.

"Seems our friend here has an issue with us," Stellan said loud enough for us to hear him. "Why don't you boys take him for a little reminder?"

Jameson's hand was on the butt of his gun, but he'd not pulled it out yet.

Thatcher came up behind him. "Pull it out," he said, leaning in close to him. "I dare you."

The shudder than ran through Jameson as he paled even further would be entertaining if I wasn't fighting the urge to look back and make sure Briar had gotten out of the way. She wasn't my problem, and she'd asked for this shit, messing with a man like Jameson.

"I said I'd have it to you next week," he stuttered, his eyes swinging from Stellan to me.

Stellan tilted his head slightly to the left. "Did I say you could speak?"

The other guests were leaving. I saw them exiting as quickly as they could. Hopefully, they all cleared out so we could get this handled nice and tidy.

"The crazy one is gonna kill him, isn't he?" Briar's voice was too close.

What the fuck was she doing? Why hadn't she left, like a sane person?

I tensed, but didn't take my eyes off Jameson.

"You need to leave," I said through clenched teeth.

"I'm not moving. There are too many guns drawn."

"No one is going to shoot you," I replied, annoyed. "Everyone else is leaving. Go with the crowd."

She sighed. "Listen, handsome. I know you don't like me. I can see it in your eyes. So, excuse me if I don't trust you to protect me."

This woman. Seriously? I didn't have time for this. My focus had to stay on the scene in front of me. If she wanted to stay here and put herself in danger, then it wasn't my problem. I'd warned her.

"I have my gun," she said, still too fucking close to me.

"You'd be dead before you could pull it out of that ridiculous, shiny purse of yours if someone decided to take you out."

She let out a soft laugh that went directly to my cock. Dammit.

"Do you underestimate all women?" she asked.

Jameson's eyes swung over in my direction again, and I saw the jealous flicker in them as he took in Briar's close proximity to me. He thought she was working with us. I only had time to read his expression before his hand tightened its grip on the gun. He pulled it out with more speed than I'd expected. Fortunately, I was still faster.

Turning, I wrapped an arm around the frustrating woman behind me and took her down to the floor with me as the gunshot rang out, flying over our heads. I recognized the silenced shot that came next and the thump of the body that followed. I knew they hadn't killed Jameson, but Thatcher had put him down. We would get our money, and then he'd die.

Running my hands over Briar's body, I tensed the moment I saw the blood oozing from the silky fabric on her shoulder. *Motherfucker.* Sitting up, I moved the dress back gently to see how bad the damage was.

"He shot me," she whispered. The shock in her tone was better than her being hysterical.

"Grazed you," I corrected, feeling relief. "You're gonna be fine."

She let out a long, steady breath. "You're sure? It hurts like hell."

I nodded. "Positive," I replied, pulling my shirttail from my pants and ripping a long strip from the expensive shirt, then taking it to wrap around her wound to help stop the bleeding.

"Get her to Maeme's," Stellan ordered as he walked up behind me. "Have Drew check her out."

Standing up, I turned to see what had taken place behind me. Thatcher and Jameson were already gone. The party had cleared out. Guns would do that. Everyone had run but Briar. She was stupid or fucking stubborn. Perhaps both.

• FOUR •

"We've arrived at the dungeon."

BRIAR

Clenching my teeth tightly, I tried not to make a sound as the pain in my shoulder throbbed. Resting my head back on the black leather seat, I closed my eyes and focused on breathing. This wasn't my biggest problem. It was a minor inconvenience. The fact that I was in an expensive SUV with a member of the Southern Mafia was my real problem. I needed to get fixed up and back to Dovie, then figure out what we were going to do next. We didn't need to move again so soon. It cost too much money.

"Take me to the hospital," I told Storm Kingston as he pulled out of the parking lot.

"No," he replied.

Great. He was going to argue with an injured woman. He really didn't like me.

"I have good insurance. Just drop me off at the door," I lied.

"We don't take this kind of thing to the hospital. We handle it ourselves."

I inhaled deeply through my nose, wishing I had something to drink. Anything to take the edge off. "I'm sure you all keep it to yourselves, but I'm not one of you. I want to go to a real doctor."

"Drew is a real doctor. He's on the board at the hospital you want me to take you to."

The annoyance in his tone pissed me off. What did he have to be annoyed about? I was the one who had been shot.

I winced, then opened my eyes to look over at him in the driver's seat. He was so stupid hot; it was unfair. His jawline was chiseled, his lashes too long, his mouth almost too wide; a small scar on his right cheekbone didn't take away from his looks at all. It only added to the sexiness.

"What if I don't want to go to the dark dungeons of yours to see a doctor?"

He smirked, but didn't look over at me. "Then, you should have left when I told you to."

I sucked in a breath and waited a second for the shooting pain to ease some. This doctor he was determined to take me to had better have some pain meds. If he thought he was going to stitch me up without giving me something first, he was very wrong.

"I'm realizing my mistake," I replied tightly.

"A little too late for that," he pointed out, glancing over at me. He frowned then and reached over to open the glove compartment. The silver flask he pulled out had a *K* engraved on it. "Here. Drink some of this."

I reached out to take it with my good arm, but when I tried to move my other arm so I could open it, I let out a small cry before I could stop it.

"Fuck," he muttered, snatching the flask from my hands, opening it up, then handing it back to me.

I took it, watching him closely. Either I was delirious from the pain and blood loss or he was concerned. For me. His hands tightened on the steering wheel as he sped up. Huh. Just like I'd expected. Storm wasn't cold with shut-off emotions. He might kill and torture people, but they weren't innocent. If they were stupid enough to get mixed up with the Mafia, then they asked for it by pissing them off. Like Jameson.

"Is he dead?" I asked.

"Jameson? No. But you'll need to find a new sugar daddy. He won't be available any longer," he said with sarcasm dripping from his words.

"He owed y'all money."

Storm nodded his head once.

"For someone so successful, he isn't very smart," I said, then took a long pull from the whiskey inside the flask.

"Yet you were fucking him."

The disapproval in his tone should bother me, but like I had already figured out, Storm was basically good. Even in this world he was a part of, he had some morals.

"And you kill people," I replied, needing to point out his faults too.

He shook his head as a humorless, hard laugh came from his chest. "Not the same. I only kill those who deserve it."

"It's still murder. A crime in the eyes of God and the law."

"Adultery is also a crime in the eyes of God and frowned on by the law."

The urge to defend myself was so strong that I had to literally bite my tongue to stay quiet. This wasn't something I needed to be talking about. I'd say the wrong thing and let it slip about Dovie. No one could be trusted with that. Especially a man who clearly had his opinion of me set.

"How much longer?" I asked him, wishing the whiskey were helping the pain.

He turned down a country road I'd never been on before. "Five minutes," he replied. "Doctor will be there when we arrive. He's already prepped the room."

Impressive. "I need a ride home. Does Uber come out this way?" I asked closing my eyes.

"One of us will drive you."

I shook my head slightly, unable to do more than that. "No. I don't want y'all knowing where I live."

A deep rumble in his chest had me snapping my eyes open and looking at him. He glanced at me, then turned his attention back to the road.

"We knew where you lived before we stepped into that bar months ago."

I gritted my teeth. "I've moved."

"Yeah, we know."

Scowling at him, I couldn't decide if he was lying or not. "And why is that? Are you stalking me?"

"Don't flatter yourself. I don't give a shit, but King does. He doesn't trust you, and he'll likely keep eyes on you for years to make sure your scumbag father is dead."

They were watching me? Did they know about Dovie? Shit!

"He's dead. I swear to God."

Storm shrugged. "I believe you. King normally would trust that, but when it comes to his woman, he isn't stable. He's insanely protective of her, and I think, deep down, he wants Roger to be alive so he can be the one to kill him."

Great. I'd killed a man. Gotten his sorry ass off this planet, and now, I was being stalked by the dang Mafia because of it. I didn't need that kind of attention on me. On us.

Storm slowed the vehicle and turned right onto a driveway. The large white gothic-style house with a fabulous wraparound porch was lit up inside and out. It reminded me of something from a commercial about summer days, with kids running around in the yard and the perfect mother standing on the porch, smiling with a tray of lemonade and cookies in her hands.

"We've arrived at the dungeon," he said, cutting his eyes at me before opening his door and climbing out.

I started to reach for the door and let out a small, strangled sound. That hurt like a son of a bitch. How was I going to play the guitar? I had to make money somehow. Sure, I had things that Jameson had given me that I could sell, but it wouldn't be enough, and now, I wasn't so sure it was all real. Had he bought me knockoffs?

This was a mess, and I needed to text Dovie. It had been well over an hour since I'd checked on her. But I couldn't even open the freaking door. How was I going to get my phone out of my purse and text?

The door opened then, and Storm held out his hand to me. I stared at it, then lifted my eyes to his face. God, that face. I needed to stop looking at it.

"Take a long drink first," he suggested, nodding to the flask I'd stuck between my legs to hold it.

I did as he'd said, and the burn from the amber liquid didn't even compare to the pain in my shoulder. Once I felt the light-headed sensation, I stopped and held it out to him. When he took it, I inhaled deeply, then decided to make this quick. Like ripping a Band-Aid off.

Sitting up, I swung my legs over and started to get out when I lost my balance. Storm's arms were around me. A musk, mixed with tobacco, scent met my nose, and I leaned in closer to inhale deeper.

Was this cologne or just him? I wanted a bottle of it.

"Are you trying to fall on your face? I'd have thought someone like you would protect her prized possession a little more than that."

His words snapped me out of the momentary haze I'd been in from the smell that clung to his body.

Jerking back from him, I straightened and glared at him. "Just take me to the doctor."

He kept his hand wrapped around my arm as if he needed to steady me. "Gladly. Can you walk without falling?"

"Yes!" I sneered.

He let go of me slowly, as if testing that statement. I motioned with my good arm for him to lead the way. His jaw ticced like he was clenching his teeth before he turned and headed toward the steps leading up to the porch. If I wasn't in so much pain, I would stop and appreciate the flower gardens as we walked past several. Seeing as I was concentrating on keeping myself upright, I didn't do that.

The front door opened, and a petite, older woman with platinum-blonde hair styled in a short bob stepped outside. The pink apron she wore with white eyelet piping made her appear like the grandmother in one of those commercials I'd imagined earlier.

Where were we?

"Storm Kingston, I know you're not leaving an injured woman to just walk by herself," the woman said in a stern voice as she looked at Storm. When her eyes shifted to me, her gaze softened. "Poor thing. We will get you fixed up." Then, she waved a hand toward me as she glared at Storm. "Get yourself over there and help her. She's in a mess of pain. Look at how pale that pretty face is."

Storm sighed as he turned around to me. "Might as well let me help you. She's not gonna let this go any other way."

I looked from him back to her. Was this his grandmother? She was too old to be his mother.

"I'm fine," I explained. "He tried to help me. I told him I didn't need it."

She narrowed her eyes. "Well, that's not true. Even a man can see it. At least a smart one like Storm. There is no shame in admitting you need some help," she said as she walked down the stairs, headed straight for me.

Storm stepped back, letting her pass with an amused grin tugging at his mouth.

"Come now," she said, wrapping an arm around my waist.

I was several inches taller than her, but the way she held on to me with more strength than I'd expected made her appear as if she could pick me up if needed to, which was silly.

I glanced up at Storm as we passed him, and he continued to look as if this was amusing.

"Briar, meet Maeme. We all do what she says. Might as well accept that she will get her way and go with it."

"That's a straight-up lie, and the good Lord knows it. Like right this minute, there are at least two of my boys in the kitchen, eating the cookies I told them not to touch. They don't listen to nothing. Not one thing."

Walking up the stairs hurt more than I'd expected, but when we reached the top of them, I caught my breath and tried to breathe through the pulsing ache until it eased into discomfort. Once it did, I looked down at her.

"Boys?" I asked, curious as to who she was to Storm.

She nodded. "Yes, boys. The lot of them."

"Is Storm your grandson?"

She smiled. "You could say that. They all are even if not by blood. Family isn't just about blood. A bond is a bond, and family is family. Don't matter how, just means they are."

I had no idea what that meant. I didn't ask for clarification because I felt like I wasn't supposed to understand it.

"Doc D is gonna fix you right up," she said.

I began to notice the house we were in. This was lovely. So bright and welcoming. We started to walk toward a hallway, and Storm moved past us to open a door, then stood back. I glanced at him. He was looking at my shoulder. I had not checked it out on purpose. Seeing blood didn't bother me unless it was mine. Then, I got a little lightheaded. The whiskey had done enough of that.

"Do I need to take her down the stairs?" Storm asked. "I don't want her falling and taking you with her."

Maeme huffed. "As if I haven't helped a bleeding one of you down these stairs before. She don't weigh even half of you, and I have handled that just fine. But to be safe, go before us in case anything happens. I don't want her any more hurt than she already is."

Storm nodded and did as he had been told.

I would not be the reason this nice woman got hurt. Focusing hard on the stairs, I went down them carefully. I couldn't believe I was in some stranger's house, going into their basement to get stitched up from a gunshot wound. Part of me kept thinking I was going to wake up at any minute.

"Thatch called. He's underground with the bastard. We gotta go," a male voice called from the top of the stairs.

Storm lifted his eyes to look past us. "Go on. I'll be there shortly."

"He took a shot at you. You sure you don't want at him first?" the guy asked.

Storm's gaze dropped to me. "Wasn't me he was shooting at."

I stilled. Wait, had Jameson meant to shoot me? Was that what he was saying?

"Thatch said he was. Didn't mean to hit her."

Storm shook his head. "No, he meant to hit her. He thought she was working with us. I saw his eyes before he pulled the gun," he finished, looking back at the guy behind us.

"Fucker," the guy muttered.

"Get going, Sebastian. We got this handled here," Maeme ordered.

Sebastian Shephard. Thatcher's younger brother. I'd done my own research on the Georgia branch of the Southern Mafia months ago. I was sure I didn't know who they all were, but the ones who had dated important people or come from wealthy families in the horse racing world were easier to find out about.

We reached the bottom stair, and Maeme held out a hand to Storm. "Come help her into the room. I'm gonna make a quick call."

Storm moved forward, and a small lift of his eyebrows, as if daring me to argue with Maeme, was the only interaction we had before he wrapped an arm around my waist. That smell was back. God, that was wonderful.

• FIVE •

"I've got better shit to do."

STORM

With my arms crossed over my chest, I stared at the television, not truly watching the car race on it. My entire concentration was on the room where Briar was with Drew and Maeme. She'd barely made a sound. Mostly, Maeme was soothing her, and Drew was explaining what he was doing, but nothing from Briar. I'd have thought Drew had given her something to knock her out if Maeme wasn't currently telling her it was almost over.

I refused to be impressed that she hadn't cried out or even whimpered from the pain. My sisters would have been yelling the house down. It was hard to look at her and not forget that she wasn't some stunning beauty that belonged on covers of magazines. The demons from her past had set up root in her and weren't going anywhere. She was dangerous. There was nothing good inside her.

But damn if she wasn't fucking tough as hell too. That must have come with the other bad shit inside her.

"I have to get home. I can't stay here." Her first words.

I turned to look at the door.

"You need to be looked after. Is there someone at home who can keep an eye on you? Help you?"

She said nothing.

"Then, you need to stay here. I have plenty of rooms."

"NO!" she replied, sounding panicked. "I have to go home."

"Well now—" Maeme started, then stopped abruptly.

"I have someone who can stay with me. He's a friend. I'll call him. I just need to go home." She walked out the door, then stopped, grabbing the frame to steady herself.

I started to move and go to her, but stopped myself. If she wanted to be fucking stubborn, then she could see just how much she needed help. I was sure she had a miles-long contact list of men she could call to come help her. The thought soured my mouth.

"If that's really what you want to do, then I won't force you to stay," Maeme said, but the worry in her face was clear. She didn't want Briar to leave.

"It's what I want," she said, moving again. She only took three steps before she swayed on her feet.

This time, I moved because there was no doorframe for her to grab on to. Wrapping an arm around her waist, I pulled her against my side. I expected her to fight me, but she laid her head on me and let out a deep sigh. When her legs started to give out, I knew she wasn't going to be able to stand, even with my help. Bending, I scooped her up in my arms and turned back to a very concerned Maeme.

"I've got her. I'll take her home and make sure she has someone there to take care of her."

"I'm fine. I can walk," Briar argued but barely moved.

"Yeah, sure looks like it," I replied, then headed for the stairs.

"I need to follow up on it in a week," Drew called out.

"She'll be here," I told him. Even if I had to go to her fucking apartment and get her myself.

"I'm fine," she muttered, but her eyes were closed.

I tore my gaze off her face. Dangerous. Lethal. Even with those eyes of hers closed, she could make a man stupid. I'd love to say it was her cheekbones or the thick lashes, but it was the mouth. The lips. Jesus H. Christ, the things I wanted to do with that mouth.

Not happening. NEVER happening.

"Dov waiting on me," she slurred.

"She's on some strong pain meds," Drew informed me.

No shit. I'd figured that out. And what the hell kinda name was Dov? Was he some poor sap that didn't have the money for her to date, but she kept around as a friend? She probably used him for things she needed done. Like fixing her car or changing her light bulbs.

"I need to get to Dov," she said, fighting to open her eyes.

"I'm getting to him as fast as I fucking can," I said, glaring straight ahead as I headed through the house and then out to the Escalade.

Jerking the car door open, I bumped her shoulder, and a small cry came from her.

"Sorry," I told her, then laid her down in the back seat more carefully. I didn't like her, but I hadn't meant to hurt her either. I wasn't a mean bastard.

Her face scrunched up as if in pain, but then it eased. "I like how you smell," she said sleepily.

Shut up, Briar.

"I want some to spray on my sheets."

I closed the door and took a deep breath. She was smoking hot and telling me she wanted her sheets to smell like me. I could not like her, but still want to fuck her. I wouldn't do it, but I could jerk one off later, thinking about her in the shower. Or better yet, go fuck someone else and get her out of my head.

Stalking over to the driver's side, I opened the door and climbed inside.

"You don't like me," she said so quietly that I almost didn't hear her.

"I don't," I agreed.

" 'Cause I date rich men?"

I backed up and then headed out of the driveway before responding, "You fuck rich, married men, then use it against them for a buyout to get money from them. It's fucking disgusting."

She didn't respond, and I thought she'd finally fallen asleep. I tried to think about Jameson in the cellars under the Shephard property. What we needed to get from him and how we'd handle him. But images of Briar, naked in my bed with her head buried in my sheets, smelling them, were taunting me. I'd never seen her naked, but I already knew she'd be exquisite.

"You don't know me," she said, breaking the silence.

"I know enough."

Why was I arguing with a drugged female?

"Yeah, you do. No one can ever know more."

What the fuck was that supposed to mean? She'd been molested by her own father. That was fucked up. But she'd gotten away. She'd saved herself. I respected that. I did. I even respected the fact that she'd killed the sick bastard. But that didn't give her an excuse to be some shallow, lying, cheating slut. There was so much potential. Even if she didn't look like a centerfold, she was talented. Really fucking talented.

"I wish you liked me."

I squeezed the steering wheel so tightly that my knuckles turned white. Why wasn't she passed out? I didn't want to talk to her.

"I was good once."

Then, be good now.

I bit the inside of my jaw to keep from responding. I wasn't going to do this with her. She was high on her pain meds. She'd probably remember nothing that she said tomorrow.

"You would have liked me back then."

I reached for the volume and turned the radio up to drown out her ramblings. Listening to her be vulnerable wasn't safe for my common sense. Not coming from that mouth. I had to get her to fucking Dov and get back to the cellars. Forget tonight happened and try to forget this woman.

If she tried to say more, I couldn't hear her over George Strait. When I finally pulled into her apartment complex, I'd found without her help since King was still keeping tabs on her every move, I glanced back to see she was asleep. Damn, she was beautiful. The urge to pull her into my arms and just watch her sleep was tempting, which meant I had to get her away from me. Far away.

Getting out of the vehicle, I closed the door and then opened hers to ease her out until I could pick her up. She didn't open her eyes, but she did nuzzle her nose into my chest and sigh contentedly.

Scowling, I stalked to the front of the upscale apartment building. A security guard studied me, then saw Briar in my arms and stepped forward to open the door. I started to go past him when I realized a card was required to get into the elevator.

"I need in the elevator," I told him.

He held out his arms as if I were going to hand over Briar to him. I didn't.

"I've been told to deliver Miss Landry to her apartment," he informed me.

"I'm capable of taking her to Dov," I replied, being sure to drop the man's name who was supposed to be up there, waiting on her.

The security guard frowned. "Dov"—he paused, as if unsure about that name—"informed me that no one was to come up that elevator with Miss Landry. Just me. I can't let you inside."

Fucking hell. Why wasn't this Dov down here to get her?

Holding on to her tighter, I realized I was ready to fight this man over something that wasn't my damn business. I had no right to Briar or her safety, and I didn't want it. What I needed to do was get the fuck away from her before she messed with my head any more than she was already doing.

"Fine," I snarled, shoving her into the man's arms. "Take her. I've got better shit to do."

He was gentle as he held her, keeping her slightly away from his chest. She was safe. I could see it in his expression as he studied her with worry. I wasn't needed here. I should leave. Walk away.

He lifted his gaze to mine. "I need to make sure you're outside and the doors are secure before I take her upstairs."

Of course he did. I might be some deranged man, obsessed with Briar, ready to chase him inside the elevator. Nope. Not that guy. I was the one who had saved her life and brought her home. Nothing more.

Turning, I walked outside of the apartment, deciding then and there I wasn't the one who would come get her for that checkup that Drew wanted. One of the others could deal with her. I was done.

· SIX ·

We needed to start packing.

BRIAR

Dovie was curled up beside me in bed, asleep, when I woke up this morning. For a moment, I was confused until I moved, and the pain in my shoulder brought it all back to me. The party, Jameson, the gunshot, and Storm. I just wasn't sure how I had gotten in bed. The last thing I remembered was texting Dovie that I had been hurt and needed Maurice, our nighttime security guard, to help me up to the apartment when I arrived. Hopefully, that was what had happened. I'd fallen asleep while Storm was driving me home.

Trying to make coffee with one hand was more complicated than I would have imagined. At least it was distracting me from all the things slowly coming back to me that I wanted to forget. Mostly what I'd said to Storm in his SUV until he turned up the radio. Thank God for that. Except I hadn't been able to stay awake when I wasn't talking, and now, I wasn't sure if Maurice had brought me upstairs or if Storm had.

Dovie's footsteps alerted me that she was walking into the kitchen. I spun around to see her sleepy expression.

Her eyes went to the sling my arm was in, and then she signed, "What happened?"

I walked over and pulled out a chair from the table and motioned for her to sit while I took the seat across from it. She did as I'd asked without question, then stared up at me, waiting.

"Jameson was—or is—in trouble with some dangerous men. They came to get him at the party, and he thought I was with them and shot me, but one of the men realized it before it happened and moved me out of the way, but the bullet grazed my shoulder. I'm stitched up, and it did cut into some tissue, but mostly, I'm just sore, and it burns. Nothing serious." It all came out in a rush, but I'd been trying to reassure her.

Her eyes were wide as she stared at me. "He shot at you?" she signed, clearly horrified.

I nodded. "Yep. But it's fine. I promise."

"We need to move. He can come here and shoot you again," she signed.

I doubted he was still breathing. "Those men who came to get him are taking care of him. He won't be a problem. But I do think it might be best if we move. I'm sorry about that. I know we've not been here that long."

She stood up, shoving her chair back. "We need to move today," she signed, looking panicked.

"We can't move today. I signed a six-month lease. I'll have to find someone to sublet to or see if there is any way I can buy myself out of it. Then, I've got to figure out where we are headed next."

Dovie looked toward the door to the apartment as if someone were going to burst through at any moment and shoot me. I shouldn't have told her, but I also didn't think it was smart to lie to her. She had to know the truth if I was going to keep us safe. Much like me, her childhood had been taken from her at an early age, and that wasn't something you could get back. Once your innocence was gone, it never returned.

"Who brought me inside last night?" I asked her.

She looked back at me and signed, "M," which was her short answer for Maurice.

I nodded, relieved.

"You can't play the guitar with your arm like that," she signed.

"I know. I'm going to sell the things that Jameson gave me. That should help for a while. As long as they aren't knockoffs."

From now on, I was going to have my gifts checked for authenticity before continuing an arrangement with a man. If I had to do this, then I needed to make sure I would have the payoff in the end.

"We could live somewhere less expensive," Dovie signed. "You don't have to do this anymore. You can perform in bars for money."

I shook my head. "That's not enough."

It would be enough to live, but not enough to stay somewhere with security like this, and it wouldn't pay for the help I wanted to get her when she turned eighteen.

Roger had taken her innocence. He'd left her with the same demons I fought daily. I'd be damned if he was going to take her voice too. She'd get it back. I'd do everything I could to make sure of it. That was something I could get back for her, and I would do it. If I had to continue dating wealthy men I knew I had no future with, then so be it. There was no saving me. Not anymore.

But Dovie, I could give her another life, and I would.

"I can keep myself safe. We can go far away. Out of the South. Somewhere they'll never find me."

There was no "they" anymore. Just her mother. But telling her that I'd killed Roger was more than she needed to know. She didn't need to know I was capable of taking a life. She wasn't old enough for that kind of information yet.

My phone rang, and I slid my hand into the pocket of my sweatpants to get it out. *Front-desk security* lit the screen.

"Hello?" I said, clutching the phone tighter than necessary.

"Miss Landry, it's Dan. You have a visitor. A Mrs. …" He paused.

"Maeme," the familiar voice said in the background.

My eyes shot to Dovie.

"Uh, Maeme," Dan, the daytime security guard, said.

I couldn't turn that nice woman away, but I also wasn't letting her see Dovie. Maeme seemed sweet, but she had the Southern

Mafia in her house, calling them her boys, with a doctor's office in her basement with legit hospital equipment in it. She was a part of them even if she seemed like a perfect Southern grandmother.

"Yes, uh, send her up. Thank you, Dan," I replied, ending the call and pointing to Dovie's bedroom door. "Go get inside the closet. Take a book and don't come out until I come to get you."

"Who is that?" she signed, not moving.

I put my hand on her back and began pushing her toward her room as I scanned the one we were in for any sign of a teenage girl. "I think she's the grandmother of one of those dangerous guys or all of them, but she was nice to me. She's who took care of me and got the doctor to stitch me up. She's here to check on me. That's all. Stay hidden."

Dovie didn't look convinced, but she nodded, then went into her room.

"Lock the door," I called out when she closed the door.

When I heard the click of the lock, I hurried back to the living room and did a quick check of things. I grabbed a pair of Dovie's fluffy pink socks and stuffed them under the sofa, although those could have been mine. After straightening the throw over the chair, I ran my hands through my hair just as the doorbell rang.

This was fine. She wasn't here to search my apartment. She was checking on me. I took a deep breath and forced myself to relax before going to open the door.

Maeme stood on the other side with a basket in one hand and a friendly smile. "Good morning," she said, stepping past me to come inside. "I came to check on the patient and bring some baked goods. There's also a container of my chicken salad and fresh croissants, along with a cucumber pasta salad."

She'd brought me food.

A real smile curled my lips as I looked at the basket and back to her face. "Thank you. That's so kind of you."

"You're welcome. Now, let me see that shoulder," she said, walking over to the end table in the living room and setting the basket down. "I know Drew is gonna check on it in a week, but I didn't want you leaving last night, as you well know. I wasn't gonna be able to rest my mind until I laid eyes on you and made sure you were okay. I also brought you some eight-hundred-milligram ibuprofen for the pain. They won't make you feel all drugged, but they will kill the pain. I suspect you're hurting real bad this morning."

She was moving my shirt over and pulling back the bandage as she spoke. I stood there and let her because I didn't imagine many people argued with this woman.

"Looks good. But then Drew is the best," she said, stepping back from me. "Now, let me take this food to the kitchen. I'll put the cold stuff away and fix you some breakfast. The blueberry muffins in here are nice and warm still."

She started in the direction of the kitchen. "This way?" she asked, not slowing down.

"Uh, yes," I replied, then hurried after her. I hadn't checked the kitchen for things that might be Dovie's.

"Looks like you made some fresh coffee. I hope you like yours strong. I need me a cup too. I prefer it to be thick enough to eat with a spoon." She laughed. "Not really, but that's what Gabriel, that was my husband, used to say about my coffee. He liked his weak for such a powerful man."

The box of Lucky Charms sat on the counter, along with the strawberry Pop-Tarts that were Dovie's favorite. But adults ate those things too. It wasn't a real clue that I didn't live alone.

Maeme picked up the Pop-Tarts and looked at me disapprovingly before setting them back down. "This is not real food. I'm glad I brought you some muffins if this is what you were gonna eat. Even my apple pie is better than eating this."

She tsked, then opened the basket and began to unload all the things she'd mentioned, along with some cupcakes, cookies, pound cake, and what looked like banana pudding. Dovie was going to think she'd died and gone to heaven with all this.

"Maeme," I said in disbelief. "This is a lot. You didn't have to do all this."

"Are you going to eat it?" she asked me.

"Yes," I replied quickly.

"Then, that's what matters. I like to cook and make food for others. Lord knows you could eat some more food. If you're eating Pop-Tarts and still that skinny, you must have a hell of a metabolism."

I hadn't touched a Pop-Tart in years, but I wasn't telling her that. Just like I couldn't eat all the sweets she'd brought. Although I was tasting one of everything before Dovie enjoyed it all.

Maeme opened the fridge and put the salads inside. She didn't seem to notice the strawberry milk, sodas, the M&M's yogurt, string cheese, and Lunchables that Dovie loved. She was going to think I had the appetite of a child.

When she straightened and closed the door to the fridge, she looked around at the cabinets. "Now, we just need coffee cups."

I walked over to the right one before she started going through them to see how few dishes we had. When you moved a lot, you didn't keep real dishes and cook wear. We had the bare minimum. Including coffee cups. My collection of cups from every city we had ever visited was one of the few things I let myself keep. The box I used to pack them was tucked away in the pantry.

Taking down two cups, I handed one I had bought at a Luby's in Fort Worth to Maeme while I kept one from Café Du Monde in New Orleans to use. She didn't seem to notice the cups as she filled my cup, then her own.

"Do you doctor yours up?" she asked me.

I grinned and reached for a packet of sweetener, then opened the fridge to get out my sugar-free caramel creamer.

"I see that you do," she replied, walking over to the table.

She sat down in the chair that Dovie had been in earlier, then took a drink from her Luby's cup.

"Now, tell me what it is you do for a living. This is a nice apartment complex. Good and safe." There was only approval in her tone.

I finished stirring my coffee before looking at her. Had Storm not told her about my singing or the men I dated? Did she just want to hear it from me?

"I play guitar and sing at a place not far from here, called Highwater," I explained.

She raised her eyebrows. "You play and sing? I'd love to hear it."

I laughed, then took another sip of my coffee, hoping she didn't demand I perform for her now.

"Why were you with Jameson Chester? He's engaged to Sol Mercer, is he not?"

I shouldn't be surprised by her direct line of questioning. It still threw me off guard though. I hadn't thought she'd just ask me about it like this. I blinked several times, then decided that with Maeme, I would have to be as honest as I could without telling her about Dovie. She would keep pressing until she thought she knew the whole story, and I needed her to leave. Dovie and I had things to get done today. Now that so many people seemed to know where I lived, moving had just been put first on my list of things I needed to do.

I set my cup on the table and looked Maeme in the eyes. "Yes, he is engaged. However, I was unaware of that when he asked me out. In fact, we had been dating for a couple of weeks before I found out about Sol. Should I have stayed with him? No. But I did. It was a mistake I believe I paid for."

Maeme studied me, then took a drink of her coffee. "You stayed because he was wealthy." It wasn't a question, and we both knew it.

"Yes," I confirmed.

She set her cup down on the table. "Well, that was easy enough. You're not one to make excuses, are you?"

"I believe making excuses for yourself is lying to yourself. And the one person I never want to lie to is me."

She raised her eyebrows slightly. "But lying to others is okay?"

I licked my lips before replying, "Everyone lies about something. To protect themselves. To protect someone they love. Not everyone can handle your truth, and it's up to you to decide who deserves it and who does not."

The corner of Maeme's mouth twitched. "I see. That's a way to look at it."

"Am I wrong?" I asked her.

We both knew she had her own secrets.

"No, Briar. I can't say that you are. But then to protect someone I loved, I would do much worse than tell a lie."

I nodded my head. "As would I."

Maeme let out a small laugh and stood up. "I'm glad to see you're doing well this morning and that you have somewhere safe to live. Storm assured me you did, but I needed to see it for myself. You take care of that wound, and it will heal up nicely," she said, then walked over to pick up the empty basket. "Enjoy the food and rest. When you're better, I'll be sure to come hear you play, wherever that might be," she replied.

"Highwater," I repeated since she hadn't heard me earlier or had forgotten.

She gave me an amused look as she hung the basket on her arm. "We both know you won't be sticking around here for long."

I opened my mouth and closed it, unsure how to respond to that.

"At least finish all the food before you take off. It would be a shame to waste it. Especially my banana pudding. I have grown men fighting over it every Tuesday." She winked and headed for the door.

When she opened it, I found my voice. "Thank you."

She paused, and I realized she was looking at the Converse that Dovie had left beside the door. Tensing, I waited. It wasn't like they couldn't be mine … well, Dovie's foot was a few sizes bigger, but Maeme wouldn't study a pair of shoes that closely. Would she?

"If you find yourself needing to leave sooner rather than later," she said, turning back to me, "you'll find that the lease you signed here won't be an issue. In fact, I would bet that it no longer exists."

I stared at her, trying to figure out what she was telling me. How did the lease no longer exist?

She set the basket down beside the Converse. "I'll just leave this too. It will hold a good bit of food. Would be a shame to run off and leave it," she said, then nodded her head before opening the door and walking out of it.

I waited until I heard the elevator ding before letting out a breath I had been holding. Had she suspected anything? Did she know I wasn't alone? And what had she meant about my lease? None of this made me comfortable. We weren't safe if someone with her power found out about Dovie. She was a nice woman, but I couldn't trust her. I couldn't trust anyone.

We needed to start packing.

· SEVEN ·

"It isn't like she's committing a crime."

STORM

Sunday lunch was always loud. Maeme made a spread of food, and whoever could be there in the family came to eat. Her long dining room table was full, along with the table in the kitchen and the seats at the bar. Several of us hadn't been to bed in over twenty-eight hours, yet we had shown up for the meal.

The money Jameson had owed us was collected, and he was sent away, beaten with a warning, which surprised me. I'd thought Stellan would kill him.

His decision had been made because Jameson hadn't actually shot at one of us and Briar Landry wasn't ours to protect. Then, there was the fact that his death wouldn't have gone unnoticed. We'd have had to clean that up, and it would have taken a lot of strings to have it swept under the rug. Some that Stellan hadn't felt was worth wasting our time on.

I'd be lying if I said my thoughts hadn't kept going to Briar and her safety. I didn't want to give a fuck, but there was a solid chance he'd go after her again. Even though I'd made it very clear to him that she had nothing to do with us.

My vehemence that she'd been innocent in all of it though might have been a little too intense. Either Jameson would fear for his life if he went after her or he would be livid, believing she had hooked up with me and I was protecting her. I felt like I should at least warn her that he was alive. She didn't need him showing up, unannounced.

When Mandilyn, Stellan's wife, followed my mother out of the dining room, he looked at Maeme, who was the only woman left at the table. King; his father, Ronan; Wells, who had been my best friend, growing up; and his father, Roland, also remained. Thatcher sat to the right of his father, and Sebastian was in the kitchen, talking to the oldest of my two younger sisters, Lela.

Although most of us were not related by blood, we were something more than that. Our families went back generations inside what we referred to as the family. In the Georgia branch of the family, we were made up of four families. The Shephards, the Salazars, the Joneses, and of course my family, the Kingstons. Some of our extended family bled into other branches. For example, my first cousin, Huck, was the boss's main protection in Ocala, Florida. Huck's father had been my dad's brother, but he'd been killed years ago. Then, Stellan's brother was over at the Mississippi branch while his son, Levi, worked directly for the boss in Ocala. Once you were locked into the family, you never left.

"You went to Briar Landry's apartment yesterday morning," Stellan said to Maeme.

That caught my attention, and I stopped the spoonful of peanut butter pie I was about to put in my mouth to swing my gaze over to Maeme. Her eyebrows were raised, and she was looking at Stellan as if he had asked her a question that was none of his business.

"And?" she replied.

Stellan leaned back in his chair and sighed. "No need to get snippy with me. I was just curious as to why you felt you needed to get her lease canceled."

Maeme placed her glass of sweet tea back on the table beside her plate. "We don't discuss business at my dinner table. You know the rules."

Only Maeme got away with talking to Stellan as if he wasn't in charge of all that went on in the Georgia branch.

"Briar Landry isn't business. Not ours at least. But you went to her place, and I would like to know why you involved yourself in her personal life."

Maeme straightened her back, which was normally a warning that she was not happy. She glared at Stellan. "The girl had been shot at because of us. I wanted to make sure she was okay and take her some food. As for her lease, the bastard who'd shot her might go back to finish the job. I just made sure she was free to go if she wanted to. I wasn't aware it was information I needed to run by you."

Stellan would have been in one of our faces if we'd spoken to him like that. But with Maeme, he looked mildly frustrated. As if this was a pointless and exhausting conversation he wished he hadn't started. "Fine. I'm sorry I brought it up."

Maeme stood up then, taking her empty plate as she did so. "Someone needed to check on her. You all believe she's a gold-digging tramp. It took me five minutes in her presence to read her. She's not what she seems, but she wants everyone to think so. It isn't like she's committing a crime."

Stellan held up a hand. "So, you don't think she's a gold digger then? What is she, Maeme?"

Maeme's eyes cut to me briefly before she looked back at Stellan. "A fighter. A damn good one. And the fight that is in her is fueled by something stronger than the dollar." She started to head in the direction of the door.

"She has affairs with rich men, then makes them pay her to keep her mouth shut. What else are we supposed to think?" Stellan called out.

"Judging a book by its cover, Stellan? You're too old to be that stupid," she replied, then walked out.

Stellan rolled his eyes. "She's found herself another fucking stray. Better hide the silver if she intends to bring this one home too."

"If she brings Briar here, I will keep her busy," Thatcher said with a smirk.

"She's not coming here. She refused to stay one night. My guess is, she's already packed up and run again," I replied, trying not to scowl at Thatcher.

"She's not left town yet. I'd know if she had," King told us as he stood up.

"You still keeping tabs on her?" Roland asked.

He nodded. "Until I'm sure she isn't lying about killing that son of a bitch."

"She killed him," Thatcher drawled. "It's in her eyes. The demons that come with it."

"What the hell do you know about seeing shit in people's eyes?" Wells asked, amused.

Thatcher's gaze swung to him. "Enough to know you're a goddamn pussy."

"Boys." Stellan's firm voice stopped whatever else Thatcher was about to say. "It's Sunday. We've had a busy weekend. Let it go."

Everyone knew he was saving Wells's ass. Thatcher had never been a fan of Wells, but he'd managed not to kill him over the years.

Ronan leaned over to say something to Stellan, and the rest of the room seemed to calm. King left to go find Rumor, who had taken their baby girl to nurse earlier. Thatcher followed him out, but I knew he was leaving the house.

The conversation about Briar was over, but I was still thinking about it. I hoped she was gone. Away from Jameson. Not that it was my job to warn her, but someone needed to.

Standing, I followed Thatcher's exit. I didn't like Briar Landry, but that didn't mean I wanted her dead. She deserved to know the man who had tried to kill her was alive. After that, she was on her own.

• 48 •

• EIGHT •

The blond Greek god could leave now.

BRIAR

Finishing my first set onstage at Highwater, I made my way down to the bar, where Bash Highwater, the owner and my boss, was standing by Mick, one of the bartenders working tonight. Mick was a good-looking guy around thirty while the other bartender tonight, Sunshine, was mid-twenties with big boobs and blonde hair. Bash was very selective with his bartenders. They all had to be efficient and attractive. I was almost positive he was screwing around with Sunshine. The possessive look she gave him was a dead giveaway. Not that it was my business, but I noticed these things.

"Thirsty?" Mick asked as I stepped up to the back of the bar.

"Yes," I replied with a smile.

He grabbed a glass from the cooler and added ice, then filled it with water before handing it to me.

"Thank you," I told him before gulping it down.

"When are you gonna do one of your originals again?" he asked while he worked on filling two mugs with beer on tap.

I shrugged. "Don't know. I think the crowd prefers what they know."

And I wouldn't be here much longer. That was why I'd come down here instead of to the back for my break. I needed to speak with Bash. Let him know tomorrow night would be my last.

"That one you did about the sawdust was a hit. You should do more of your own stuff."

I loved writing my own music, but typically, I sang it in the safety of my home. Dovie was my only audience, and she loved whatever I wrote. It was safe to sing my songs to her. I wasn't so brave about doing it to a crowd full of folks who just wanted to hear me cover their favorites while they drank, danced, and flirted the night away.

"Briar," Bash said in greeting when he turned and realized I was there. "You are killing it up there tonight. I swear our crowds are bigger when you're scheduled onstage."

Bash was a nice guy. Mid-forties, very charismatic, successful at keeping the bar his father had built and made popular forty years ago going strong. I hated letting him down. I enjoyed working here, and that wasn't always the case with jobs like this. I'd dealt with bosses who thought I was theirs to paw at and who said inappropriate things to me. Bash wasn't like that at all. It would be hard to find another bar like this one. And if we went north, like Dovie had said we should—and she was probably right—I was worried finding a bar who wanted a country singer for entertainment might be more difficult to find. I was sure they had them, but not like they did in the South.

"Thanks, but ladies' drinks for five dollars on Sunday nights might have something to do with the crowd," I pointed out.

He waved a hand as if that meant nothing. "I've been doing ladies' five-dollar drinks on Sundays for years. Sure, it brings folks in, but when you're onstage, it's at least forty percent busier."

"He's not lying," Mick added.

This only made it harder to tell Bash I had to quit. He seemed too happy about the crowd, which he should be. There were just as many men here as women and their drinks weren't on sale. Not to mention the food that was coming out of the kitchen constantly.

My tip jar onstage was already full, and I had two more sets tonight. I doubted I'd ever find a job as good as this one again.

"Here's your dirty martini. Just the way you like it," Sunshine said, pressing her chest against Bash's arm as she held out his drink to him.

He winked at her. "Thanks."

Yep, they were so fucking.

I cut my eyes to Mick, who gave me a look like he was thinking the same thing. I bit my bottom lip to keep from smiling. I didn't want them to know we were onto them.

"Briar."

The deep voice behind me caused me to stiffen as my heart sped up. I knew that voice, but why was he here?

My eyes widened as I stared at Mick, who was frowning as he looked over my shoulder. I had to turn around before Mick thought he needed to protect me. No reason to get him or Bash killed for pissing off the Southern Mafia.

Slowly, I turned around to see Storm Kingston standing there. The black T-shirt he was wearing stretched over his chest, leaving little to the imagination on just how cut he was. His biceps almost looked like the sleeves were too small. Lifting my eyes, I realized I was holding my breath. His hazel eyes were hard as he stared at me. Always so disapproving, yet it didn't take away from the way the honey color drew me in. I wanted to study them closer. He hadn't shaved in a few days, and the way it made his masculine jawline appear, I fought the urge to reach out and run my hand over it.

My memory hadn't been exaggerating it. Storm was a god. One who disliked me immensely. That snapped me out of my moment of lust.

"Storm," I said, then cleared my throat, realizing I'd sounded a little strangled. "What can I do for you?" That last bit sounded friendly enough.

"We need to talk," he said, then glanced at the men behind me. "Alone."

Great. So, he hadn't just come in to get a drink and listen to the music. He was here with more crap I had to be concerned with. I immediately thought of Dovie at the apartment, alone. Sure, Maurice was working security downstairs, but that wasn't going to stop someone if they wanted to get to me. Not really.

"Sure," I said in a fake bright tone, then looked back at the others watching me closely. "I'll be backstage for a few, but I won't be late for my next set."

Bash nodded his head, but he kept his eyes on Storm. Did he know who he was? He seemed unsure about letting me go.

"Nice to see your father's place is still thriving," Storm said to him.

That answered my question.

"I do my best," Bash replied. "I was unaware you knew my best performer." The cautious way he spoke to Storm made me wonder just how he knew him.

"There aren't many gorgeous females in Georgia I don't know," Storm said with a crooked grin that was meant to ease Bash's concern, but seemed so out of place on him. At least the Storm that I knew. He was always scowling.

Bash let out a nervous chuckle. "Yes, I imagine you do."

His eyes shifted back to me then, as if he wanted to warn me. It was possible Bash thought I didn't know who and what Storm was.

Reaching up, I touched Storm's arm affectionately and smiled at Bash. Storm's arm flexed under my touch, but he didn't jerk it away.

"We won't be long," I told them, then turned my head up to look at Storm. "Follow me."

I didn't wait to see if he was behind me as I made my way to the door that led backstage. I knew he could keep up just fine. The people in our path seemed to part as we walked by. Was it just Storm's commanding presence, or was he scowling again, looking like he might shoot someone who didn't move? Probably the latter.

Stepping through the door, I kept going until I made it to the dressing room I used on nights I worked. I left it open for

Storm to follow me inside, knowing he'd close it behind himself. Crossing my arms over my chest, I turned to look at him. His broad back was to me, and good Lord, his ass in a pair of jeans was fantastic. Jerking my eyes off his bottom half before I ended up admiring his muscular thighs, I watched as he locked the door before facing me.

"I've got ten minutes left on break," I informed him.

He studied the room for a moment before looking back at me again, as if searching for something. "You need to leave town."

I was already planning on it, but having him tell me that I needed to annoyed me. "And why do you think I should be taking direction from you?" My tone was snarky, but he seemed to bring out the worst in me.

"Jameson is injured, but he's not dead. You've got maybe a week before he's moving around again."

I felt the blood drain from my face as I stared at him. I hadn't thought this was what he'd come to say. Jameson being alive was something I'd stopped worrying about. I had been sure that they killed him.

"But he shot at you," I said, my voice giving away my fear.

Storm shook his head. "No. He shot at you. That's not reason enoough for us to kill the heir to one of the biggest whiskey distributers in the South and Sol Mercer's fiancé."

Panic was rising in my chest. Dovie wasn't safe. I had to get her out of this town, this state, now.

"I thought the Mafia wasn't afraid of anyone," I blurted.

Sure, I wasn't their concern, but didn't they kill people and ask questions later? Why let Jameson live?

"We aren't. We just know when a battle is worth it. This one isn't."

Ouch. Okay, that was fair. No reason to bring on that kind of attention over me. Someone they didn't like or trust.

"Right," I muttered as my mind raced as to what I needed to do next.

I couldn't go back on that stage. Not with Dovie at home, alone.

"Is that all then?" I asked him when he didn't move to leave or say more.

He nodded. "Yeah. I felt like you should be warned."

"Why?" I asked before I could stop myself.

When he didn't respond right away, I started to think he wasn't going to, but he lifted one of his large, tanned hands and ran his thumb over his lower lip as he studied me. That one move, although my life was in danger and I had to go save Dovie, made my body tingle. Especially the area between my legs.

"I don't like you, but that doesn't mean you deserve to die. I debated not coming. Letting your fate lay where it might. But unlike you, I do have a conscience. I wouldn't be able to look at myself in the mirror, knowing I did nothing. I've warned you, and now, it's on you what you do next."

It wasn't like this was the first time that Storm had said things to me that stung, but it didn't make it any less painful. I said nothing, but nodded my head. I didn't trust my voice. I needed a moment alone to regroup and make a plan. The blond Greek god could leave now.

As if he'd read my mind, he turned and walked back to the door. I watched as he opened it and closed it. Not once even glancing at me again. Reaching into my back pocket, I pulled out my phone and texted Dovie.

> Are you good?

That was my typical question. I didn't want to alarm her with, *Put a chair in front of the door, go get my spare gun from under the floorboard in my room, and hide in the closet.* That would have been a little dramatic, but right now, I'd feel better if she did just that.

> Yep! Watching season four of Never Have I Ever.

• SIZZLING •

A small smile tugged my lips. I didn't care for the show. I thought it was silly, but I was glad Dovie was watching something age-appropriate for once. When she'd been on a *Sons of Anarchy* kick, I had hated it and felt like I was failing as a ... whatever I was to her. The stepsister who had stolen her from abusive parents and kept her on the run to protect her. Not really a title you could share with people.

I paused my finger, hovering over the keys, wanting to tell her to finish packing up her things, but knowing that would have her asking questions that I wasn't going to answer with her there alone. She'd be terrified.

I was supposed to. But not anymore.

The dots appeared immediately, telling me she was typing.

Smart girl. She'd been on the run with me for too long. She knew the signs.

Dots, then ...

UGH! I was not telling her this over a text.

> Watch your show and stop being a brat. I'll be there soon.

More dots.

> Fine, but I'm getting the big knife from the kitchen and putting a chair under the door. Knock when you get here.

A bitter smile touched my lips. I hated that she knew this life. But it was better than the one I'd taken her from.

> Okay.

I wasn't about to tell her not to. I'd feel better, knowing she was on alert.

The guitar I used here wasn't mine. It was one that Bash supplied. He wanted me to use a flashy one onstage, and mine was nice, but it wasn't anything like the one he had me use. I didn't have to go back to get anything, and although I needed to tell Bash I was leaving and why, I didn't have time. I'd text him and apologize that way. It was a shitty thing to do, but Dovie came first.

Grabbing my purse, I slung it over my shoulder, then headed for the door. When I opened it, I came face-to-face with Bash. Shit. He looked at my purse, then back to me.

"What's wrong?" he asked.

"It's an emergency. I have to go," I explained. "I am really sorry about this."

"Are you in danger, Briar? I know who Storm Kingston is. Do you?"

I nodded. It was a yes to both questions after all.

He ran a hand through his hair and let out a heavy sigh. "Shit. Okay. What can I do to help you? I know Stellan Shephard because my father worked with him some and Stellan helped him with a uh, situation, years ago. It's how he got the money to open this place. But I'm not tight with them. They're not people you get tight with."

I nodded again. "Yeah, I know. It's not them that my issue is with, if that makes you feel better. Storm came to warn me—that's all. They won't be back here, but I-I have to go. As in leave town. I thought I had more time, but I don't."

"Jesus," he muttered. "Okay, right. At least let me go get your tips and pay you what I owe you. If you're running, you need money."

Yes, I did. But I had to hurry. "I don't have much time."

Bash pulled out his wallet, and I watched as he took out a small stack of one-hundred-dollar bills, then held them out to me. "Take this then."

I shook my head. "That's too much."

It was at least two thousand, maybe more. He owed me a thousand, max.

"Take it," he demanded, shoving it into my hand. "You need it."

I hesitated for a moment, then wrapped my fingers around the cash. "Thank you. I'll pay you back one day. I swear it."

He shook his head. "Just when it's safe, come on back. Your job will be waiting on you."

I'd never be able to come back, but I didn't say that. I gave him a smile I didn't feel. "Thank you."

"Anytime. Go. Be safe. Call me if there is anything I can do to help."

I started to go, but stopped and threw my arms around him and hugged him briefly. It was rare that men helped me without wanting something in return. The emotion clogging my throat at his willingness to help surprised me. I wasn't used to it.

Letting him go, I stepped back and turned to head out the back exit. I was going to miss this place, but I'd move on and find something new. I always did.

• NINE •

With all this caffeine and sugar, I might just make it to Tampa tonight.

BRIAR

I couldn't reach the basket filled with the food Maeme had given us. I really wanted another muffin. But I also needed coffee.

Dovie was sound asleep in the passenger seat of the Honda Accord I'd traded in my Jeep for back in Jacksonville. That was painful. I'd been wanting a Jeep for years, and when I bought that eight months ago, it had made me giddy. But driving around in a candy-apple-red Jeep stood out, and I needed to blend in. So, gray Honda Accord it was.

At the last minute, I'd decided against going north and headed south instead. But not the real South. The Florida south. I figured we could keep driving all the way to Key West. Find a little bungalow or house boat to rent. I'd be able to find a singing gig easy enough there. Or perhaps Miami would be better. It was bigger and easier for us to get lost in. Right now, I just needed to get some more miles between us and Atlanta before I felt safe enough to stop and get rest. A few more coffees, maybe two muffins, and I'd be good to go for at least six more hours.

I'd turned off the audiobook we'd been listening to when Dovie fell asleep. I didn't want her to miss any of it, but it had helped keep me awake. Maybe if I stopped for coffee and got another muffin out of the basket, I could load another audiobook and start it instead. A good story might keep me going for eight hours. I wasn't big into reading like Dovie, but there was something to be said for an audiobook. I liked it. Dovie had told me I would. She knew the real reason I wasn't a big reader was because I struggled with the words. Labeling myself as dyslexic had always felt off because when it came to music, I could write it all day. Something about the notes and the melody made sense to me. But reading words on paper, nope.

My phone began to ring, and I reached for it, seeing a number I didn't recognize. I stared at it, unsure if I should answer or not, but seeing as it wasn't Jameson's number or even one with that area code, I decided to see who it was. If it was him, I'd hang up before he could track me. If that was even a thing with cell phones. I wasn't sure. I'd need to get a new one when we got to wherever we were going. But for now, I had to use what I had.

"Hello?" I said, not talking too loud. I didn't want to wake Dovie.

"Where are you?" Storm's voice came over the line.

My head was in battle with the rest of my body. While my brain knew to be annoyed with this rude, intrusive man, my body began to warm up and come alive from his deep, husky voice. Stupid body.

"Uh, I don't see how this is your business."

When he'd left my former dressing room, hadn't he made it very clear that I should leave town and he no longer cared what I did?

"Maybe not, but King is pissed. The tracker on your vehicle is in Jacksonville, Florida, at a dealership."

What?!

"Tracker?!" I caught myself before shouting and ended up hissing the word instead.

"You knew he was keeping tabs on you," Storm sounded as if this made sense.

"I'm sorry. A man I do not know had a tracker on my Jeep. I have the right to be angry."

Storm sighed. "He's going to find you, and you can make this easy or hard. I'm just warning you that you don't want an angry King. He's got a temper."

Gripping the phone tightly, I glared at the road ahead of me. "I am getting out of town, like you suggested. I was unaware I had to check in with *King*. The man who was my father is dead. Very dead. Bottom-of-the-ocean dead. I swear my life on it. He can stop watching my every move." I glanced over at Dovie, who was thankfully still asleep.

"Why are you whispering?" Storm asked, catching me off guard.

Did he pay attention to everything?

"I'm not."

"Yeah, you are. Who is with you?" The distrust in his tone was clear.

"Not Roger, if that's what you're thinking," I replied, disgusted at the thought.

Silence.

Had he hung up?

"King is not someone you lie to, Briar. He's pulled a gun on Sebastian for letting Rumor wear his fucking hoodie because she was cold. When it comes to Rumor, he is not sane. He'll put a bullet in your head and go eat his Maeme's banana pudding in the same damn hour."

His Maeme? So, was she King's grandmother? I shook my head. Why did I care?

"I am not lying," I said through clenched teeth.

"Then, who is with you?" he demanded again.

I glanced at Dovie.

"A friend." That was all he was getting.

"Who?"

"Not your business. But it is not Roger. The fact that he's swimming with the sharks makes that impossible."

"He will find you. It'll be easier if you just tell me where you are."

Putting on my blinker, I got over to exit. "Somewhere south of Jacksonville."

"Florida is a big state. Be more specific."

I had Jameson to worry about. I didn't need the freaking Mafia hating me too. I looked around at the hotels and gas stations for some sign of where I was.

"Leesburg," I said when I saw it on a bank sign.

"Are you staying there?" he asked.

I pulled into a service station. "No. I am getting gas, coffee, and going to pee."

"Where are you headed?"

Cutting off the engine, I saw Dovie start to stretch. This conversation needed to end.

"Look, I don't know. I am just going. Probably Miami. Maybe the Keys. But I am done talking about this. I've got to go," I said firmly, then ended the call before turning my phone completely off.

Dovie squinted, then rubbed her eyes before sitting up. "Where are we?" she signed.

"Leesburg, wherever that is. I need to fuel up and take a bathroom break. Go on in and use the toilet, then get you something to eat inside or from the basket."

She yawned, then nodded, reaching for the door handle. There were no questions in her expression, and the sleepy look on her face said she had just woken up. She'd not heard the conversation on the phone. Small blessings. Not that I got very many of those, if any.

I watched as she made her way to the store before filling up. I didn't like her being out of sight, but then we weren't being followed, and if the Mafia had even lost their trail on me, then we were safe from Jameson. It only took thirty-seven dollars to fill the tank, and that right there made having to give up my Jeep less painful. At least I was gonna save money on gas.

After we both used the restroom and picked out several unhealthy snacks in case we ran out of food in the basket, I got a large coffee and paid for everything, and we headed back out to the car. It really was a boring car, but it didn't draw attention. With a sigh, I climbed inside and got my things situated. Dovie was already opening the bag of chocolate mints she'd bought, and I held out my hand for one. She placed two in my palm, then popped one in her mouth.

We were ready to keep going. With all this caffeine and sugar, I might just make it to Tampa tonight.

"Want to listen to more of the book?" I asked her.

She nodded and picked up her phone to press play.

"Hand me a muffin," I told her.

She rolled her eyes but reached for it and unwrapped it, then handed it to me. I took a large, dramatic bite that made her smile before pulling back out onto the highway.

I struggled to keep my thoughts on the audiobook this time though. The call from Storm kept replaying through my head. His tone had made it clear that calling me was the last thing he wanted to do. I was something he wished he could get rid of completely. For the first time in my adult life, I'd met a man who didn't want anything to do with me. I was so used to them falling all over themselves to get my attention, and the one time I met a man who stirred things inside me, he couldn't stand the sight of me. Figured.

Let him hate me. It was better for both of us. My lies served a purpose, and he didn't deserve the truth. Human lie detector, my ass. He hadn't read my lies. Only the truths.

I finished off my muffin, then took a drink of my coffee.

Storm Kingston was the sexiest man I'd ever met, but he was an asshole. I had to stop letting thoughts of him into my head. Maybe this time, wherever we ended up, I could find someone I was interested in. Someone I liked. A good guy. Sure, I needed him to have money, but there wasn't a rule that said I had to use a man.

What if I fell in love or at least had feelings for a wealthy man? An available one? Someone who would take care of Dovie and me? That didn't sound so bad. Maybe then we could stop running.

When I glanced over at her, she was smiling at whatever was happening in the book that I had lost interest in. Seeing the enjoyment on her face as she listened and ate her candy made all the bad I'd done okay. It had been for a reason. Her. If there was a god, surely, he'd see that. He was supposed to be just and forgiving, right? I thought I'd heard that somewhere. Or maybe I had made it up.

• TEN •

"When it comes to the Shephard brothers, it's Thatcher who gets the pussies wet."

STORM

"Jameson got arrested for assaulting a security guard," Sebastian said as he walked into the lounge room in the Shephards' stables.

I set the glass of whiskey I had been drinking down and looked over at him. "Are you serious?"

He nodded, grinning. "Very. I'm sure he's already out on bail, but he's gonna have to go to court over it. Guess what security guard it was."

I inhaled sharply through my nose. "The one at Briar's former apartment building."

He nodded. "Yep. Security footage showed him losing his shit when he was told she no longer lived there. Damn, that's funny."

I took a drink. Maybe I'd find humor in it if King wasn't hell-bent on tracking her down. Roger was dead. She wasn't lying about killing him. Why couldn't he let it go? If Rumor knew he was still tracking her, she'd be pissed. And I wanted to not have to hear Briar Landry's name so I could stop thinking about her.

King stalked into the room, looking more relaxed than the last time I'd spoken to him. Maybe he'd decided to let it go after all. Or he'd just fucked Rumor and he was relaxed and sated.

"You're in a better mood," I pointed out.

He opened the fridge and grabbed a bottle of water. "It's a good day. The jockey we got riding Bloodline is a hell of a lot better on him than Carmen was at Preakness," he said, then took a long drink from the water in his hand.

"Yeah, I saw him out this morning. Small guy, but that always makes for a good jockey," Sebastian said.

"It's a her," King said. "Young too. But, damn, she can ride. Even better that she's a local. That shit never happens. Fantastic jockey who isn't full of herself, and we don't have to fly her ass around. Anyway, I'm done for the day here. Going home to my girls."

He hadn't mentioned Briar, which seemed odd, and I should be fucking thankful. Maybe her name would stop popping up around here, and I could get that face of hers out of my head.

"Letting the Briar thing go, huh?" It just came out of my mouth before I could stop it. I was supposed to be getting her out of my head, not asking about her.

He took another drink, then shook his head. "Not until I am positive the bastard is dead. Huck sent one of his guys out and tracked her down. Found her at a hotel in Tampa and got a tracker put on her new car."

I frowned. "How did they track her that fast?"

"They asked the car dealership where her Jeep was and about the woman who had traded it in and what car she'd bought. Then, they started in Leesburg, like you'd said, and headed south until they saw the car and followed it to a Hilton in Tampa."

None of this surprised me. If I had taken a moment to think about it, I'd have figured it out.

"She's traveling with a girl though. Young teenager from what Huck's guys said. It sounds fucking sketchy, which leads me to believe she lied about something, and if it's Roger, I will be the first to know." King headed for the door. "Check on the jockey in a bit, yeah, Sebastian?" he asked.

"On it," he called out with a salute.

I finished off my whiskey, trying to figure out why she had a teenage girl with her. Not that this mattered to me, but I was fucking curious. King was right. Something was definitely off. Didn't add up.

"Your wheels are turning. You got that look on your face," Sebastian said, breaking into my thoughts.

I shrugged. "Nothing important."

"Bullshit."

I shot him an annoyed glance before taking my phone out of my pocket to check the last few texts I'd ignored.

"The fucking hot redhead has gotten under your skin. King is trying to find a man who is dead by tracking her, but you, you're hoping she's not what she appears to be. Admit it."

I didn't look up from my text. Two were from women I could use to get the edge off. Neither were redheads though, and right now, I was thinking that might be what it took.

"She did call you the hot one," he said.

Why had Thatcher told him that? Yeah, she'd called me hot more than once, and maybe I liked it, but that was it.

"Because I am," I replied.

Sebastian chuckled. "King's the hot one, but now that he's married off and a daddy, I'm gonna have to say I get that title now."

"Keep dreaming," I drawled. "When it comes to the Shephard brothers, it's Thatcher who gets the pussies wet."

"Sure, the fucked-up ones with daddy issues. They're into psychos."

"They all got daddy issues," I told him, barely glancing up in his direction. "Learn to slap an ass until it's red and how to call them ugly names, then you might be competition for your big brother."

He sighed. "There is so much truth to that, that I won't argue."

With a smirk, I sent a text to Laurel. She was a strawberry-blonde who served drinks at the strip club we went to in Atlanta regularly. Close enough to red. It wasn't the dark copper of Briar's hair, but in the dark, that didn't really matter. I headed for the door.

"Where are you going?" Sebastian called out.

"To get my dick sucked."

"Wait up! You headed to the club?"

"Yeah," I replied, not stopping.

"Let me check on the new jockey, and I'll go with you."

"Hurry," I shot back as I stopped at my leather jacket I'd left hanging on the hook and took out my pack of Reds before heading to the truck outside.

I'd get my fill of tits and ass while sinking my dick in a couple of mouths and pussies. This Briar Landry shit in my head would be forgotten by the time the sun came up tomorrow.

Lighting up the cigarette I'd stuck between my lips, I waited for Sebastian to talk to the jockey. He needed to speed this shit up. I wasn't in the mood to get stuck in rush-hour traffic. Leaning against the truck, I crossed my ankles and inhaled deeply. If only this took the edge off like it once had. Now, it was only a habit.

Sebastian tilted his head, and I could see a smile curl his lips. He was fucking flirting. Shaking my head, I finished the cigarette, then tossed it down before covering it with my boot.

Looking back out at Sebastian, I lifted my hands up and yelled, "You coming or not?"

He turned his head and looked over my way, then nodded.

Rolling my eyes, I jerked open the truck door and climbed inside. Sebastian and his Casanova ways were entertaining at times, but right now, I was ready to go. He loved charming a female almost as much as he loved fucking them. They always fell for his clean-cut look, love of books, how he could quote lines from literature, his expensive sports cars, and how he gave them his complete attention. Knowing the bastard was just trying to fuck them.

He said his goodbyes to the jockey and jogged toward the truck. She must not be pretty enough to keep his attention if he still wanted to go to the club. Rolling down the window, I lit up another cigarette as he climbed in the passenger seat.

"Not gonna fuck that one, huh?" I asked.

He shrugged. "No, not that one. She's not worth pissing Dad off."

I nodded. Smart. If she was that good with Bloodline that King was impressed, then Sebastian fucking her and tossing her would end up with us losing a jockey. It wouldn't be the first time it had happened.

"Is she hot enough to get Thatcher's attention? Because he won't give a rat's ass about pissing off your dad."

Sebastian chuckled. "Not Capri. He'd never go there. She's not his type."

Now, he had my attention.

"You know her?"

He shrugged. "Not really. She's our age, and she grew up in town, but she was homeschooled. Her dad is the minister at the Methodist church. I dated a friend of hers once years ago. Anyway, she's the religious sort. She does volunteer work, sings at her church in the choir and shit. Real sweet though."

I grinned and took another pull from the cigarette. He was right. Thatcher and his demons wouldn't get anywhere near her. She'd try to pray for his soul or some shit. The idea was funny though.

• ELEVEN •

"I see it's real nice and friendly down here in Miami."

BRIAR

This was my first night playing at my new job. We'd made it to Miami two weeks ago, and I'd decided, for now, we needed to stay here, where hiding was easy. Dovie was tucked safely in our new apartment; although it didn't have a security guard, it was in a nice area. There was a burger place right across the street in a little shopping complex that also had a bookstore. Dovie loved going to eat there, and then we'd go to the bookstore, where she would spend hours.

The stack of bills that Bash had given me came to three thousand two hundred dollars. Way more than he'd owed me, and I would pay him back. It had given me time to get settled in with Dovie and make sure staying here was the right move. I could already tell that the beach bar I had gotten a job at got a lot of bikers. The place was nice. Clean and classy even. The fact that it was full of mostly bikers was odd, but this was Miami, and life was different down here.

Paradise Brew also didn't sound like a place where men and women in leather and tattoos wanted to hang out. Pepper Abe was the owner, and although she was young and attractive, she was feisty. I'd seen her talk to some of these rough-looking men like they were children. I liked her. She had their respect, and I would be lying if I said I wasn't envious of her. No one treated her like she was just a piece of ass they wanted to own or control. They treated her as if she were an equal.

I wondered how she did that. She was a beautiful woman, and men had to see that. I wished I knew her trick. She owned and ran a bar on the beach. Yep, in my next life, I wanted to be Pepper Abe. Someone who didn't get by on their looks.

"It'll be a packed house tonight. Saturdays are always big. The Judgment comes in and fills the place up. Your tips should be great. The boys are good about tipping," Pepper said, walking backstage with a bottle of water in her hand that she held out to me.

"What's The Judgment?" I asked, confused.

She waved a hand. "Sorry. I forget you're new to town. The Judgment MC. They're a biker club. The biggest one in Florida."

My eyes widened. "Like a real biker club?" I asked.

She grinned. "Yeah, but you'll be fine. There isn't a one of them that would cause any trouble here. Sure, they're gonna make a few catcalls and stupid shit like that because, well, you're stunning, but Micah, my older brother, is their VP, and he'd have their head on a stick if they even tried. When he and his wife, Dolly, get back from their trip to Europe, you'll meet them. Now, if you need anything, just let me know. Give me a wave, whatever."

I felt better about this biker thing now that I knew they weren't about to stand up and start shooting at each other. Her brother was their VP. That explained her clientele.

She gave me a thumbs-up and turned to leave. I picked up my guitar. Pepper had said she didn't mind if I used my own, and I was looking forward to playing onstage with it again. Opening the water, I took a long drink as I listened to Pepper announce tonight's entertainment.

There were some cheers and a few shouts about how it'd better not be Swift-type shit from some deep, rough-sounding voices, but Pepper simply told them to shut up and stop being dicks or she'd remind them where the exit was.

I was nothing like Swift, but that didn't mean I was against her music. She was incredibly talented. I'd just grown up listening to Loretta Lynn, June Carter, Tanya Tucker, Tammy Wynette, and of course Dolly Parton. I was country to my roots, but not the way most country singers were today. There was a twang in my voice that I didn't try to change.

Taking a deep, steady breath, I slid the strap of my Fender over my shoulder and made my way out the door and up onto the stage. At first, the place went silent, and I knew this was my cue to take control of the room.

"Hey, y'all," I said, smiling out at the mix of bikers, some business-looking people, and possibly some vacationers.

It was definitely heavy on the folks with leather vests on though. Several shouted out different greetings. There was one marriage proposal by a biker, and someone else yelled out their number.

"I see it's real nice and friendly down here in Miami," I said, using my flirting skills as I ran my fingers over the strings. "I grew up in the deep South, if my accent didn't already give that away, and my favorites are the classics. But I'm also open to requests, so feel free to come right on up with one at any time. But to get us started, I'll pull one out that I think can get any crowd warmed up."

More shouts and whistles. I blocked it easily enough as I strummed the first chord of "Coal Miner's Daughter." By the time I was on the second line of the song, three couples had made their way out to the dance floor. Smiling, I lifted my eyes to look back at Pepper, who stood at the bar with her arms crossed over her chest, grinning. She gave me a nod and held up the glass of beer in her hand.

I was gonna be okay here.

When I had walked in a week ago and asked to speak to the manager and Pepper walked out, I'd been worried. I wasn't used to working with women. Men I could get to do things easily. But women were another thing. Pepper didn't hire me immediately, like most men did. She walked to the back and brought a guitar out, then handed it to me.

"Show me what you got," she'd said and stood back, waiting on me to do just that.

I'd been so surprised at first, but it only took me a moment to gather myself. When I started singing, her eyes lit up. I felt a real sense of accomplishment. When she'd hired me, it had been because of my voice, not my looks. There was a power in that. One I wasn't used to.

I moved on to "Before He Cheats," "Jolene," "My Church," "Strawberry Wine," "Suds in the Bucket," and then finished the first set with "Mama Tried." When I stepped back, the bar erupted in clapping and shouting.

"I'll be back shortly. It's time for a drink," I said over the noise and turned to head down the stairs.

Pepper came walking through the crowd, looking thrilled.

I hadn't let her down, and it felt really good.

When she reached me, she put her arm around my shoulders. "Dear God, woman, you can sing. You were good when you sang for me last week, but seeing you work a crowd like that? You held back on me. Just wow. Come on. Drinks on me," she said, leading me through the crowd and shoving at a few arms of men who tried to come close enough to talk to me. They all obeyed her too.

"What's your poison?" she asked me as we reached the bar.

I normally only drank water since I had to drive, but it was early, and just one wouldn't hurt. I felt like celebrating. "Jack Daniel's," I told her.

"On the rocks?"

I nodded.

She turned to the bartender. "Fix her up."

Then, she looked back at me. "That hip thing you do and the way you walk around the stage, batting those lashes of yours, is a talent I want. You are a complete package up there."

I laughed at her description. I'd never really had female friends in my life. Or any friends really. I moved too much. Dovie was my only friend and family.

"Thanks," I replied. "I guess I don't see myself that way."

Pepper raised her eyebrows. "What way?"

I shrugged. "Like you're describing."

"Have you looked in a mirror? Should we go do that now?"

I laughed again, feeling embarrassed. "No. I … I'm aware of how I look. I just haven't ever thought about the other stuff being … that impressive. I love music. Singing, playing the guitar. Writing songs. But that doesn't make me good at it. I mean, I can carry a tune but …"

Pepper picked up our drinks from the bar and handed me one. "I'm going to have someone video it. You need to see yourself. You are too good to be singing at my little bar, but I'll keep you! I might have a riot from this bunch if I talk you into going somewhere else. And as for those songs you write, why don't you sing them here?"

"Hey, Pep, we expecting problems?" a burly man with a leather vest, tattoos, and long hair in a ponytail asked as he stepped up in front of us, stopping me from having to answer that question.

I wasn't ready to sing my original stuff here just yet. I wanted to get the feel of things first.

Pepper set her drink down and straightened. "No. Why?"

He nodded his head toward the door. "Couple of Hughes men just walked in."

Pepper visibly relaxed, and she let out a sigh. "Probably here for a drink," she replied. "Must have business in town."

She took my arm. "I don't want to leave you here to get proposed to and mauled. Come with me. I need to go greet our honored guests," she said the latter with sarcasm.

I walked with her over to the three men who were taking a seat at a table toward the middle of the room. It was as if the rest of the crowd had backed away to give them plenty of space. Were they cops? I studied them. One was huge. Tall with wide shoulders. The other two weren't as large, but one of them was covered in tattoos and looked more like the bikers here, where the other two stood out.

"Huck Kingston," she said, and my ears instantly perked up. "Didn't know you were in town. Hope it's for pleasure and you're not about to do something that'll make a mess in my bar."

The massive man turned. His eyes went from Pepper to me, and then they narrowed before he looked back at Pepper. "Not today," he replied. "Stopped by as a favor to my cousin. We were in town, and he asked me to check out things here." His eyes swung back to me.

Cousin. He was Storm's cousin. Kingston. But how had he known I was here? Fucking Mafia.

I stepped forward and smiled a little too brightly. "Y'all are just everywhere, aren't you? I can't seem to get free of you. Tell Storm that I am just fine, but thanks for stalking me so efficiently."

Huck cocked an eyebrow as he studied me for a moment. "Huh," he said, then shook his head before looking back at Pepper. "Seems I misunderstood the reason I was asked to stop by. I wasn't given all the details. We'll have a round and whatever special you have tonight in the kitchen."

Pepper looked at me, then nodded. "All right then. Kye, Six, good to see you both. How's that baby boy of yours, Kye?"

The blond guy grinned. "He's fucking awesome."

Pepper chuckled. "Glad to hear it. I'll fix y'all up with the best we got in the back tonight."

She nodded her head for me to follow her as she moved from the table. When we were far enough away, she leaned close to me. "How do you know them?"

"Who? The Mafia? Because technically, I don't know those guys, but I know the cousin he's referring to. He's in Georgia though. I assume those guys are here in Florida."

Pepper nodded. "Yeah. So, you aren't in trouble with them, are you? Because if so, I know someone who can fix it. I've got connections to the boss, and when I say boss, I mean, THE BOSS. The one who runs all of the Southern Mafia. The Florida branch is the main one. It's run by Blaise Hughes, and he controls the entire bunch. Even those hotheads in Louisiana."

How many states was the Southern Mafia in? They were clearly larger than I'd realized. Maybe I should have gone north. I wonder how far north I'd have to go to get away from them.

I shook my head. "No. I've done nothing to any of them. They just wanted a man dead, and he was already dead. King Salazar isn't sure I'm telling the truth, so he's watching me."

Pepper's gaze watched me steadily. "You're not hiding anyone from them, are you?"

"No. The man they want dead is very dead. I would have happily handed him over to them if he were alive. He was a sick bastard."

She took a deep breath. "All right. But you're sure he's dead? You've seen his dead body? Because you do not want them to think you're lying to them."

I swallowed hard and glanced around before looking back at her. "He's dead."

"How did you know him? Why did they come after you to find him?"

I wished she'd let this go, but she was being careful. Making sure I wasn't about to be an issue for her. I understood that. "He was my father."

She sucked in a breath. "But you wanted him dead?"

I nodded.

"You can see why they might not believe you though, and if he's not dead—"

"*I* killed him, Pepper."

She stared at me for several moments, and I knew my admission might get me fired. I waited, and she finally let out a long breath.

"Well, okay then." She blinked a few times. "It's time to get back up there."

I didn't move. "You aren't firing me?"

She frowned. "Why would I do that?"

I wanted to laugh, but I didn't. "Because of what I just told you."

Pepper pointed her finger and swung it around the room. "I grew up with this. Bikers. My dad was one. My brother is one. You killed a man who deserved it. Not a reason for me to fire you. Clearly, you can hold your own, and that's good to know."

TWELVE

"No man drives over ten hours for tomatoes."

STORM

There was no fucking reason I should be here. Not one. King wasn't asking, and he hadn't even mentioned anything about her in the past two weeks since Huck had come to check things out. To see if this was in fact where Briar Landry was working. When he'd gotten her location, it had been too close to coincidental that of all the bars in Miami, Briar had found herself a gig at Pepper Abe's place.

Pepper's connection to Blaise Hughes was through her brother and Blaise Hughes's father-in-law, the president of The Judgment MC. When Blaise had hooked up with his now wife, it had been a given that The Judgment was now under the family's protection. They'd been a powerful MC before, but with Blaise standing behind them, they were now untouchable on both sides of the law.

Huck had found no reason for concern and even suggested Pepper seemed protective of Briar. Was there no one that woman couldn't charm? Jesus, she was dangerous and sexy as fuck. No, I wasn't going there. She wasn't using that voodoo shit on me. Reeling me in and choking me out. The line of men she'd wrung dry and walked away from was probably endless.

I should turn and go back to Georgia. Standing outside Paradise Brew, I glared at the building as if it had offended me just by being here. She was in there. The tracker on her car had brought me here, and it was currently parked in the back. I hadn't told anyone where I was going. If they knew, I'd never hear the end of it. Especially from Thatcher. Even though the fucker would have come with me if he'd known.

I swung my gaze over the parking lot. So many damn bikes. Harleys mostly, but there were a few Indian Chiefs and one Black Shadow, which surprised me. Pulling out a cigarette, I stuck it between my teeth and lit it. I'd driven six hundred fifty miles. I was going in that damn bar, but not yet. First, I had to take the edge off and figure out why the fuck I'd gotten in my Jeep and driven south at four this morning. I'd checked into a hotel, taken a shower, and tried to talk myself into not doing this. It had failed.

Telling myself it was because I wanted to be sure Briar wasn't using people that the family protected wasn't a lie. But I knew I was also worried she was gonna fuck with the wrong man here and get a bullet between her eyes. Why had she had to come here? And to a damn biker bar? Was she asking for more trouble? I wasn't her keeper, and I hated the fact that I couldn't seem to shut it off.

"You standing outside my bar, looking at it like you might just burn it down, for a reason?"

Turning, I saw Pepper Abe walking toward me in a pair of tight jeans, boots, and a black halter top. She might look like a pretty picture, but I knew just how lethal she was. She'd been raised around bikers.

"How you doing, Pepper?" I asked, finishing up the cigarette.

She cocked an eyebrow at me. "I'm just fine. Saw you in my security cameras and thought to myself, *Looks like Storm Kingston might be lost*. This is a long way from Madison."

I smirked and dropped the butt of my Red before stepping on it. "Or I might just be wanting some of those fried green tomatoes you serve up here."

She let out an amused laugh. "Bullshit. No man drives over ten hours for tomatoes. But my entertainment now, I can see how she could bring a man that far away from home. What you got going on with Briar? First Huck, now you."

I rolled my eyes and shook my head. "Not got shit going on with her. Just making sure she's not causing problems here."

The corner of Pepper's mouth lifted, showing a dimple. "Is that so? Well, seeing as she has brought in a crowd every night she's been here, my sales are up almost forty-five percent, and the tips that these fuckers are dishing out to not only her, but also my servers, I'd say she's the opposite of trouble."

Of course she's got the business up. I'd witnessed her perform. Still burned in my damn head.

"She's good at what she does. Manipulative, charming. You can't trust her."

Pepper visibly tensed. "Sounds like someone is bitter. What, she didn't fall for your lines? Left town before you got her in your bed?"

Not an image I needed. Briar in my bed was one I'd let myself imagine more than once.

"My pockets aren't deep enough for her, and I'm not married. I'm not her type."

Pepper let out a bark of laughter. "Oh, your pockets are deep. Can't bullshit me on that. With more money and power than any one man needs. But sounds like you're calling Briar a gold digger, and if that were the case, she'd have latched on to you real damn quick."

"You don't know her," I clipped.

"No. Seems *you* don't know her," she said, then pointed a red fingernail at me. "Stay the fuck out of my bar if you're going in there to upset my entertainment."

I should leave. Get back on the road and head north.

"Just stopping by for a drink and food," I replied.

She looked at me as if she didn't believe me.

"I swear I'm not here to cause a problem."

With a rise and fall of her shoulders, she gave me one last once-over. "Fine. Keep it that way. Either go inside or leave. Stop standing outside like some psycho."

I held up my hands. "Going inside," I assured her before starting toward the entrance.

She didn't follow me, and I glanced back to see her walking back around the building, where she'd emerged from.

When I reached the heavy wooden double doors, I pushed the right side open, and before I even stepped inside, I heard her. That voice. She was singing familiar lyrics that I'd never heard a woman sing. She changed the "her" to "he" as her smooth Southern voice, with just the right amount of country twang, sang about whiskey glasses.

The dance floor was covered with couples, tables were full, and the place was fucking packed. My gaze did a quick sweep of the room before they locked on the stage. Briar was grinning at some stupid fucker as she did a slow roll of her hips before moving to the other side as if she owned the room and knew it. From what I could see, she was right. I stood there, unable to take my eyes off her. It had been almost eight months since I'd seen her perform. Just like the first time, I was completely captured and wishing like fuck I weren't.

"Mr. Kingston?" a female voice said beside me.

"Yeah?" I replied, not taking my eyes off Briar.

"Pepper sent me to show you to a table."

Of course she had. Probably in the back, behind a wall. I nodded and tore my gaze off Briar for a moment to see a petite blonde with her hair high in a ponytail, wearing the same black crop top Pepper was with the words *Paradise Brew* stretched over her chest. She did a small pucker with her red-painted lips, and I knew she was trying to draw attention to them.

"Thanks," I said, then turned back to see Briar finish the song.

The moment her eyes locked on me, I saw the smile on her face falter only slightly.

I gave her a small tilt of my head, then smirked, unable to stop myself. I'd shaken her up by being here. Why did that feel so damn good?

" 'Girl Crush,' " someone shouted from the crowd.

Briar quickly recovered from seeing me, and that smile of hers that could make anyone lose focus spread over her face. "All right then," she replied. "One more for this set, and then I gotta get me a drink, y'all."

"I got you a drink right here, baby!" some fucking biker called out.

She winked in his direction before she slid the guitar off her shoulders and set it in a stand, then walked over to a keyboard I hadn't noticed sitting to the left of the stage behind her. She could play the fucking piano too? I stopped following the waitress as I waited to see just how well Briar could play yet another instrument.

Her fingers began to slide over the keys, and the music filled the place just before she leaned forward and began singing in her thick, sexy voice. Her eyes closed as she continued, and the rest of the place went silent. As if they were all afraid they'd miss something. I watched those pink lips and her bare, tanned shoulder lift as she felt the music.

"Jesus," I muttered.

"Mr. Kingston?" the waitress said, touching my arm and reminding me that I was supposed to be following her to my table.

I jerked my eyes off Briar and blinked, trying to refocus from whatever haze she'd just put me in. "Sorry," I told the girl waiting on me.

She gave me a tight smile. "No worries. She's good."

Good wasn't the right word for it. Fucking magical was more accurate, but I didn't say that. I remained silent as I followed her to the table that was empty, right in the middle of tables covered up with bikers.

Well played, Pepper.

"What can I get you to drink?" the blonde asked as I took a seat.

"Maker's, straight," I replied.

She nodded and turned to head back to the bar. My eyes swung back to the stage just as Briar stepped down and made her way into the crowd. I didn't have to see her to know she was headed to me. Probably pissed off, and I realized I was looking forward to it. She'd be brave here with all her fans surrounding her. That mouth of hers snapping off at me. Forgetting the performance I'd just witnessed was going to be a slight inconvenience.

• THIRTEEN •

"I'm not ole-lady material."

BRIAR

What the hell was Storm doing here? It wasn't like I'd done anything wrong. I hadn't even started dating anyone. The money coming in from the tips and my cut of the house take on nights I worked was the best I'd ever made. Sure, it wasn't what I would get from a wealthy asshole, but this was enough for now. Dovie was happy here. I had more time with her. We could go out and not worry about being seen. I wasn't going to mess this up.

Trying to keep a smile and respond to the customers as I walked through them to get back to the table I had seen him sit at was difficult. I was on a mission, and until I knew the reason Storm was here, I wasn't in the mood to chat.

"I want to hear that song you sang last Friday. The one you wrote," a woman said from the lap of Country, one of The Judgment members.

I'd seen her here before, but I didn't know her name. Country had a new one with him every week. It was hard to keep up.

" 'Tangled,' " the woman across from her said.

"All right," I replied while still moving.

"You think about that marriage proposal?" Tex, another Judgment guy, asked as I passed him.

I patted his chest. "I'm not ole-lady material. I told you that." I was learning their lingo as well as their names.

His hand came over mine, holding it to his impressive pecs. "Don't know until you try."

I laughed, pulling my hand free and shaking my head. "Not tonight, Tex."

"Leave her be, Tex!" Pepper shouted out from the bar.

I managed to smile and nod at the next few before I finally got to the table where Storm sat, leaning back in his chair with a glass of whiskey in one hand and the other crossed over his chest, watching me.

Let the wet panties commence. Damn him and his sexy-ass face.

Might as well get this over with. He'd come over six hundred miles for a reason.

Pulling out a chair across from him, I took a seat just as Pepper appeared at my side, setting my ice water down in front of me.

"You got time to talk to this one?" she asked me point-blank.

I lifted my eyes to her and nodded. "Yeah."

She swung her eyes to Storm. "Keep it quick. She's got another set in fifteen, and she needs a break."

Storm looked amused but nodded his head once before those hazel eyes of his shifted back to me. He lifted his hand to place the glass to his lips and took a sip, his eyes never leaving me. I fought the urge to squirm in my seat. Even his hands were sexy. Large, veiny, tanned. I bet they were rough from working with the horses.

"You got Pepper fooled real nice, don't you?" he drawled, breaking the silence.

I glared at him, no longer focused on his hands. "What do you want, Storm? Or did you just come here to degrade me and call me names? I'd have thought by now, that would have gotten old. Lost its entertainment value."

He chuckled and set his glass down, then leaned forward, putting his elbows on the table. "Just thought I'd come to make sure you're not fucking over a friend."

I leaned forward and narrowed my eyes. "I'm an excellent employee."

The corner of his mouth twitched. "Until you get what you want and bolt."

Inhaling sharply, I moved back some, not liking how close we were. I could smell him, and he smelled damn good. I didn't need that reminder.

"What I want is for you to leave me alone. I'm aware how Pepper is connected to … y'all. And I assure you that I want no trouble with any of you. If you'd all stop showing up here and let me just get on with my life, that would be great."

A twenty-dollar bill landed on the table in front of me. I lifted my eyes to see Brick, one of the larger members of The Judgment, standing there, looking down at me.

"My ole woman wants you to sing 'Stand by Your Man.'"

Goldie, his wife, was one of my favorite women in The Judgment. She was friendly, bubbly, and always smiling. The two of them didn't seem like they fit. He was so grumpy, and she was the complete opposite. But when he looked at her, the worship in his gaze was clear. I had found myself longing for that more than once. To have a man look at me that way. I'd never know what it felt like, but I couldn't help the way my heart squeezed when I saw them together.

"First one I'll sing in the next set," I told him, but moved the twenty back toward him. "No need for this. I'll happily do it for Goldie."

"Take it," he said with a bark to his tone I was used to.

"I don't—"

"I said, take it," he interrupted me, turning and walking off.

With a sigh, I took the twenty and folded it up before looking back at Storm. He seemed to be trying to read my thoughts with the way his eyes were locked on me so intently.

"What?" I snapped.

He took another drink, then licked his bottom lip. "Just trying to figure out why you didn't snatch up that money since that seems to be your goal in life."

My stomach twisted as a sour feeling burned my throat. Why did I let this man and his hateful words bother me so much? He wasn't important to me, and I didn't need his approval.

I pushed back my chair and stood up, tucking the twenty into my pocket. "If that is all you need, then I'll be heading on back. Don't choke on your food," I said, getting the hell away from him before he could say anything more.

I couldn't go onstage angry. I had to get away from everyone and calm down before I had to walk back out there.

He was gone before my next set ended. Thankful that I didn't have to feel his judgmental, disgusted gaze on me, I began to enjoy the night. I had even done two of my own songs and put my backup drum track on for "Honky Tonk Women," which had the entire place cheering and filling the dance floor.

By the time I finished my last set, it was almost one. Pepper sent her guys through doing last call and clearing the place out as I took my tip jar and went through straightening and counting the money backstage. It had been a good night if you left out the fact that Storm had shown up to try and ruin things.

Heels on the hardwood floor caught my attention, and I looked up to see Pepper walk around the corner. She was smiling, clearly pleased with the night's success. By my third set, the kitchen had run out of fried pickles, fries, and tonight's special—the pulled pork coleslaw burger.

She held up a roll of bills. "This was left for you," she said, then held it out.

Reaching out, I took what looked like a hundred-dollar bill wrapped around a few more bills. Curious, I unrolled it to find there were five hundreds. Frowning, I looked up at her. "I think someone made a mistake."

She shook her head. "Don't think so. It's a hundred for every set tonight."

I looked back at the money. "This can't be a tip."

"Oh, but it is, and you're taking it."

"Who in their right mind would leave me this kind of tip?"

Pepper sat down beside me on the edge of the back of the stage, then crossed her legs. "One Storm Kingston."

"*What?*" I asked incredulously. "He left during my second set. This can't be from him." Then there was the fact that he hated me.

"It's from him. He put it in my hands himself. Said to make sure you got it. And he didn't leave during your second set. He just moved to the back."

"What back?"

I could see the entire room from the stage. If he'd been in the back, I would have seen him.

"My office. He watched from the screens, and before you say anything, I let him because he had left you five hundred dollars. Not to mention the way he was looking at you like you were his favorite snack."

I let out a laugh. "Storm hates me. Loathes me. This?" I held up the money. "This was some kind of bribe to get you to let him back there." I stood up, starting to seethe. "He's up to something. He doesn't want me here. I don't think he even wants me breathing and walking the earth. But mark my words: This money was not for me. It was for something else."

Pepper leaned forward, resting her elbows on her thighs as she studied me. "You sure about that? Because I'm real damn good at reading men, and that one couldn't take his eyes off you."

"I am positive. All he did was make degrading comments when we spoke. I don't know why he was here, but it wasn't for me." Then, I held up the money. "And I don't want this. Take it." I shoved it into her hand and bent down to pick up the real tips I'd made.

I was going home to take a hot bubble bath and drink an entire bottle of wine.

"I'm not keeping this money. If you won't take it, I'll make sure he gets it back," she said slowly, then stood up. "If you're sure."

I nodded emphatically. "Very!"

"Go on home. Get some rest. You were incredible tonight," she told me.

"Thanks. I need to go grab my things from the dressing room, and then I'll head out. See you in two days," I said, lifting a hand in a small wave.

"Drive safe," she replied, then turned and walked back toward the bar with the five hundred dollars Storm had left me.

Asshole. Why would he do that? How was that supposed to insult me? I knew he'd had a purpose, but for the life of me, I couldn't figure it out.

Taking my time, I got my things together, downed a bottle of water, made sure my tips were safely tucked in my purse, and slid my gun into the waist of my jeans before heading for the side door. Not that I'd ever had trouble here, but it was best to be safe. The front door would be locked, and I was parked closer to the front of the side entrance. The door wasn't locked yet, but I knew at least two of The Judgment guys would stay until Pepper was locked up and safely in her car, headed home. I had yet to meet her older brother, but I already knew he was very protective of her. His club made that very clear with the way they all seemed to be her personal bodyguards.

Stepping outside, I started toward my car when the dark figure leaning against it caused me to freeze. My hand went to the butt of my gun just as the man's head turned, and the moonlight hit Storm's face. Relief and annoyance collided into me as my hand let go of my gun, dropping back to my side.

"That's a real good way to get shot," I called out, not moving in his direction.

"I took my chances," he replied, staying there against my car as if he owned it.

I had to get in my car to leave. His blocking me was one more strike against him tonight.

"What do you want, Storm? To call me some more names? Please get it over with so I can go home," I said, then started heading in his direction again.

"You refused my tip," he said as I got closer.

"That wasn't a tip. No one tips that much. It was some weird, twisted thing that I can't figure out the purpose of at the moment, but I'm tired, and you are standing in the way of me and a bubble bath."

He didn't move. Of course not. That would be the polite thing to do, but Storm was an asshole.

"You're talented. Real fucking talented. You should be making a hell of a lot more than that."

Okay. I paused. Was that a real compliment, or was he about to turn it around and make a snarky comment about me being a gold digger?

"You owned that crowd with ease, like nothing I'd ever seen. You should be packing out civic centers and football stadiums, not singing at bars."

Now, I was completely thrown off guard. He looked serious. But I knew better. He was leading up to something mean.

I shook my head and placed a hand on my hip. "Sure, I'm the next Taylor Swift. Now, can you move so I can go home?"

The corner of his full mouth tilted up, and his eyes seemed to heat. Even in the darkness, I could see them change. A stir in my stomach was followed by a flutter. I blinked, trying not to fall for this. He was going to slap me with something cruel at any moment.

Did he know I struggled with how gorgeous he was? That my stupid body reacted to him even though my head knew better? God, I hoped not.

"Your problem is, you don't see it," he said, pushing away from the car and taking a step toward me, closing the distance. "All you see is what the mirror and men tell you. That you're stunning. Men throw themselves at you. But your looks have nothing on that voice."

When was he going to lay the smackdown and tell me I was a slut or whore or whatever? I was in need of that right now because the way he was making me feel, all warm and needy, was not good. I was letting my guard down, and that was a big no-no.

I swallowed hard and tried to take a step back, but my legs wouldn't move. They were glued to the ground they stood on. Every breath I took, his scent filled my senses, making it hard to concentrate.

"You want millions, then make them. Use that talent of yours and be an independent woman who makes her money honestly."

His voice was deep and husky, but the words were what snapped me out of whatever this was. He lifted his hand and ran a finger down the side of my cheek, trailing along my jawline, then into my hair. I was trembling. Damn this man.

Reaching up, I wrapped my hand around his wrist and pulled at it, trying to get it off me. His arm flexed, but that was the only sign that he even acknowledged my attempt at removing his hand.

"I'm sure that between those smooth, silky thighs is the hottest, sweetest pussy I've ever tasted," he said as his fingers tightened in my hair, slightly pulling it with the action.

I stared up at him and watched his jaw clench as he held me there.

"This goddamn face," he snarled angrily. "No man should have to endure this kind of temptation."

"I'm not ..." My words came out in a breathy gasp, but I wasn't sure what it was I meant to say.

Every time he tugged at my hair, the area between my thighs he'd mentioned throbbed.

"You're not what?" he asked in a sardonic tone, tilting his head to one side.

I opened and closed my mouth. I was struggling to keep a clear thought. He took a step closer, and then with a hard jerk of my hair, he turned me around until my back was against the car, and he was towering over me. A cry left me from the pain, but he didn't ease up his hold. I felt his hand slide over my waist and slowly toward my back, making my knees weak from the rough feel of his callous palm. When the heavy metal from my gun was eased out, I tensed as fear began to slip into this needy lust haze he'd pulled me into.

My eyes followed his hand as he took my gun and placed it on the hood of my car behind me.

"You didn't answer my question," he said, cupping the side of my face gently before gripping my chin almost too roughly. His heated gaze stared down at my mouth as his hold got tighter. "I hate this mouth," he growled. "It's too goddamn full and pink. Always so *fucking pink*. Taunting me. Making me ache to see these fat lips wrapped around my cock while I hear you choke on it."

A whimper escaped me. My body felt like it was on fire. This was not normal, and what he was doing wasn't okay. No man had ever talked to me like this. Yes, he was being a little too rough, but it was just enough to cause excitement. The edge of fear only seemed to heighten the emotion.

I should stop him. Scream. Get away. But my body was completely against that course of action. My panties were soaked, and I was aching so badly that I was having to fight myself to keep from rubbing against him.

"I want to kill. Rip off heads. Slice off every fucking dick that's getting off right now to thoughts of you," he snarled, tightening his hold on my hair even more, then pulling my head back so that my neck was exposed and he was all I could see.

Sucking in a breath, I trembled as he stepped closer to me, letting go of my chin and running his hand down the front of my chest, stomach, going until he found the edge of my miniskirt. My mouth fell open on a gasp as his hand shoved between my thighs, and two fingers slid inside my panties. Both my knees buckled, and I moaned from the sheer pleasure. The ache that had built was now a pulsing need.

"That's a real fucking wet cunt." He lowered his head until his forehead was resting against mine. "All that for me? Does a little pain make this pussy cream? Hmmm?"

The two fingers he slid over my slick folds thrust inside me hard, and I grabbed both his arms as a cry ripped from me. My hips rocked against his hand, wanting his fingers deeper. Needing them to move. To fuck me.

"That's it, little siren. Lead me to my own fucking destruction." His voice was hoarse, and I could hear his fast and heavy breathing. He wanted this too.

"You'd like to ride my cock like that, wouldn't you? I'd split you in two," he said just as his teeth grazed my neck. "This pussy is too tight. You've not had a real man's dick inside you."

He bit down then on the tender skin at the curve of my neck. The sharp sting only seemed to make me crazier.

"Oh God," I breathed, bucking harder against him.

"Not even close," he replied before he began to lick where he'd bitten.

Staring up at the sky, I was helpless to whatever this man wanted to do to me. The orgasm building inside me was growing stronger, and it was all that mattered. His mouth moved over my heated skin. He didn't kiss me, but then he licked me like an animal. I wanted to feel him do that between my legs. Have him bite my thighs.

"Good little pussy," he groaned. "I bet you'd like to straddle my face and fuck it. Let my tongue lick that clit until you're screaming my name."

His free hand jerked my shirt up and tugged my bra down until my right breast was free. When his teeth clamped down on my nipple, I threw my head back as the climax consumed me. He started sucking hard, only making it prolong the blissful release that was coursing through me.

My nails were cutting into his biceps, I realized as I slowly began to come back to myself. The nighttime sky came into focus again, and Storm slid his fingers out of me. Part of me was horrified at what I'd just done, and the other part wanted to grab his hand and force it back between my legs for more.

I gulped in air, my eyes on him, not sure what he was going to do next. He lifted his two fingers to his mouth, then began to lick them slowly while his eyes stayed on me. Good God. I shuddered, feeling my body began to stir again.

When he finished licking them, he stuck them in his mouth and sucked hard. I made a sound. I thought it was a moan, but I couldn't be sure. I was completely focused on Storm sucking me from his fingers.

"Tight and sweet. Like honey. Maybe I was wrong after all. If you fuck anything like you just took my fingers, then perhaps that is your biggest talent."

My head jerked back as if he'd just slapped me, and he might as well have done just that. Grabbing my skirt, I shoved it back down and found my balance as I straightened.

"Bastard," I ground out as the shame of all I had just let him do to me sank in.

He chuckled. He actually fucking laughed.

"What? You use it for your gain all the time. I was just saying I understand it now. But then I didn't fuck you, so I can't be sure."

I was going to shoot him. "Shut up," I snapped, taking my gun from the car and jerking the door to my car open.

What had I been thinking? This man had never once been nice to me. But he could get me to ride his hand like a damn porn star in less than five minutes.

"Ah, little siren," he drawled. "Did you think that me getting a taste of that pussy was going to change my opinion of you?" He made a tsking sound. "Silly girl. I've had a lot of sweet pussy. Yours wasn't the first, and it won't be the last."

I hated him. I hated everything about him. Slamming the car door closed, I realized I was shaking as I put my foot on the brakes and pressed the button to turn it on. Never again. I would never ever get near him again. We wouldn't even breathe the same air.

Fool me once, shame on you. Fool me twice, and I'll cut your dick off. But it wouldn't come to that. Because he was dead to me.

FOURTEEN

We might need to get a new jockey.

STORM

"When are you going to tell me why you're in such a fucking bad mood?" Sebastian said, setting a beer down in front of me before he sat down on the sofa across from me with his own.

"I'm not in a bad mood," I replied, picking up the beer and taking a long pull from the bottle.

"Yeah, you are," he replied. "You've been snarling and scowling for three days."

I took another drink, not wanting to talk about this. He was right, but I wasn't going to admit it. If I did that, I would have to admit why, and I preferred to lie to myself. It was easier than remembering. That look on her face. Goddammit! I slammed my beer down with more force than necessary, and I could feel Sebastian's eyes on me. I'd just proven his point.

Shoving my fingers in my hair, I sighed heavily. "Guess I'm not sleeping great," I muttered.

"Yeah, sure, that's it. I mean, we often go forty-eight hours without sleep, and you always act like a complete asshole." Sarcasm dripped from his words.

I dropped my hands and leaned back on the sofa. Sebastian stared at me while he took a drink from his bottle. He was waiting on an explanation, and normally, I told him everything. Once, that had been Wells, but things had changed when we became adults, leaving our youth behind. Wells was self-absorbed, and the older we got, the more I realized he was never going to care about anything more than his own needs.

Sure, we would always be friends. We lived the same life. We'd grown up in it. But no one would ever be as important to Wells as he was to himself. It was hard to trust someone that was like that with your secrets. When life got real and our biggest problem wasn't stealing our dad's whiskey or getting laid, Sebastian and I had become tighter. If I was going into a dangerous situation and I had to choose, it would be Sebastian I wanted at my side.

"I'm messed up in the head about some shit. I'm working it out," I finally said, knowing he wasn't going to let this go.

He raised an eyebrow and took a sip. "That shit happen to be a smoking hot redhead?"

I cut my gaze from the bottle in my hand to him.

He shrugged. "Good guess?"

I shook my head and stood up. "No."

"Ah, denial. That's not gonna snap you out of beast mode. Admit it. Face it. Then figure out how to get over it or ... not."

I swung my eyes back to him. "What's that supposed to mean?"

Sebastian grinned. "Exactly what I said. Whatever happened on your little jaunt to Miami fucked with you. Accept whatever it was that happened and move on. If you can't move on, then go get some more."

He had no idea what he was talking about. He meant well, but he read too many fucking books. Life was more complicated.

"Nope," I replied as I started for the door again.

If I went to get some more, I wasn't sure I could stop. The image of Briar coming on my hand as her tight cunt squeezed my fingers with her orgasm was burned into my brain. The taste of her pussy was taunting me. Reminding me how much better it would be straight from the source. There was nothing as fucking beautiful as that woman getting off.

I was tense all over again. Thinking about her seemed to do that to me. The craving to go back to her, tie her up, and get my mouth all over her body was getting stronger with every breath I took. She'd probably point her gun at my head, and that image only made my cock harder.

Once I stalked outside, I took several deep breaths, trying to think about anything other than those blue eyes looking up at me, full of want. Hearing her sexy little cries and moans. MOTHERFUCKER! I closed my eyes tightly, fisting my hands at my sides, and willed myself to think of anything else.

Horses, knives, Maeme's fried chicken …

"Excuse me. Storm, right?" a female voice asked.

My eyes snapped back open to see the new jockey, Capri, I thought Sebastian had called her.

"Yeah?" I asked.

She jumped, and I realized I'd barked out the word. I hadn't meant to, but she needed to get tougher if she was gonna work here. I didn't have time to worry about some shy, soft-spoken minister's daughter.

"I, uh, I was wondering if you, knew, um …" She was stammering, and that just annoyed me more.

"I don't have all fucking day." The words came out before I could stop them.

Her eyes widened, and she paled. Sighing, I started to apologize when my entire body was shoved back against the wall with enough force to take my breath. My defense instincts immediately kicked in, and my hand was on the butt of my Glock when I realized who had just body-slammed me into a brick wall.

The unhinged gleam in Thatcher's eyes wasn't new. He always seemed a little unsettled, but right now, there was a feral threat in his expression that I'd never witnessed before.

What the fuck was wrong with him?

"Leave," he ground out in a hollow tone.

"You've got me up against the fucking wall, man. Where the hell you want me to go?"

"Thatch!" Sebastian's voice didn't mask his alarm.

No one wanted to set Thatcher off. We were never sure about what triggered him. When he'd been a teenager, he'd broken a guy's neck, and to this day, we didn't know why. He refused to tell anyone, and because of Stellan and the family, he hadn't gone to prison. But for a moment, he'd been real close to being put behind bars.

His hold on me eased, and I watched him closely, making sure he wasn't about to pull his gun or knife next.

He pointed toward the truck parked closest to us. "Leave," he repeated.

"Thatch, what the fucking hell, man?" Sebastian asked, sounding as confused as I was.

He shifted his crazed stare to his brother, then back to me. "Don't ever speak to her like that again."

Oh. Oh. *Oh fucking hell.* My eyes widened, and I simply nodded, not sure if saying what I was thinking would end up with him snapping my neck or slicing my throat.

"Thatcher?" The tiny, petite jockey called his name, and he tensed even more, then turned and stalked off. Not toward her, but in the direction of the main house.

"What did you say?" Sebastian asked me in a low voice, not wanting Thatcher to hear him and come back to finish what he had started.

I shrugged, then glanced over at the jockey, who was frozen in her spot. "I'm sorry," I told her. "I'm having a bad day, but I shouldn't have snapped at you."

She nodded, wringing her hands nervously in front of her. "It's fine. We all have bad days." The sincerity on her face was real. There was a kindness there. Sweet. She was sweet and innocent-looking.

I looked at Sebastian, and I could tell he was thinking the same thing I was. If Thatcher had some weird thing for her, then she was in deeper shit than any of us.

"Uh, Capri, do you know my brother? I mean, have you dealt with him while working here?" he asked her.

She was silent, and I could see the anxiety slowly creeping up into her features. She looked ready to run. This girl was not Thatcher's type. Not even close.

"Not much."

"Not much," Sebastian repeated, not sounding convinced.

She shook her head, then sighed as her shoulders dropped some. "We were friends once. It was a long time ago."

Sebastian's eyebrows flew up, and he pointed toward the direction Thatcher had gone. "You were friends with him? Thatcher? My crazy-as-fuck older brother?"

The clear disbelief in his tone echoed in my head as I stood there in shock.

She smiled then. A soft smile that lit up her face. It wasn't that she was plain or anything. She was pretty. The wholesome kind of pretty. But when she smiled, it transformed her face. The kind you stopped and looked twice at. Her eyes seemed to dance with amusement, as if she had some private joke that we weren't privy to.

"He's not crazy," she said. "Maybe a little intense at times."

"At times?" Sebastian asked, then let out a laugh.

She lifted her shoulders slightly. "Maybe it's you that doesn't know him."

"Sweetheart, I've lived with him my entire life. I know him better than anyone. And …" He paused and looked to make sure Thatcher was gone from sight before continuing, "He is an unpredictable, sadistic motherfucker. Whatever friendship you think you had with him once, forget it. Stay clear of him, okay? He's not stable. Never has been. Just stick to working with Bloodline and go back home. No interacting with him."

She nodded. "That's easy enough. He doesn't really talk to me."

Sebastian looked at me, then back at her. "He just slammed a friend against a fucking wall for snapping at you."

She sighed and held up her hands. "I have no clue why he did that. Like I said, he really doesn't speak to me. Our friendship was brief, and I thought he had forgotten about it and me … until that just happened."

We might need to get a new jockey. That would be easier than asking Thatcher about his connection to her. King was gonna be upset over it since he was so pumped this one was working out so well. But King could deal with Thatcher if he wanted to. He seemed to not fear him more than the rest of us.

She waved then, and I looked to see JB, one of our best stable hands, walking from the stables with one of the new thoroughbreds we were currently boarding. "There he is. I'm sorry about that," she said to me. "I need to go. That was who I was looking for."

We both stood there as she ran over to JB, who was grinning at her like a fucking idiot. That was a nightmare just waiting to happen. If I was right and Thatcher had any kind of thing for the sweet little jockey, JB's days might be numbered.

"You need to talk to your dad," I told Sebastian.

"No shit," he muttered. "Preferably before Thatcher kills JB."

"You don't think he's got a … thing for her? I mean, she's a minister's daughter, and she's … nice and good and shit."

Sebastian shook his head, still looking like he'd walked into the twilight zone. "I fucking hope not. For Capri's sake."

"And JB's," I added as they laughed, walking side by side out to the corral.

"That too," he agreed.

When he started in the direction of his house, I stood there, wondering how the hell this was gonna play out until my own problems came back to me. At least for a moment, I'd forgotten *her*.

FIFTEEN

"Save yourself. I'm vile."

BRIAR

Slowing the treadmill until I was no longer running, I reached for my water bottle and took a sip. I was slightly out of breath, but then I'd run harder the past few days and longer than I normally did. Glancing over at the kickboxing class happening in one of the other rooms in the gym, I wondered if I needed to try that. The more I exerted myself, the less energy I had to stew over Storm freaking Kingston.

Turning off the treadmill, I grabbed my towel and stepped off, drying the sweat from my face. I needed to get back up to our apartment and get a shower. Dovie and I had plans for dinner and a movie. One of the books she loved had just been released in the theaters, and she was pumped about it. We were going to go have some Thai, then head over for the late viewing. Having all these things so close to our apartment complex was nice. As was this gym, which came with the amenities.

"Excuse me," a deep voice said.

I dropped the towel from my face to find an attractive guy, about thirty maybe, with deep brown eyes, smiling down at me. He was tall. I liked tall. NO! I was off men. No more. They always led to me and Dovie running.

"Hello," I said, trying to be polite when I should just bolt.

"You're new here," he pointed out.

I nodded. "Yep."

His grin grew, and he looked a little shy, which I highly doubted. He was easy on the eyes with a nice body and clean-cut-looking, and I noticed two other women in the room watching us. He had a fan club, it would seem.

"I'm Ajani Michel. I live on the fourth floor," he said, holding out his hand.

I slipped mine into his and immediately thought about how much smaller his hand was than Storm's.

Not going there, Briar! Who cares how large that asshole's hand is or how it feels? UGH! Snap out of it.

"Briar Landry," I replied, leaving out that I lived on the second floor. Not his business. I didn't trust men. For good reason.

"There's no ring," he said as he glanced down at my hand, and I slipped it free.

I shook my head, giving him a tight smile. "Not made that mistake yet," I quipped. And I never would.

He chuckled. "Spoken like a man."

I shrugged. "Or a smart woman."

He laughed again. "Aside from your aversion to marriage, how do you feel about dinner? With me?"

And there it was. I had known it was coming. The interest was in his eyes.

"As nice as that sounds, I am currently off men and women. Dating in general."

He let out a deep sigh. "Damn. Bad experience?"

"You could say that," I replied.

He tilted his head to the side. "What about something less date-like? How do you feel about baseball?"

I licked my lips. "I feel like it's a good thing to watch when you want to go to sleep."

Another laugh.

Yes, I am a riot. Just laugh and continue to push this.

"Noted. No baseball. How about music? Concerts?"

He wasn't going to let this go, and I needed to get upstairs. My night was booked.

"You seem really nice, and"—I glanced around to see at least three women looking this way now—"there is a gym full of women who would be thrilled to go out with you. I bet they'd even sit through a baseball game, awake. But this one"—I pointed to myself—"is a mess. Complete disaster. I've got more baggage than anyone should have. The last five relationships I had were because the men were rich and I'm a gold digger. Run away, Ajani. Save yourself. I'm vile," I told him, then flashed him one real smile because I'd just made myself want to laugh before walking past him and toward the exit.

When I reached our apartment door, I pulled out the key and swiped it, then went inside. Dovie was already dressed in a pair of green shorts and a T-shirt that had *The Floor Is Lava* on the front. We'd bought it at a thrift store last summer. It was one of her favorites.

"I'll be ready in twenty minutes," I told her.

She held up the book in her hand to show me, which translated to, "I'm not in a hurry. I have a book to read."

"Okay, make that thirty then," I called out as I hurried to the bathroom.

We both knew that it was going to take me a solid forty minutes, but Dovie was good with the lie.

Dovie covered her mouth to keep from spitting her food and then coughed before taking a drink of her soda.

"I think it'll keep him away. Don't you?" I asked.

I had just told her about the man in the gym and what I'd said to him while she had a mouthful of pad thai in her mouth.

She swallowed, then signed, "What did he say next?"

"Nothing. I left him there before he could respond. But really, what could he say to that?"

Dovie's grin spread across her face as she twisted more noodles around her fork. She refused to eat her pad thai with chopsticks, no matter how hard I tried to convince her how much more fun it made the meal.

"I work Saturday night, of course, but I was thinking we'd drive to the beach that morning and do beachy things."

She laid her fork down and signed, "Beachy things?"

"Yes. Beachy things. Eat ice cream, lie out on the sand, eat seafood, go buy ugly shirts from the gift shops. The tie-dyed ones that match. That kind of thing."

She shook her head. "No to the shirts. But I like the other stuff."

"What about slightly tacky shirts that match?" I suggested.

She mouthed the word, *No*, then stuck a spoonful of noodles in her mouth.

"Oh, come on. Can you even say you've been to the beach if you don't buy the shirt? We can get cropped ones that are tacky and sexy. All at the same time."

She shook her head while she chewed.

"You used to be more fun," I told her. "You know, back before puberty hit."

She swallowed her food, then stuck out her tongue at me.

"It's true. Back in the day, when you'd wear matching shirts with me, dance in the car while going down the road, drink those slushies that turned our mouths blue. Those were the days."

She put her fork down, then signed, "I'll still drink the slushies."

I placed a hand over my heart dramatically. "Small blessings! We will go get one and take it to the movies with us."

She scrunched her nose at me. "Not there."

"See! I knew it! You will drink one, but you're too cool to let people see your blue mouth."

She was smiling as she stuck more pad thai in her mouth.

When I had first found her, she never smiled. I had worked so hard at getting her to smile. Then, one day, she broke out into a huge grin when we were in a Laundromat, washing what little clothes we had, and "Pump Up the Jam" came on the radio they had playing. I dropped the basket I was holding and grabbed Dovie's hand and spun her around, then began to dance. Sure, people stopped what they were doing to watch, but I didn't care.

Dovie watched me for a minute, and then she began smiling just before she started to dance with me.

It was a day I would never forget. I'd felt like I had done something of worth. I had unleashed Dovie's smile on the world.

"What are you thinking about?" she signed. "You got that far-off look on your face."

I leaned in toward her. "That dance party we had at the Laundromat that time. Do you remember?"

Her eyes lit up, and then she nodded.

"Want to have one now? I can put 'Pump Up the Jam' on my phone," I told her, holding it up and wiggling my eyebrows.

She grabbed my phone and tucked it in her pocket, shaking her head.

"You spoil all the fun," I grumbled, putting a bite into my mouth, but I was smiling.

If nothing else I did in this world was worth much, I knew I had done one thing right. I had given Dovie another life. It might not be the best one, but it was better than the one we'd both survived. And I'd do whatever I had to in order to make sure her future was nothing like mine. Which was why I had come up with an idea. One I hadn't thought of until two nights ago, when I'd overheard a conversation at the bar.

SIXTEEN

"I'd bet my left nut he's dead, and the songbird killed him, just like she said."

STORM

The blood on my hands wasn't mine. It rarely was. King tossed a towel toward me as I reached the Escalade. Catching it, I wiped myself clean.

Tonight was King's first time back doing the dirty work since his little girl had been born. He'd been different. There had been more caution in his actions when he'd once thought second, acted first. If Thatcher hadn't arrived with his reckless insanity, things could have gone bad.

"We weren't supposed to kill. Just warn," King said as Thatcher jerked open the passenger door to climb inside.

"You prefer I let them shoot your ass?" he asked in a sardonic tone.

He wasn't wrong.

This was supposed to have been a regular debt-collecting run. The Morse brothers owned a chain of service stations across Georgia and Alabama. They'd gotten in a bind financially, and one of their sons had gotten mixed up with a gang in Atlanta. When Joe Morse came to ask Stellan for help with both things, we stepped in for the price of four hundred grand. That money was due yesterday. They were given their warning by a call from Stellan. The twenty-four hours were up, and we came for the next step of the process. It was a more intense warning.

However, Joe Morse's two security men were flanking each side of the desk where he sat and pointed a gun at me and King. I was weighing the options, but my hand was on the butt of my Glock when Thatcher walked in, a pistol in each hand, taking out both men, then going straight up to Joe, not stopping until he had both barrels against his forehead.

Joe Morse was alive, but he'd cried, pissed his pants, and when we'd walked away, I'd heard him retching in his office.

The money was in a leather bag in the back of the Escalade, and our job was done, but there were two dead bodies left inside. I'd taken their guns from them and checked them for any wires, hence the blood on my hands.

"They weren't going to kill us. That would have been a deadly move on Morse's part, and he knew it," King argued. "Then, you came walking in like fucking Doc Holliday, both guns blazing, putting bullets between their eyes. Jesus, Thatch," he said angrily as he headed to the driver's seat.

"We got the money. Job done," Thatcher said, leaning back in his seat. "And since we're making comparisons, I thought it was more of a Wyatt Earp move than Doc."

"Doc Holliday was the psycho," King replied.

I kept my mouth shut.

King and Wilder Jones had grown up with Thatcher. They were as close as you could be to Thatcher, and they were the only two who talked to him like that. Sebastian did at times, but even his brother didn't push too hard. Seeing as how Wells, Sebastian, and I were the younger group, we had grown up tight, looking up to the older three, but not really in their circle of trust. Until we all took our place in the family. Still didn't make me or Wells comfortable with Thatcher.

Once I was settled in the back seat, I dropped the bloodstained towel in the black trash bag we kept in the back for things like this.

"You were supposed to stay outside and keep watch," King told him as he started the engine.

Thatcher let out an amused laugh. "You've gone soft, King. Got to toughen up, fucker, if you want to stay alive for that baby and wife of yours."

"I've not gone soft," King snarled.

"Shiiit," Thatcher drawled. "Until tonight, I can't think of a time a man pointed a gun at your head and you didn't take him out yourself."

"I was giving them time to back down," he argued.

"I gave them fucking time. I counted to ten," Thatcher replied.

King shook his head and pulled out onto the street, and we drove down the long drive that led to the Morse mansion.

"Storm was the only one going for his gun," Thatcher pointed out. "You didn't even move to go in that direction. Storm couldn't take them both out at the same time, so I did what I needed to."

King lifted his eyes to the rearview mirror to look at me.

I shrugged. "Gun was pointed at my head," I replied.

He let out a sigh and looked back at the road.

Thatcher stretched in his seat, then turned his head toward King. "Heard our murderous little songbird asked for a fake identity. She needs birth certificate, Social, school records, all kinds of shit."

What the fuck? I leaned forward and noticed King stiffen.

"Briar Landry is asking for this? Who did she ask?" King demanded.

"She talked to Abe's sister. Seems the sister called her brother in for a favor, and Abe contacted Walsh, who went to Blaise. Boss called Wilder today with the order."

"Blaise told him to do this?" King asked, sounded pissed.

"Yep."

"I knew she was fucking lying!" he roared, hitting the steering wheel.

"Easy," Thatcher said with a chuckle. "It's not for her. It's for some teenager. Briar can't fucking pass for a fifteen-year-old kid, no matter what paperwork she has. She's helping someone, it would seem."

The teenage girl that had been in her car? What the fuck was Briar up to? Had she kidnapped someone? Would she do that?

"You're quiet back there," Thatcher said. "Thought you'd be interested in this little turn of events."

I leaned back as my mind ran through every scenario I could. None of them looking good. "Why is Blaise helping a criminal?" I finally asked.

Thatcher turned to look back at me with a smirk twisting his lips. "Criminal? You're mighty judgmental. Fucking men over for money isn't a crime. It's brilliant."

"If this isn't about Roger Ball, it doesn't affect me," King finally said. "But I want to know who the identity is for. If it's connected to him, it could lead to him."

"If he's alive," Thatcher added.

"Yeah, that," King muttered.

"I'd bet my left nut he's dead, and the songbird killed him, just like she said," Thatcher said. "Regardless, Wilder couldn't give us details. He isn't authorized. He said he was just relaying the message and King could do with it what he wanted."

"Why didn't he call me, and why are you just now telling me?" King snapped.

Thatcher rolled down the window as he lit up a cigarette. "Because he didn't trust you not to go running to Miami, and I knew we had a job to handle tonight. So, I waited." He took a long draw, then glanced back at King. "Now, you know. Go south if you must, but it's a waste of fucking time."

King sighed heavily. "Cosette has a doctor's appointment tomorrow. The last time they had to give her shots, Rumor cried more than Cosi. I have to be there. Besides, if what's her name, Melissa or whatever, runs, I'll know. The tracker is on her car."

"Briar," I corrected before I could stop myself.

Hearing him call her Melissa annoyed me. Sure, she'd been born with the name, but she'd escaped that life and tried to wipe it clean. Least he could do was respect her name change.

King looked up at me in the rearview mirror again. "Whatever. Does it matter what I call her?"

"Oh, to him it most certainly does," Thatcher replied with his cigarette clamped between his teeth.

"You got a thing for her?" King asked.

"No," I said firmly.

"He just wants to fuck the hell out of her," Thatcher added. "But then so do I. I'm just not moody as fuck about it."

My hands fisted at the thought of Thatcher touching her.

King rolled his eyes and looked back at the road. He reached for the radio and turned the music up.

I had some time. While King was dealing with his baby girl and wife, I could make a little visit to Miami first. What I was going to do when I got there, I wasn't sure, but I needed to find out what she was up to. I wished I could forget Briar but if she was about to get herself into trouble, I … I just needed to know what kind of trouble and why. Maybe then I could let it fucking go.

I'd fought going back for over a week now, and it was getting more difficult. There was a real good chance she'd pull her pistol out the moment she set eyes on me. I was prepared for her to hate me. I'd asked for it with the way I treated her last time. That had been more for my benefit than hers, and at the time, I'd thought her ego could take it. But the hurt look in her eyes was still replaying in my head. Damn if it wasn't fucking me up. I didn't want to give a shit about her, but Thatcher was right. I did want to fuck her. I knew if I did, it wouldn't fix anything. That wasn't the kind of woman you got out of your system. She was the kind that took your soul.

SEVENTEEN

"Wasting your time. She requires deeper pockets."

BRIAR

A flat tire. Shit! I had to be at work in an hour, and I was going to go get some groceries first. Staring at the offending tire, I tried to think through my options. I didn't have many. Changing a tire wasn't something I'd ever had to do. Maybe I could pull up a YouTube video on how to do it.

"Need some help, neighbor?" a male voice asked behind me.

Turning, I saw Ajani Michel, Mr. Fourth Floor, walking up to me. I guessed taking help where it was offered was my only option.

"I thought I told you to run. Save yourself," I replied in a teasing tone.

He gave me a small shrug. "I like to take chances. I'm a rebel like that."

Great. He was still giving me a flirty smile. I hadn't scared him off even a little bit. Fine. He was a man, and I had a flat tire.

I pointed at my tire. "Seems I do have a slight problem."

Ajani studied the tire for a moment, then gave me a cocky grin. "You got a spare?"

I nodded. "That I do have. The knowledge on what to do with it though I don't have."

"Then, it's your lucky day. I've changed many," he said, then waved a hand toward my trunk. "Want to pop that open so I can see what we have to work with?"

I wasn't going to have time to get groceries, but I would make it to work on time. I could just order a pizza for Dovie's dinner. I'd hoped to get her something from the deli that was a little bit healthier, but this would have to do.

"You're a lifesaver," I said, taking my key from my pocket and pressing the button that sent the trunk slowly lifting.

"Eh, well, I didn't say I was gonna do it for free."

Of course not. I tried to hold my smile. "What's your price?" I asked, already knowing he wasn't about to give me a dollar amount. My warning speech of crazy hadn't fazed him in the least.

"Dinner," he replied.

I nodded. "Okay then, you want me to order you a pizza, or do you prefer Thai? Because I know a really good place not far from here. I can pick it up and bring it to you."

His grin spread as he looked at me through his lashes. I was sure this worked with most women. He knew what he was doing clearly. But he was dealing with a pro, and I wasn't biting.

"With you. I'll take you to dinner."

I placed a hand on my hip. "Do I need to remind you of all my faults?"

"Not necessary. They're all up here," he said, tapping his temple with his pointer finger.

I needed my tire changed, and if it meant dinner with the man, then so be it. "Well, if you're willing to chance it."

He did a quick scan of my body. "Definitely willing to take that chance."

One meal wouldn't kill me.

I waved a hand at the car. "Then, please work your magic."

"That won't be necessary," a familiar deep voice came from my left.

I jerked my gaze from the car to see Storm walking toward us. I tensed immediately. The fact that the sight of him in a pair of faded jeans and another snug-fitting T-shirt—this one was blue—made my body tingle annoyed me to no end. I should accept that he made all female bodies tingle. It was something that was a given. But I could ignore it. I was stronger than that.

"Excuse me," Ajani replied.

Storm cut his eyes to the other man. "I'm certain I spoke clearly."

Ajani turned to me. "Briar? Is this a friend of yours?"

I was about to say no, but I stopped myself. Ajani did not need to die today, and he had no idea who he was dealing with.

I forced a smile. "You could call him that."

Ajani frowned and looked back at Storm. "We've got things covered."

Oh sweet Jesus. Ajani was gonna get himself killed over a stupid dinner date.

I stepped between the two of them before Storm decided to do something illegal. "Really, Ajani. Storm is here to help. I wasn't expecting him so soon. But thank you for offering to help me. I really do appreciate it."

Ajani looked over my shoulder, his jaw clenched, then back to me. "If you're sure."

I nodded. "Yes. Very." So sure.

For real, dude, you need to run for your life. No joke.

He stood there, not leaving, like he needed to be doing. Why couldn't he read my mind?

Look into my eyes, Ajani, and see that you are walking a line you do not want to walk for a woman who has no interest in you.

"You're not wealthy enough for her," Storm told him. "Wasting your time. She requires deeper pockets."

I pressed my lips together and inhaled, trying to keep from turning around and slapping his stupid, handsome face. If it wasn't for my fear of what he'd do if Ajani said or did the wrong thing, I'd shove him and tell him to go to hell or wherever he had come from.

"She mentioned that already," Ajani replied. "But I think she'd find that I have more than enough to keep her attention."

Stunned by my neighbor's quick response, I stared at him. He was making this a situation, and we did not need a situation. Not today and not because of me.

"You don't. Now, go," Storm replied, sounding bored by the conversation.

Ajani looked back at me and took a step back toward Storm.

"Thanks again, but Storm will handle it now."

He wasn't happy about it, but my moving closer to Storm had been enough to finally make him give up and go. When he turned around to walk away, I wanted to sigh in relief.

"You're welcome," Storm said too close to my ear.

Narrowing my eyes, I turned to glare at him. "For what?"

He nodded his head toward Ajani's retreating form. "Getting rid of him."

"Maybe I wanted his help!" I hissed angrily.

Storm looked down at me as if I were being ridiculous. "He's never gonna have enough money to get your interest," he replied, then glanced back at my flat before turning to look at it closer.

Crossing my arms over my chest, I tore my eyes off his backside and focused on the burger place we liked so much across the street.

"Someone sliced it."

Storm's words caught my attention, and I swung my gaze back to him. He was walking around the car to the other side.

"What?" I asked incredulously.

"You got a sliced one on this side too."

"As in someone took a knife to it?" I asked, needing clarification.

He nodded his head once. "Yeah. You fucking someone's man?"

"NO!" I spat angrily, stalking over to the car to get a closer inspection.

Who would have done this? I hadn't made any enemies here. But I had enemies. My gaze scanned the parking lot. Had I been found? No. This place was too big. I had left no paper trails.

"Briar," Storm said, and I looked back at him.

Panic starting to build in my chest. I didn't want to leave here. I would have all the paperwork Dovie needed soon. She'd have a new identity. She could go to school. Eventually get a job. Have a life.

"Who do you think would have had a reason to do this?" he asked.

A humorless laugh bubbled from my chest. "You want a list?"

He scowled, looking back at the tire in front of him before making his way back around the car toward me. "What about the neighbor?"

Taken aback, I shook my head. "Ajani? I barely know him. Met him once in the gym."

His steady, intent gaze made a slow scan of the parking lot. "Doesn't mean he wouldn't do something stupid to get you to go out with him."

"Storm, two of my tires are sliced. That is a threat. He wouldn't have done that to get my attention."

Storm shrugged. "Men can be idiots when they want something bad enough."

I didn't have time for this. "Why are you here?" I asked him.

"Checking on things," he replied as if that were obvious.

I held up my hands. "Well, here I am. Happy?"

His brows drew together, but he said nothing.

"Listen, I need to get to work. I have two flat tires and only one spare. I've got to call Pepper."

"I'll drive you," he told me.

I glanced back at the apartment. I needed to talk to Dovie. Explain things and make sure she didn't open the door or leave tonight. The pizza. Crap. I couldn't order her pizza.

Chewing on my bottom lip, I tried to figure out what I was going to tell Storm. Sure, I needed a ride, but before work came Dovie.

I'd not told Pepper who Dovie was or even given her a name. I just said it was someone who needed saving and I couldn't say more. She'd trusted me and agreed to help me with the new identity. I owed her a lot. Which meant I couldn't *not* show up tonight.

"I have to run up to my apartment real quick. I won't be long," I told him.

"I'll go with you."

"No," I blurted.

He raised an eyebrow at me. I swallowed, thinking through this. I had to come up with a reason why he couldn't.

"I'll just be a second, and I'd rather you not know my apartment number." Which wasn't a lie.

"Two twenty-nine," he replied without pause.

Shit. Did they know everything? No, they didn't. They had no idea about Dovie. Just my location at all times, it seemed.

"Stalker," I muttered.

"Don't flatter yourself."

With a roll of my eyes, I decided I'd have to just text Dovie. There were eggs in the fridge. She could make an egg sandwich or a grilled cheese and heat up the can of tomato soup to go with it. It wasn't the best dinner, but it would have to do.

"I'm running out of time," I said. "Let's just go."

He studied me for a moment, as if he was going to insist we go to my apartment, but finally, he turned and headed toward a matte-black Jeep. It was new and expensive. The kind of Jeep I would never be able to afford.

When the locks on the doors clicked, he headed for the driver's side, and I went to climb in the passenger seat. Once we were inside, I glared straight ahead.

"This doesn't change the fact that I hate you. I just need to get to work," I clarified.

He backed out of the parking space. "I don't particularly like you either."

I'd done nothing to this man! Nothing. "Glad we can agree on something."

He didn't say anything more, and I remained silent. No need to talk and pretend like we were anything more than enemies. Even if his scent had saturated this Jeep, and it was hard not to think about how his fingers inside of me had felt. When his body had been pressed against mine.

UGH! No, no, no, no. I was not that weak. He had humiliated me.

My hands fisted in my lap, and I tried to think of anything other than him. If the damn vehicle didn't smell so freaking good, I could.

Drive faster, asshole.

EIGHTEEN

"The lot think they're in love with her."

STORM

"Back again. They must not have decent bars in Georgia," Pepper Abe said as she stood on the back side of the bar with two bottles of whiskey in her hands.

"Just in town. Thought I'd drop in."

The corner of her lips curled up, and then she turned to put the bottles on the shelf behind her.

When I had brought Briar in earlier, I hadn't gotten out of the Jeep. I waited until she was outside, and then I went back to her apartment and did a closer inspection on her car. I'd spent very little time near it earlier, just enough to get done what I needed to, but I noticed something that I wanted to check more closely without her around to see me do it. The tracking device was still in place, but another one had been added, along with a wiretap inside the vehicle. The devices weren't ours. They were cheaper and easier to spot if you knew what you were looking for.

I'd debated on taking them or leaving them so as not to alert whoever had put them there that they'd been found. Leaving them for now seemed like the best idea, but then that meant I couldn't let Briar out of my sight.

SIZZLING

She had just taken the stage for her second set when I arrived, and the furious gleam in her eye when she spotted me was brief, but I didn't miss it.

The angrier she was at me, the harder it made it for me not to throw her against a wall and fuck her until I was sated. Which part of me feared I'd never be when it came to her. Sated, that was. It made me hard as a damn rock, even thinking about it. She'd liked it when I was rough with her. That tight pussy of hers had literally been soaked. She had a redheaded temper, and I liked it.

Pepper turned back around. "So, it's business then and not the gorgeous woman on my stage?"

Both.

"Not my type." Fucking lie.

Pepper let out a cackle. "She is everyone's type. Heck, even I think I'd be tempted to swing that way if she asked. At least when she's up there singing."

Not an image I needed. My hand tightened around my glass, and I took a drink in hopes of cooling down. I didn't want to see Briar with someone else, but the thought of her and sex always got me worked up.

Unable to help myself, I turned to look at Briar onstage. She winked at someone as the words to the song flowed easily from her, as if the song had been written just for her. It hadn't been, but she sure made it seem that way. Somehow, she managed to make the entire room think she was up there for them. She drew you in and held you there with her.

"Another beer, please, Pep," a tall blond biker said, leaning against the bar as he continued to watch Briar sing.

"You came without a woman tonight. Not like you, Country," Pepper said to the man.

"Got my eyes on something better." He grinned and turned to pick up his beer as Pepper slid it across to him.

"You and every other single man in here," she replied.

"Ah, Pep, but it's me. I got this smile and all this charm."

• 119 •

I wondered how big of an issue it would be with Blaise if I killed one of his father-in-law's men.

"She's not gonna date a biker. Let it go," Pepper informed him.

He smirked, putting the beer to his lips. "She might."

"She won't." The clipped words came from me before I could stop them.

"And who are you?" the guy asked, giving me a challenging look.

"A Kingston. Go back to your seat." Pepper's tone had a warning in it that the guy didn't miss.

"As in—" the guy started.

"Yes," Pepper snapped.

He took a step back and nodded his head once before turning and walking away. Clearly, he'd met Huck.

"Don't start anything with them. The lot think they're in love with her. Brings in business. If you got something to handle with Briar, then do it elsewhere," Pepper told me.

I held up my drink. "Just here for this."

"Uh-huh," she replied with a twist of her mouth, then turned to walk down the bar to take someone else's order.

The place was clearing out as Briar made her way toward me. I'd eventually moved to a back table and ordered food tonight. Every chance she could, she shot me a warning look. It had become amusing as fuck. She walked past the servers cleaning up with her determined glare locked on me.

"Why are you here?" she demanded.

I stood up and pushed in my chair. "To take you home."

She blinked at me as if taken off guard for a moment, but then she recovered quickly. "Pepper is giving me a ride. You can leave now."

"Not the best idea, seeing as how your car has a tracker we didn't put on it and is wired."

I hadn't planned to blurt that out just yet, but she'd started talking about getting a ride with Pepper, and, well, it'd come out.

A flash of unease lit her face. "What?" she asked, her voice just above a whisper.

Got your attention now, little siren.

"My guess is, it's the ones who sliced your tires. You need me because, right now, you're not safe."

She paled, and her eyes widened. "I don't need you," she said with more grit than she appeared to have at the moment. "I can take care of myself."

No, she couldn't. She had a gun, but whoever was watching her probably knew that. It wasn't some stranger. They'd tracked her down and gone to the trouble of wiring her car. I needed to know who the fuck it was, and when I knew, I would take them from this world. Staying close to her, I'd find them soon enough.

I took a step toward her. "You can hate me, but I'm not leaving you until I know who it is that's fucking with you."

Her shoulders stiffened. "It's not Roger, if that's what you're thinking."

I had thought for a brief second that it could be. I never questioned my lie detector, but with this woman, I wasn't positive it was working one hundred percent. I couldn't help but wonder if that pretty face of hers had distracted me. But even if it had and the motherfucker wasn't dead like she'd claimed, I wasn't ready to alert King. I didn't trust him with her. No matter how much her life choices pissed me off, I was finding it impossible not to want to protect her. If she'd lied to King, then he'd make her pay for it, and I wasn't letting that happen. Admitting I'd go that far to protect her shocked the hell out of me, but I would. The idea of anyone hurting her seemed to send me into a blind rage.

"Like I said, I'm not leaving."

Anger, frustration, even fear flashed in her ocean-blue eyes. "You're not coming inside my apartment."

I walked past her. "I've got my Jeep," I replied, although if I wanted in her fucking apartment, I would go inside.

"Where is King? I want to talk to him. I'm over him sending you here. This needs to end."

The thought of her talking to King made me uncomfortable. It wasn't going to happen.

"King isn't someone you need to piss off. Keep your distance."

She waved a hand at me. "And you? Y'all are just alike, yet I keep getting you in my face all the time."

I turned back around, leveling her with my stare. She needed to understand this. "King and I are not alike."

Placing both her hands on her hips, she scowled. "Is that so?"

I took two long strides until I was so close to her that our bodies were almost touching. Towering over her, I inhaled her sweet, heady scent and wished like hell I hadn't. "King doesn't care if you live or die. I do."

She sucked in a breath as she stared up at me.

"Now, get your goddamn shit, and let's go." I spun around and started stalking away from her, needing to calm down. Get her scent out of my fucking nose.

"Why do you care?" she blurted out.

I didn't look back at her, but I stopped. "I just do," I bit out, then continued on toward the exit.

Verbalizing the way I felt about her wasn't something I was ready to face just yet. I had too much other shit going off in my head, making me do things I'd never imagined I'd do. All because of her.

Why did she have to be so fucking difficult? Jesus, I was helping her. Couldn't she just shut up and let me? I didn't want to feel this unhinged. I didn't want to give a flying fuck, but she'd managed to get under my skin and make me overlook what she was. Just like every other man she'd manipulated and controlled. I was weak where she was concerned, and I couldn't be weak. I had to handle this. Figure out what was happening and fix it, then get the hell away from this woman. Before I did something really fucking stupid.

NINETEEN

"Were you watching me?"

BRIAR

Standing at the window of my apartment, I stared down at the black Jeep parked so it was facing the building. I was sure he knew exactly which windows were mine, so I stood back in the shadows with the lights off. The last thing I wanted was for him to think I was looking at him. God knew that man's ego was already the size of Mount Rushmore.

We hadn't spoken in the car on the drive here. But now, I had a million questions. Simple ones, like: How was I going to get my car fixed tomorrow? When could I get groceries? How long did he plan on sleeping in his Jeep outside my apartment? What had he meant when he said he cared? Okay, that one was the main one that kept running through my head.

I'd thought he was stalking me for King, but now … I didn't think he was. In fact, I wondered if King even knew he was here.

Thankfully, Dovie had been in bed when I got home. She was most nights, but every once in a while, she'd be on the sofa, locked into some TV series or reading a book. I had almost told Pepper about her. I wanted to believe I could trust Pepper, but in the end, I knew I couldn't. I was the only person I trusted with Dovie's safety.

Pepper had trusted me though. Most people wouldn't have agreed to help get me a fake identity for a fifteen-year-old without knowing the details. Dovie was a minor. I could have kidnapped her for all Pepper knew.

I dropped the strand of hair I'd been twirling around my finger and turned to walk over to my bed. It was almost three, and I needed some sleep. I just hoped I could shut my brain off long enough to get some.

A car door closing had me spinning back around and rushing back to the window. I could see Storm walking over to the building. Scanning the parking lot, I looked for a sign of anyone else, but I didn't see movement. Was he coming up here? Glancing back at my door, I knew Dovie would hear him if he came inside. He wouldn't know to be quiet, and what if she came out of her room instead of hiding? If she thought I was in trouble, she'd try to help me.

If he was headed this way, I had to stop him.

Hurrying down the hall, I unbolted the door, moved the chain, and then unlocked the doorknob before I could open it and step outside into the hallway. Looking both ways, I saw no one. I didn't let the door close behind me because it would automatically lock. I hadn't taken the time to get the keys, afraid of Storm banging on my door at any moment.

But he wasn't here. Maybe he'd gone inside to the gym to pee? Was it even unlocked at this time? I didn't know what to do. If he did show up and knock on the door, Dovie would wake up. I could always tell her to hide, but what if Storm noticed something that clued him in that I wasn't alone?

I continued to stand there in the dark hallway, alone, waiting. There was no sound on this floor. Wherever Storm had gone, it wasn't here. I should go back inside and lock back up. It had been enough time that if he was coming, he'd have already been here.

The slam of a door startled me, and I jumped, letting the door behind me slip, then click shut. Shit! I grabbed the handle and turned, already knowing it was going to be locked. I'd have to knock until I woke Dovie up and likely wake my neighbors in the process. Just perfect.

"Briar?" Storm's voice was both a relief and an annoyance.

I was stuck outside my apartment because of him. The slamming door had to have been the stairwell closing. Of course he couldn't take the elevator. That would be too quiet.

"What?!" I hissed under my breath, turning to glare at him.

"Why are you in the hallway?" he asked, his eyes slowly trailing down my body, making me very conscious of what I was wearing. Something I hadn't thought of when I came running out into the hall.

"Because of you!" I said through clenched teeth.

His eyes were currently on my chest, and, dammit, I could feel my nipples harden.

"Me?" he asked, lifting his gaze back to my face.

The heated look in his eyes scattered my brain for a moment, and I forgot what we were talking about.

"Briar?" he said again, and I tried to clear my head.

He had asked me something. What was it?

Oh, the hallway. Yes. That had been the question.

"You …" I paused, not wanting to stammer over my words or sound breathless. "You came inside. I thought you were coming up here, and I didn't want you waking my neighbors, knocking on the door."

He tilted his head to the side slightly. "Were you watching me?"

I swallowed, then nodded, lifting my chin higher. It wasn't like I was being a voyeur. I had just wanted to make sure he didn't come inside—which he had!

"I was checking to make sure you were staying outside, where you belong."

"I hadn't planned on knocking on your door. I was doing a sweep of the place." He nodded his head toward my door. "You can go to bed now."

Crossing my arms over my chest, I huffed, hating that I was about to tell him what I'd done. He'd no doubt laugh at me. But what did I care?

"When the stairwell door slammed, I was startled, and my door closed. Locking me out."

He raised both his eyebrows. "You can't get inside your apartment?"

"Not until my landlord is awake tomorrow." Which was a lie.

"Guess you're stuck sleeping in my Jeep then."

Frowning, I shook my head. I was knocking on this door the moment he left until Dovie heard it and let me inside.

"I'll wait right here. Or go down to the common room and sleep on the sofa."

His eyes dropped back to my body. "Dressed like that?"

Okay, he had a point. I wouldn't be sleeping in either place, but I just needed him to leave. Then, I'd fix this. No one but him would get a view of me in my cropped red camisole and matching red shorts that barely covered my ass. I just wished he'd stop looking at me like that. He was never touching me again. I had learned my lesson.

"Just go," I urged him.

He shook his head. "No. You're coming with me."

Like hell I was.

"No thank you."

He grinned then and cocked an eyebrow. "No thank you? I didn't offer you a drink. I'm taking you to my Jeep until morning. Unless you'd rather I take you to a hotel."

I shook my head. "No. I am staying here."

"My Jeep it is then."

"I'm not going to your Jeep."

"You're not staying out here alone."

I took a deep breath, trying not to lose my temper and scream at this man. "I am okay here. You're outside watching, right? I will be fine. Go back outside and do your stalker thingy."

He turned and leaned up against the wall beside my door.

"What are you doing?" I asked in frustration.

"Waiting here with you."

"You're serious?"

"Very."

"Why are you being so stubborn?"

He turned his honey-colored eyes my way and let them slowly drift down my body. "Because, Briar, you're out here, barely dressed, looking like a goddamn centerfold. I will not leave you alone for one of your neighbors to walk out and see you like this."

I was ignoring the centerfold comment. I. Was. Ignoring. It. I didn't care that he thought I looked like one.

I do not care. I wouldn't care. But clearly, my body did because it was very aware of the man.

"And you being out here with me keeps any one seeing me dressed like this, how?"

Storm smirked in response, and good Lord, now, my panties were damp.

"I'll cover you."

The image of him covering me wasn't helping. My imagination was working overtime on that one. I had to get a grip.

"I'll go to the gym locker rooms. They have benches. I need to use the restroom anyway." If they were unlocked, that was.

He waved a hand. "Lead the way."

"Are you following me?"

"Yep."

Okay, fine. It wasn't like he was going to go into the ladies' locker room with me.

I went over to the elevator, and we waited in silence for it to open. Stepping inside, I was very aware he was behind me and that my butt cheeks were slightly visible in these bottoms. I didn't know if he was looking, but the thought that he could be made me get goose bumps.

The doors closed, and he stood on the other side of the elevator, as if getting too close to me would somehow taint him. I ignored it the best I could, and when the doors opened up again, I bolted out of them.

"The gym is this way. I have it from here," I told him, striding off, hoping he'd go outside to his Jeep.

The heavy footsteps behind me told me otherwise.

Stopping at the gym door, I spun around and threw up my arms. "What are you doing?" I demanded.

"Following you."

I rolled my eyes. "I can see that. I meant, why are you not going back outside?"

He leaned forward and pushed the door behind me open. "Because anyone could be inside here." Then, he nodded his head for me to enter.

I went in the direction of the women's locker room and held out my hands as I walked. "See, it's empty."

He said nothing, and I bit back a groan as I shoved the door to the locker room open and went inside. If I stayed in here long enough, then maybe he would leave.

The door didn't close behind me, and I closed my eyes with a sigh. He'd come inside the flipping locker room.

"I am perfectly fine in here," I told him.

He walked past me and then began looking around the place. In toilet and shower stalls. I stood there, trying not to watch him but it was hard. This whole protective thing he was doing had clearly messed with my head. I liked it, and I didn't need to like anything about Storm Kingston. Not one damn thing.

When he seemed satisfied that we were alone, he walked over toward one of the hardwood benches and sat down, leaning back against the wall and propping his right ankle on his left knee, as if he was planning on staying awhile. If I was going to get back into my apartment, he had to go back to his Jeep.

"You are staying?" I asked, already knowing this answer.

"I am."

Tired of being annoyed and just tired in general, I walked over and sat down on the other end of the bench, as far away from him as possible.

"You should sing more of your original stuff," he said, turning his head to look down the bench at me.

It wasn't like I hadn't heard this before, but when he said it, I felt a jolt of pride. That wasn't something I felt too often or ever. The elation that came with it was like a high I wished I could ride awhile.

"Shame you would rather use your body to make money when you're so damn talented."

And there it was. The end of the high. Why couldn't he let that go? Leave it in my past, where I was trying to put it and close the door on it.

"We can't all be honorable members of organized crime," I replied sarcastically, giving him a hateful smile.

The amused gleam in his eye and upturned corners of his mouth made me momentarily forget that I hated him. It was really difficult to dislike a man who looked like that, and I was sure he knew it. Asshole.

"I don't deceive anyone," he said to me.

"No, you just kill them."

The deep laugh that came from him made my stomach flutter. It was an intoxicating sound. One I wanted to hear more of.

"Only if they deserve it."

I straightened and shifted my body toward him. "The men I've deceived didn't deserve it? They were cheaters."

He raised his eyebrows. "Only because you seduced them."

This time, I laughed. "I absolutely did not. They always approached me first."

Storm ran the pad of his thumb over his lower lip, and the movement distracted me. I felt my breathing hitch as I tried to tear my gaze off his stupid, beautiful face. It was hard, and I was failing.

"All it takes is one smile. One moment of your attention, and they're seduced."

Trying like hell to control my breathing as I lifted my gaze from his mouth to meet his eyes, I swallowed hard. Getting worked up over this man was a mistake. He'd say something cruel at any moment. He was disgusted by me.

"That sounds like a them problem," I said, a little too breathy.

"Maybe, but you know the power you wield over a man. You use it to your advantage knowing you're only in it for the money."

My hands tightened in my lap, and I jerked my eyes off him and glared at the wall of lockers. "For someone who has never known what it's like to be hungry, homeless, and desperate, you sure are judgmental." I surprised myself by saying that. Admitting it. I never gave excuses for my behavior, yet here I was, doing it to this man because I didn't like hearing the disapproval in his tone.

"You're right. I don't," he agreed. "But again, with a talent like yours, you had another way to make money. Not everyone has that. You do."

And it wasn't enough! He had no idea how much money was required for staying on the run. Keeping Dovie safe. Making sure she had everything she needed while unable to give her any kind of education since I struggled to read a freaking menu at a restaurant. He had never raised a kid. Those were things I couldn't say to him.

"I'm giving that a try now. I'll let you know how it goes since you have such a strong opinion on the subject." And it was going well, but only because of the thousands I'd put away that wealthy men had given me.

"You're not currently looking for a new sugar daddy?" he asked, sounding slightly surprised.

I turned my head back to look at him. "Why? You offering?" I asked with a flirty smile I knew would piss him off.

His face was smug when he replied, "I've never had to pay for a hot fuck."

Hearing him say *fuck* made me feel flushed.

I did my best to remain unaffected as I lifted a shoulder. "I never asked for money. They just gave it to me."

"Don't kid yourself. You asked. They knew they had one flex to keep you as their side piece, and they used it. Their wealth."

Letting out a sigh, I laid my head back and rested it on the wall, staring up at the ceiling. "Whatever, Storm. I'm tired, and I do not have to defend my life choices to you."

He was the first person I'd ever even tried to defend myself to. Why was I doing it now? Why did I care? It wasn't like I would ever have him look at me differently. He'd never want me. Accept me. My crush, or whatever it was I seemed to harbor for him, needed to end. When I looked at him, I wanted to truly hate him. Every part of me. Right now, that was not the case.

"But you are," he replied, then stood up.

I tilted my head to watch him as he walked toward me. My body began to do that tingly thing it did when he was close to me. It was not getting the memo that this was off the table.

"I'm what?" I asked, unable to remember what it was we were talking about while he towered over me.

The smile on his face held a touch of cruelty that should be a red flag, but I was overlooking it. He was too close to think about much else.

"Stand up, Briar," he demanded in a husky tone that sent a thrill throughout my body.

I wouldn't let him control me. Not again. I'd already suffered that humiliation.

"No," I replied, not moving a muscle.

He tilted his head to the side, and his gaze traveled down my body slowly. Inhaling oxygen was a struggle. I tried to focus on that while he made his way back to my face.

"Now."

My eyes widened, and the area between my legs clenched at his order. Dammit, why was this hot? I didn't let men talk to me like this. I was the one who held the power. I decided what I would and would not do. Yet I uncrossed my legs and felt my body betray me as I did as told.

A pleased gleam lit his eye, along with the swirl of hate and desire I could see there. He lifted a hand and gently cupped my face as he seemed to drink in my features, as if he was trying to memorize them.

"Dangerous fucking beauty," he said huskily.

Breathe, Briar. I had to breathe.

He stared at my mouth so intently that I wet my lips, expecting him to kiss me. Realizing I was going to beg if he didn't. I wanted to know what that felt like. How he tasted. If it was as delicious as I imagined it would be.

His hand dropped then, and I gripped my thighs to keep from reaching out and grabbing his hand to bring it back up.

"Turn around and put your hands on the wall," he said in a low, hoarse voice.

A major red flag. I should sit my ass back down and tell him to go to hell. I should. It was what I'd do to any other man who treated me like this.

When I turned around and leaned over the bench to place my palms on the cool, smooth wall, I closed my eyes in disbelief at my own actions. Maybe I would have changed my mind and walked off, but the hiss of Storm's breath just as his hand slid over my butt stopped me from getting my act together.

My eyes flew back open, and I stared at that bare wall I was leaning against as his hands slid up to the waist of my bottoms. With a hard jerk, they were shoved down to my ankles. Storm's large, callous hand ran over my bare bottom, and then he slid a finger beneath the thin satin strip of my thong and ran it down from the top until he reached the damp achiness he had caused.

I bit down hard on my lip to keep from begging him to touch me when his finger left, but the hard slap that landed on my right butt cheek had my teeth releasing the abused lip as I cried out. That stung. Another loud smack echoed in the room, and I jerked from the contact.

"Fuck, that ass bounces nice," he snarled.

My entire body felt flushed. I fought back the moan I wanted to make. This time, when his hand made contact, it was a loud crack that had me crying out. Damn, that was hard. It was going to leave a mark. I should stop this. Get away from him because, clearly, he was one of those men who liked to hurt women while having sex.

His hands ran over my skin, then moved up my back and then around and under my camisole until both my breasts filled them. He squeezed as he pressed against me. The hard length of his erection through the denim of his jeans made me whimper. He rolled my nipples between his thumbs and forefingers, then pinched them until I was gasping. Too much.

"Does that hurt?" he asked, close to my ear.

I nodded, unable to use words.

"Good," he growled. "Bad girls need to be punished. Even if you've got the sweetest ass I've ever seen." He ran the tip of his nose over my shoulder. "And smell like a wet dream," he added.

Oh God. Why was this hot? I pressed my legs together, needing to get some relief.

"Open your legs!" he barked, reaching down and grabbing my right thigh, jerking my leg out until I was completely exposed.

A hard slap landed over my sensitive clit, and I let out a strangled sound as my fingers curled into a fist.

"Your thighs are wet," he said, running a hand over one, then the other. He let go of the breast he had been squeezing, then slid his hand over my stomach. With his open palm, he pressed me back against him. "Being punished makes you wet."

Until this moment, I hadn't known that myself.

I closed my eyes, and a whimper came out.

Storm moved behind me, and I looked back over my shoulder to see him lower his head to my bottom before his teeth sank into the bruised flesh.

I opened my mouth, but nothing came out as his tongue lapped at the spot he'd just sunk his teeth in. Lifting his gaze, he gave me a sadistic grin before doing it again in another spot. I sucked in a breath and stood there, unable to stop watching him as he began to soothe that bite with his tongue.

"Bad girls don't deserve to have their pussy eaten, but I'm gonna make an exception," he told me as he lowered himself to his knees. "Smells too good, and I want it on my face."

His hands grabbed on to my hips, and he buried his face between my legs. Throwing my head back, I let out a loud moan of pleasure just as my knees buckled. His talented tongue began to fuck me and lap at me as if I were his last meal. My climax was building, and I didn't know if I was going to be able to stand up for it. The power I felt behind it, pushing me higher, was as terrifying as it was exciting.

"Fucking sweet pussy," Storm growled as he moved a hand from my hip to my butt cheek and squeezed.

I was going to collapse. "Storm," I gasped. "I'm gonna … I can't keep standing. My legs."

His fingers dug into my flesh just before his mouth left me. That was not what I wanted him to do. That magical mouth was gone.

"Ride my face," he ordered.

I turned to see him lying down on the tiled floor on his back. When my eyes met his, I felt a tremor run through me at the sight of his face wet with … me.

I moved, not waiting for him to change his mind. Walking over to where he was lying, I placed a foot on each side of his head. He ran his hands up my calves as I lowered myself over him. When I was on my knees, he took control, grabbing my waist and pulling me down until his tongue was shoved inside of me, followed by a finger.

The moment he flicked my clit with his tongue, I lost any control I had managed to gather. Rocking my hips, I rode his mouth and fingers while the intensity began to build inside me again. Storm's other hand slid down until I felt a finger press against my back entrance, and I tensed.

A deep chuckle vibrated against me. "Easy, baby. I'm just playing."

The darkness in his voice had me panting again and taking my pleasure from him. He never pushed his fingertip inside the small, puckered, untouched-until-now hole, but the way he gently massaged it somehow made me wilder. More desperate. His name fell from my lips over and over again as a powerful orgasm slammed into me.

"Fuck yeah." Storm's deep voice made me shiver as I jerked over him. His tongue still tasting me.

Feeling weak, I slowed as the reality of what I'd done sank in.

One more swipe of his tongue, and then Storm slapped me on my right butt cheek. I managed to lift myself off him without crumpling to the floor. Standing, I moved over to the bench and sank down onto it. My panties and pajama bottoms lay on the cold tiles as if they were mocking me. Reminding me how stupid I was when it came to Storm.

"Get on the floor," Storm demanded.

My eyes snapped up to meet his face as he stood there, unzipping his pants. Was he going to fuck me? The way my vagina pulsed as if I hadn't just had a record-breaking orgasm showed exactly how weak I was when it came to this man.

He pointed at the floor as he shoved his jeans down just below his hips. I sat there, transfixed, as he pulled out a long, thick, and pierced penis. Sweet Jesus. He had a bar through the tip. How would that feel inside me? Could I feel it through a condom?

His hand slid up and down it, and I watched unable to look away.

"Floor!" he growled angrily.

I moved then. Scrambling to get up and do as I had been told.

"Take off that fucking top," he said.

Taking the hem, I slid it up and over my head with my back to him, then let it fall to the floor.

"Turn around." His command this time sounded less harsh and as if he was struggling with his breathing.

Finally feeling some power, I twisted to glance back at him before letting my full front come into view. His eyes flared, and my entire body sang with pleasure at the sight. He wanted me as badly as I did him.

"On your back. Knees bent and legs open."

He was so demanding. I went to my knees, then moved onto my bottom before lying back and getting in the position he'd asked for. He used his free hand to shove his jeans down to his ankles, and then he motioned for me to scoot closer to him with his fingers, all the while rolling his thick erection up and down with his right hand. The metal bar glistened with his pre-cum, and I was mesmerized.

Storm's eyes slowly roamed over my body as he began to jack off faster.

"I don't have a condom," he said, "so I'm gonna coat you in my cum."

Oh. Oh God. I sucked in a breath.

"I thought about letting you take it down your throat," he said through his teeth. "But I want to see it on those tits and watch it drip over your thighs and pussy."

Unable to take any more, I eased my hand down until my fingers slid between my legs. Keeping my eyes on Storm, I saw his gaze darken.

"That's it. Touch that hot little cunt. Let me see you fuck yourself."

Slipping my middle finger inside, I lifted my hips off the floor and let out a low moan as he began to pump himself harder. I'd never done this before, but damn, it was hot. Something about knowing you wanted to fuck so bad and were denying yourself.

"Motherfucker, I want to sink my dick into that sopping wet cunt," he growled as the room was filled with sounds of his heavy breathing.

When he stepped forward, the veins on his neck standing out, his jaw clenched tight, I knew he was there.

"GAH!" he shouted as the first shot of his thick white release was on my chest. The next one hit my hand as I reached my own climax. Another on my stomach, and then the last one landed on my right thigh.

I lay there, staring up at him as his gaze followed the trail of his semen on my body. Neither of us spoke for several moments. When he pulled his jeans back up and began to zip them, he finally moved back from where he'd been towering over me.

He leaned down and held out a hand to me.

I slid mine into it, realizing it was covered in both our releases. His hand wrapped around it tightly as he pulled me up. Instead of letting my hand go, he ran his over it, as if he were rubbing lotion into my skin. His eyes were locked on what he was doing.

Then, he dropped it so quickly, as if it were on fire. I stood there, waiting on him to say something about what we'd just done. We might not have had sex, but somehow, this felt more intimate. I'd never done anything like it before. Sex had been ... well, sex. This had been ... on another level.

Storm turned and stalked toward the door. I opened my mouth to ask him where he was going, but he jerked it open and left before I could form the words. The room suddenly felt cold. The heat from moments earlier had seemed to vanish with him. Wrapping my arms around my waist, I shivered.

Part of me wanted to believe he was just checking things out and was coming back. But as the silence grew louder and the chill began to settle in my bones, I knew. He'd left. Without a word.

· TWENTY ·

But that man, he was dangerous.

BRIAR

"There is a vehicle outside, changing the tires on our car," Dovie signed.

I set the brush in my hand down on the bathroom counter and walked out to see what she was talking about.

After I had taken a shower in the locker room—allowing a few tears, but not a full-blown pity party—and dressed myself, I made my way back to the apartment, and luckily, I was able to wake Dovie up easily enough. She came after my third attempt at knocking, looking sleepy and confused. I told her I'd thought I heard something, then accidentally locked myself out. She went back to bed without questions.

I hadn't gone to the window to see if Storm's black Jeep was out there since coming out of the locker room. I hadn't wanted to know. Seeing it out there now, as he stood in front of it with his arms crossed over his chest, watching the men who were changing my tires, made my chest ache. Dammit. My chest needed to stay out of this. I couldn't help my vagina betraying me, but not my heart. I didn't ever allow a man close to that.

Scowling, I turned away from the window.

Dovie was watching me closely. Too closely.

"What's wrong?" she signed.

I shook my head. "Nothing. Just glad they got here."

Although I hadn't known they were coming. She didn't need to know that though. I didn't work tonight, but I could go get Dovie and me groceries. We could go have our beach day. Anything to get away from Storm.

But there was someone tracking me. The car was wired. Crap!

I glared back at the window. I didn't want to talk to him. He wanted to protect me, but after last night, it was him I needed protecting from. I couldn't trust myself around the man, and I did not need to be feeling things in my chest about him. That was bad. Very bad. Leaving would be best even if I loved working at Pepper's bar. If I could find the trackers and wire, I could take them both off. Or I could go trade that one in and get another car without Storm knowing, and then we'd take off again. Get out of Florida. Go north, like I should have done. Leave the South behind.

I wanted a new identity for Dovie, and she deserved it, but did I have time to wait? Probably not if my tires had been sliced and there was a tracker on my car. We had to get out of here. I'd send Pepper a text and hope she didn't hate me. I didn't get to have friends, and letting myself think I could had been a weakness. I always needed to be free to run.

"Someone put a tracker on our car, and the tires were sliced. We are gonna have to leave," I told her.

She didn't look surprised. Maybe she'd already figured it out.

"Who is the hottie with the Jeep?" she signed.

Of course she'd noticed him. He was impossible not to notice.

"No one," I replied.

She gave me a look that said she knew I was full of shit.

"Okay, fine. He's a guy who … who thinks he is helping me but hates me. I don't know, honestly. It's … he's complicated."

Dovie walked back over to the window, now more curious.

"Don't let anyone see you," I warned, now worrying that Storm might have noticed her looking out earlier.

She turned back to me. "He just paid them in cash."

"Maybe he will leave," I said.

Dovie backed up farther from the window. Had he seen her? Shit.

"I think he's coming inside the building," she signed.

Double shit.

"Go hide in your closet."

She hurried in that direction without arguing with me.

Why couldn't he just leave like he had earlier? I was easy enough to cover in cum, then walk away. My chest tightened, and I realized I was grinding my teeth.

Forcing myself to relax my jaw, I scanned the room for any sign of Dovie and saw nothing that couldn't be mine. Swinging my attention back to the door, I waited for him to knock.

If I could convince him to leave the parking lot, then Dovie and I could pack up and go. I'd only agreed to pay an extra three hundred a month in rent not to sign a lease so we could go quickly if needed. Most of our things were still in boxes. We could get out of here in three hours, maybe even two. New England was sounding good. The Southern Mafia sure as hell wouldn't be there.

Three sharp raps on the door snapped my attention back to the first hurdle. Getting rid of Storm Kingston. At least with Dovie in earshot, I wouldn't do anything stupid, like allow him to touch me. Again.

Taking a deep breath, I made my way over to the door and unlocked the three separate locks before steeling myself and opening it up. Flashing a smile, I looked at Storm as if I didn't want to slap him across the face and call him names.

"Storm, what a surprise," I drawled, leaning against the door casually.

He shot me an annoyed glance, then walked past me, barely grazing my arm as he stepped inside my apartment.

"Entering uninvited. Guess you're not a vampire then. I'll have to scratch that villain off my list."

There was no amusement on his face as he took in the living room as if the secrets to my life could be found here.

Sorry, buddy. I'm smarter than that. No mantel photographs for me.

"Your tires are fixed. When do you work again?"

"I'm off the next two days."

He turned his attention to me then. "I need to handle some things in Ocala. I want you to go stay with Pepper."

My eyebrows shot up. "You want me to?" I let out a laugh. "I'm sorry. I don't remember when I started taking orders from you."

His eyes darkened. "I can think of when you took orders without that fucking sassy mouth only a couple of hours ago."

Shut up! I'd walked into that one. *Please don't let Dovie have heard that. Change of subject. Just agree and get him out of here.*

"Whatever, fine. I'll go to Pepper's."

That was too agreeable. I could see the way his eyes narrowed. Dammit, I was better at lying than this. I needed to get it together.

"Fine. Get your things, and I'll take you."

Shit. Of course he was going to make this difficult.

"I need to do some laundry, clean the toilets, and get my things together. I can take myself to Pepper's. My tires are fixed, remember? Besides, I need to call Pepper and ask if I can stay there."

"You can stay. I've already spoken to her. Get your things. The rest can wait."

I was real close to hitting him. I swear to God, this man was driving me crazy.

"I will go when I am done here."

"Get your shit. Last chance before I throw you over my shoulder and take you out of here."

UGH! What was I supposed to do now?

"Okay, listen. You have a tracker on my car. I can't go anywhere without you knowing. Please, I just need to do some things here before I go. This is my day off, and I have a list of things I want to do here."

Storm's scowl meant he was as annoyed with me as I was with him. I wasn't hiding Roger! Why couldn't they leave me alone? The man was dead, and I was going to relive the moment my bullet had gone into his head and he fell to the ground for the rest of my life. He'd deserved it, but killing someone changed you. It left a mark on your soul. I would do it again, but damn if I'd lie about something like that.

"If you weren't lying to me right now, then I might believe you. But you're hiding something. I'm real fucking hard to lie to, Briar."

My heart beat fast against my chest. Panic. I was starting to panic. He was too close to this. I'd let him get too close. Entirely too close.

Placing my hands on my hips, I tried to think of anything to get him to leave.

"What I am not hiding is Roger. IF I am hiding something else, it isn't your business. It doesn't affect you. So, leave me alone!"

He took a step toward me. "You're working for Pepper. She's our business. Someone is after you, and you're leading it right to her door."

"Then, WHY send me to her house?! Isn't that leading my danger right to her?" I was yelling. I needed to calm down, but he was making me so mad.

He didn't answer that one right away. If I wasn't so angry, I'd relish the fact that I'd turned his own words against him. But seeing as I hadn't won this yet and he was still in my apartment, I didn't have time to enjoy anything.

"Do you know who is following you? Is that it? Some spurned lover trying to scare you? Get you back?"

"It wouldn't be the first time," I lied. Until now, I had never had a man chase me down like this.

Storm's scowl deepened, as if that angered him. "Who is it then?"

I threw up my hands. "I don't know! Jameson?"

"He's out on bail. If he leaves Atlanta, he'll be found and put back behind bars."

Oh. Okay. That was news. Out on bail for what? That was not the point. I didn't care.

"I do not know!" I couldn't think of one man from my past who would follow me. But their wives ... "Maybe it isn't a man."

Storm seemed to understand my meaning without me spelling it out for him. He let out a sigh and ran his hand through his hair, muttering a curse.

"Fine. Stay here. Do whatever you want. But if you're lying about Roger, then we will find out."

He was going to leave. I'd done it. I had convinced him to go. We were going to be able to get away from here. From him.

So, why did it feel like he'd just slapped me? Because he wasn't fighting to protect me.

He wasn't protecting you, Briar. He was making sure you weren't hiding Roger.

This was never about him caring about you. He'd made you think that, or you'd let your head go there. You'd wanted it.

"You leaving now?" I snapped.

He studied me for a moment, and I thought I saw something there ... something that said this was about me. He was worried about me. He cared.

Then, he stepped around me and headed for the door. I didn't turn to watch him leave. I closed my eyes when the door clicked shut. He'd left, and I realized just how stupid I had been. I'd come so close to letting him in. Never had that happened. I'd never even been tempted. But that man, he was dangerous. A danger I couldn't allow.

After I was sure I'd gotten my emotions under control, I headed to let Dovie know it was time to pack. I hated leaving like this. Pepper deserved more from me, but I wasn't in the position to be a good person. Maybe she wouldn't hate me.

TWENTY-ONE

"She's not a prisoner in her apartment."

STORM

"Not that I don't want you here, but … why are you here exactly?" Wilder asked me as he handed me a beer before taking the seat across from me in the living room at his house in Ocala, where he lived with his wife and daughter.

Wilder had grown up in Madison with us, and his dad was still there, but Wilder had been moved to the main family branch, working directly for Blaise Hughes.

I took a long drink from the bottle. I needed to talk, and there was no one back home I could talk to about this. Hell, I wasn't even sure what to talk about. It wasn't like talking was going to fix shit. I wasn't about to admit to Wilder what I'd done. Where my head had gone with this woman. Thinking about her, I pulled out my phone and glanced at the location of Briar and her car to make sure she was still at her apartment. I'd checked at least a hundred times since I'd walked out of there earlier.

Angry at her, at myself, at the whole fucking situation, I'd gotten in my Jeep, determined I was leaving. Headed north as fast as I could, but I'd only made it to Ocala before realizing I couldn't leave. Not if she was being tracked by someone other than us. If she was fucked up with some shit that was going to get her in trouble with King, I needed to know. The knowledge that I'd protect her against my own was a little more than I was ready to admit aloud.

"It's complicated," I finally said.

Wilder looked amused as he leaned back on the sofa. "So, this is about a woman. Thatcher was right."

"Thatcher?" I asked, wondering what the hell he was talking about.

Wilder smirked and took a drink from his beer. "Yeah. Thatch called yesterday. Said you'd come south, chasing a woman. Told me to make sure you weren't doing something stupid."

Thatcher had already figured out where I was. This didn't surprise me. However, his concern for my choices did. What did he know? I'd covered my tracks carefully, but if anyone was twisted enough to even go in the direction of my choices, it would be him.

"He didn't give me all the details, but if this woman is lying to King, then you know it's gonna be bad," Wilder said.

I shook my head. "She's lying about something, but it's not Roger Ball. She killed him—or believes one hundred percent that she did."

"But you don't know what it is she's lying about?"

I sighed. "Nope. Can't figure it out."

"But you care about her." It wasn't a question.

I shrugged. "Yeah. I mean, she's the fucking hottest female I've ever seen. But she's a gold digger. Her morals are shit. That should turn me off." I shook my head. "But then she smiles at me or just looks in my direction, and I don't give a fuck. I want her. All her immoral, lying, fucked-up parts."

Wilder laughed as he took another drink.

"Nothing I said was funny," I snapped.

It was a goddamn shit show. I was someone I didn't even recognize anymore. The things she had me doing were fucked up.

"Yeah, it is," he replied. "You're talking about her morals like you're not in the Mafia. A little high and mighty there, man, don't you think?"

I scowled at him. "It's not the same."

But right now, he had no idea how spot-on he was. My morals had taken a complete nosedive into the pits of hell. I wasn't sure I would recognize them if they slapped me across the face.

"Of course it's not. You kill people, torture them. She's just taking money from horny, unfaithful scumbags. Yours is way worse."

He had no idea how much worse, but this wasn't what I'd expected from Wilder. I had thought he'd get what I was saying about her choices with men. It wasn't like I'd not fucked immoral women most of my life. But I never wanted them again. I didn't care about their safety to the point that I stalked them. If a woman ever got under my skin, I'd thought it would be one like Rumor or Wilder's wife, Oakley. They were beautiful and good. They were the kind of women you wanted to birth your children. The ones you trusted enough with your heart. Your future. They didn't make you a motherfucking lunatic.

Briar Landry was nothing like them. She was shallow. Sexy as fucking hell and funny, but she had no depth. I couldn't trust her to mother my children. She was not the kind of woman you let get a hold on you. But here I was, being someone who didn't need to father any children. My sanity was now in question, and I wondered why I'd missed this all these years. I'd never realized I could snap like I was about to do.

"Tell me to go back to Madison. Forget her." As if hearing him say it would do any good. I knew I wasn't going. I just wished like fuck I could. Be the man I had been before I tasted Briar's pussy.

Wilder frowned. "Does it matter what I say? Could you leave if I told you to?"

I stared at him. Was it that clear on my face? Could he see the madness in my eyes? How the fuck was I supposed to hide whatever she'd done to me? No one needed to know my truths right now.

"I ..." The words didn't come.

Wilder leaned forward and rested his elbows on his knees. "That's what I thought. You can't leave her. So, go back. See where this takes you."

"She's not like Oakley," I argued like that fucking mattered.

He grinned. "No, she's not. No one is as perfect as Oak. But it's not fair to measure her against another woman either. Oak's taken, and family or not, I'd put a bullet in any man who tried to take her from me."

I didn't want Oakley. That wasn't what I was saying, and he knew it. Drinking down the rest of my beer, I took out my phone and checked the tracking on Briar. Her car was still at the apartment. But she wasn't. She was moving.

"Fuck," I said, standing up.

"You going north or south?" Wilder asked.

I didn't take my eyes off the phone. "To hell," I replied.

"South it is," he said with a chuckle.

"She's headed somewhere," I told him. "But not in her car."

"She's not a prisoner in her apartment."

"No, but someone else tracked her car and wired it."

Wilder stood up. "And you left her there?" he asked incredulously.

I looked up from the phone and saw the concern in his expression.

"She refused to go with me. I figured she knew who it was and wasn't worried."

Wilder's eyes widened. "Or someone wants to get to you so they're going through her. Thought of that? When our enemies want to hurt us, they go for our weakness."

My enemies? I'd never thought of that.

"She's not my weakness."

"Is that so? Then, drive your ass on back to Madison and delete that app off your phone. Stop tracking her."

I knew that would be impossible. I had to get back to Miami. I stood there, saying nothing.

"That's what I fucking thought," Wilder drawled. "Weakness." He walked over to the desk and picked up a file. "Take this with you."

I reached out and took the folder. "What is it?"

Wilder shrugged. "The fake identity Briar ordered. I'm willing to bet that whoever that is for is the secret she's keeping."

TWENTY-TWO

"We got company."

BRIAR

The Buick was newer than the Accord had been, but I felt like a grandma, driving it. At least we had more room in the back seat and trunk. Not that we'd acquired anything new at our brief stop in Miami other than a dozen or so new books for Dovie. Finding the trackers had taken me a little longer than I had anticipated, but it was amazing how helpful YouTube could be on just about anything.

I knew Dovie had a million questions about Storm after what she'd heard in the apartment, but I'd not had time for all that when he left. We'd been on a time crunch, and once we were an hour north of Miami, I felt better about things.

Dovie had her shoes off and was curled in the passenger seat, reading a book. I glanced over at her, wondering if she was upset about running again. She hadn't complained, but she rarely did. Every time we had to go, she went with it.

"We will have to stop at a beach before we get too far north. Maybe Myrtle Beach. I bet they have fabulous tacky matching shirts there."

We had never made it to the beach, like I'd promised. I wanted to make that up to her.

Dovie glanced up from her book and shook her head.

I reached over and nudged her leg. "Come on! We'd be sooooo cute!"

She rolled her eyes, then looked back at her book. I knew she hated it when I interrupted her when she was reading, so I let her be. I was just trying to keep my thoughts away from Storm. Anything but him.

It was quite near impossible too. Damn him and his gorgeous face, body, magical tongue, and pierced penis. He was messing with my head, and I did not like it at all. He had walked out on me while I was covered in his cum! I had more self-respect than to lust over a man who treated me like a whore. I'd never felt so cheap and used in my adult life. He'd made me do things I knew I shouldn't, but couldn't manage to stop myself.

Glancing up in the rearview mirror, I almost swerved off the road when I saw a black Jeep. Dovie's head shot up, and I knew she was staring at me, but I kept my eyes on the Jeep behind me. Flat black. Just like Storm's. But I'd gotten those trackers off and left them in the parking lot. Right where the car had been parked. I was in a different car. How would he have found me this fast? Sure, he'd have figured out that I was gone eventually, but seriously? This was too fast. Impossible unless he was a mind reader.

I put on my blinker to get off at the upcoming exit. The Jeep did not, and I let out a sigh of relief. Perhaps I was just letting my imagination get the best of me. There were a lot of flat-black Jeeps out there. It wasn't exclusive to Storm.

"Hungry?" I asked Dovie, glancing at her briefly before looking behind us again.

She turned in her seat to see what I was looking at. I veered over into the exit lane, and just when I thought the Jeep was going to pass me, it moved over entirely too close to my bumper. Dammit!

"We got company," I said through clenched teeth.

Dovie's wide-eyed expression when I looked at her made me feel guilty for putting her in this situation.

But how had he found me? I'd been so careful. He was nowhere. I scanned everywhere, making sure we weren't being followed, did checks several times before pulling out of that car lot. There had been no sign of Storm or anyone who looked to be interested in me for that matter.

"I'm going to pull into the McDonald's," I told her. "Stay in the car. Duck. Keep yourself down."

"Is it the man from the apartment?" she signed.

I nodded.

She didn't ask anything else but put her book away and lowered herself to the floorboard, tucking her knees under her chin. I had to park fast and get out. Keep him away from my Buick. He'd been watching me. A small warmth tried to spread through me, and I mentally cursed at it. Clamped that shit down. I wasn't going to feel anything because he was stalking me. He wasn't doing it because he cared about me. He didn't trust me. He thought I was lying to them.

I made sure to park between two cars, keeping several full spaces between our car and the next closest parking spot. Slamming the car door, I made my way over to his Jeep as he pulled in three cars down. Closer than I wanted, but it would have to do.

He was opening his door when I grabbed it.

"Seriously?" I shouted.

Storm appeared unaffected. He smirked. "Funny meeting you here, Briar. Didn't know you had a thing for Big Macs, but you need to know there are some right there in Miami. Dozens."

I gripped the door, leaning closer to him, which was probably a bad idea. "HOW?! I detached the trackers!"

He appeared amused. "Yeah, I noticed that." Then, he grinned. "Good thing you don't leave home without your phone."

I stared at him, gaping. My phone?

"You put a tracker on my phone?" I asked in shock.

"You should know by now how thorough I am. In all things."

The way his tone dropped, I forgot for a brief moment that I was hiding Dovie in my car. From him. There was no time to get flustered or hot and bothered. This man was not nice. He was cruel. I had to keep replaying how cruel he was in my head to keep focused.

"Where are you headed this time?" he asked.

"Why do you care?" I shot back at him.

He shrugged. "Business."

Crossing my arms over my chest, I shot daggers at him. "What am I going to have to do to get rid of you?"

He stepped out of the Jeep, leaving very little space between our bodies. "You sure that's what you want?"

I raised my eyebrows, trying to move back, but being boxed in by the car beside him made that difficult. "You're the human lie detector. You tell me!"

The sardonic smile that spread across his face made my hand itch to slap him. "I think your panties are wet right now because you're thinking about early this morning." The husky sound to his voice sent a shiver through me.

They weren't, but now … DAMMIT!

"That was a mistake," I bit out. A massive one.

He leaned in close. Too close. "Sure didn't sound like it with the way you cried out my name and God's at the same time."

Placing both my hands on his chest, I tried to shove him back. I was done with this. He liked playing with me. He knew he got to me. I'd made that very clear both times he got his hands on me.

"I'm done with your sick games," I told him.

He ran his fingertips over the side of my face. "You sure? No more spreading those pretty legs and letting my mouth on that needy pussy?"

I held my breath while I mentally scolded my body for reacting. Clamping my teeth together so that I wouldn't respond.

"If you want to get rid of me, then tell me what you're lying about other than the fact you like my tongue lapping at your cunt. You prove me wrong, and I will walk away."

I was a game to him. He found humor in the fact that he could make me pant for him so easily. Everything I was disgusted him. I was feeling something for a man who had no respect for me and might actually loathe me—I wasn't sure exactly how deep his hate for me went.

His hand dropped then, and he moved so quickly that I almost lost my balance as he pushed me back into the Jeep and headed off toward … my Buick. Oh God! Scrambling up from where I'd caught myself before completely falling back into his seat, I took off running to stop him. He couldn't see Dovie. How would I explain her? I didn't trust him. He wasn't one of the good guys who would help me. He could use her to hurt me.

"STORM!" I screamed his name, realizing he was almost there and my legs weren't long enough to catch him.

He didn't slow or even glance back at me. He was there at the passenger door, looking inside, and I was helpless to stop it. I let out a cry of frustration as I took two more long strides and stopped. Staring at him, I waited.

When he finally turned to look at me, I couldn't read his expression. It looked as if he'd shut off all emotion.

"Get her out."

Horror gripped my chest. How was I going to save her now? What did I do? I had led her to this man. MEN who could use her for what? Why was he doing this? I had to think of something. We had come too far for me to mess up and let her down now.

"Why?" I asked.

I thought I could hit him hard enough to possibly knock him out. No, probably not. He was fast and smart. He dealt with bad men all the time.

"Because you're both getting in my Jeep."

"Where are we going?" I wished I could yell at Dovie to run. But where would she go that he wouldn't catch her?

"We can start with an explanation."

Shit. Shit. Shit.

I did not trust this man. I had never trusted Dovie with anyone, but especially not Storm Kingston. He'd done nothing to earn my trust. He'd done everything to make sure I didn't trust him.

"Just let us go. You know she's not Roger. That's all that concerns you."

His brows drew together. "You have a minor hiding in your car, Briar. That concerns me."

"She's with me by her own choice. I didn't kidnap her if that's what you're worried about."

He gave me a look that said he did in fact think I'd taken her against her will. What? Did he think I was abducting kids for money now? My stomach twisted at that thought. If I could take every girl from the horror Dovie had been in, that I'd been in, and run away with them, I would. The law hadn't protected us. No one had saved me. I'd be damned if I let it happen to Dovie too.

Dovie sat up in the seat, and her eyes swung to me. I could see the wide, fearful look there, and I hated Storm for putting it there. Why couldn't he just get in his Jeep and leave us alone?

Storm stepped back, and Dovie's gaze swung to his before the door slowly opened.

"It's okay," I lied to her. I didn't know if it was okay or not. I just hated for her to be so scared.

She gave Storm one more glance, then broke into a run until her arms were wrapped around me. She was trembling. Fuck him! I glared at him with all the fury boiling in my chest.

He studied us, then nodded his head toward the Jeep. "Let's go."

Not wanting to make any more of a scene than we already had, I held on to Dovie as we walked toward his Jeep. He opened up the back door.

"It's fine, I promise," I whispered in her ear before helping her climb inside.

Before following her, I turned back to him. "I will *kill you* if you do anything that puts her in harm's way. I don't *give a fuck* who you are."

His eyes flared with something I wasn't sure I read correctly, but I no longer cared. I wanted this over and to be free from Storm. Climbing inside behind Dovie, I reached over and took her hand in both of mine, holding on to it tightly.

Storm climbed in front and glanced back at us in the rearview mirror.

"What's your name?" he asked her.

She looked at me, and I signed for her to let me handle him.

"She doesn't speak."

He frowned, clearly seeing me doing sign language with her. "Is she deaf?"

"No," I replied.

Neither was she mute. Not exactly. She hadn't been born that way. It was trauma-induced.

"Why do you have her? Who is she? Where are her parents?" He shot questions at me fast.

I started to respond when a gunshot hit the side mirror on the driver's side. My side of the Jeep. Shoving Dovie down, I looked up at Storm, who was starting the Jeep and pulling out a gun from his waist at the same time.

"Get down!" he shouted at me, and I covered Dovie with my body.

The Jeep slung us to the side as he backed up fast, then spun out of the spot we'd been parked in. Dovie's entire body was shaking violently. I tried to hold on to her tighter for reassurance, but I knew she could hear my heart slamming against my chest that was pressed to her ear.

I didn't want to distract Storm since he was driving the Jeep like a maniac, not that I was complaining. Whoever had shot at us, I wanted to get as far away from them as possible. Even if it was in Storm's Jeep. That couldn't have been meant for us. They had to be shooting at Storm. Who would want Dovie and me hurt?

"We're going to be okay," I told Dovie. "I swear, I won't let anything happen to you."

"Stay down," Storm ordered as if I planned on sitting up with someone firing a gun at us.

There was a phone ringing over the speakers in the car.

A deep voice said, "Hello?"

"We were just shot at," Storm informed whoever was on the other line.

"We as in you and Briar Landry?" the man asked.

There was a pause, and I held my breath.

"Yeah," Storm replied, not saying anything about Dovie.

I let out the breath I had been holding, closing my eyes in relief.

"Where are you?" the man asked.

"We were at an exit in Port St. Lucie, at a McDonald's. Headed north now on 95. Her Buick was left there."

"I'll send some of The Judgment. They're closer. Description of the car?"

"Blue Buick Encore, I believe. Briar?"

"Yeah, Buick Encore, 2019. Full of boxes in the back seat."

"Got it," the guy replied. "Are you headed here?"

Another pause.

"No. We are headed to Madison."

He let out a sigh. "Okay, if you think that's, uh, safe."

"It is," Storm said with a hardness in his tone that hadn't been there before.

"I'll handle this. You get her north."

"Thanks," Storm replied and ended the call.

The only sound in the car was our breathing for several minutes. I stayed over Dovie as I racked my brain for who could have been shooting at us. Who would have tracked my car? Wired it? I didn't want to think this was about me, but all the clues pointed to me. Not Storm.

"We are in the clear. No one is following us. You can sit up."

I straightened, then patted Dovie's back, but she only scooted over to bury her face in my arm.

"Who is she, Briar?"

I glanced down at her as she lifted her eyes to look at me. "It's okay," I assured her. Then looked up at Storm in the rearview mirror. "She was me. Except she was younger. She wasn't old enough to run, and I couldn't leave her there to live the hell I had until she was old enough to get away."

Storm's eyes hardened as he stared back out at the road. "Roger?"

"Yes," I replied. "First time I went to kill him, I found her instead. I didn't get him that time, but I got her free."

Storm didn't say anything for several minutes.

We rode in silence. I didn't have a car. I didn't have my purse. We had nothing but Storm right now. I didn't even have my money. Everything had been in that car. I'd let this happen. Let my guard down.

"How long has she been with you?" he asked.

"Four years."

His eyes locked with me in the rearview mirror.

"Her mother is Netta. You met her. She can't live with that woman. Even if Roger is dead."

When he said nothing, I tightened my arm around her. "I won't get the law involved. If you try, we will find a way to run."

His eyes swung back up to meet mine. "When do I get the law involved in anything, Briar?"

True. He had a point.

"Will we get our things? My car?" I asked.

He nodded. "Yeah."

Relief washed over me. "Now, you know I'm not hiding Roger. Can we go once we have it?"

"Someone is after you. That gunshot wasn't meant for me. No one knew where I was. They were following you. I'd been so locked on you that I missed the fact that I wasn't the only one following you."

Dovie tensed up again.

"Could you please not?" I asked tightly, glaring at him.

It took him a moment, but he realized what I was saying, then nodded. "Sorry."

I turned my attention to look out the window. We weren't a secret anymore. Someone knew. Someone I had trusted twice, and he'd burned me. But that had been sex. He didn't respect me, but possibly, he could be trusted with this. For Dovie's sake.

"What if I had somewhere safe for the both of you to stay until we knew you could leave on your own again? Somewhere no one could get to you."

I frowned at his reflection. "I'm not moving into your house."

"No shit," he shot back at me like the idea revolted him.

Asshole.

"I'm talking about Maeme's. You remember how big her house is, and no one lives there but her. She'd love the company. You can each have a bedroom with a connected bathroom. Plenty of space."

As awesome as that sounded, I didn't think my taking Dovie into the den of the Mafia grandmother was a good idea. I also wasn't ready to add someone else to this circle of trust that was already really weak with a lot of cracks.

"I don't think that's a good idea. The less people who know, the better."

"Maeme is someone you want on your side. No one will get to Dovie that you don't want near her. Maeme would never allow it."

Having someone with that kind of power sounded almost too good to be true. I knew better than to trust things that sounded too good to be true.

"Who is Maeme exactly?" I asked. "I know she's not your grandmother."

He grinned. "For all intents and purposes, she is my grandmother."

For all intents and purposes? What the heck did that mean? Either she was or she wasn't, and what kind of grandmother was going to be able to protect us, protect Dovie?

"I need a little bit more security than your grandmother."

He chuckled. "She's not actually my grandmother. She's King's."

I'd thought that might be the case, but I had hoped it wasn't. "Oh, well then, that's a hell no."

What was he thinking, and why hadn't I known that already? I had let that woman into our apartment.

"Just let me explain. King isn't a bad person for starters. He just worships the ground his wife walks on, and he's determined to kill every fucker who ever hurt her. Rog—uh, well, you know he was at the top of that list. As for Maeme, she's his grandmother, but she's all of ours too. She's not a normal grandmother. She's a Mafia grandmother."

Dovie's head shot up, her eyes wide as she stared at me in horror.

Dammit, Storm. Did he have no control over his tongue? No ... he did not. I'd already known that.

"It's okay," I told her and touched her cheek. "I swear it is."

"Sorry," Storm said, sounding like he meant it.

"Yeah, not exactly the way I was gonna explain to her what and who you were. So, thanks for that."

"I said I was sorry."

I signed, "I knew. It's the Mafia in the South, and they have no issue with us. They wanted to kill Roger because one of their wives had been abused like we were."

The flicker of pain in her eyes from the sorrow she felt for a woman she didn't know, I understood that all too well.

"He isn't going to hurt us?" she signed.

I shook my head. "He will protect us, and right now, I think we need him."

She glanced up at him and sighed, then turned back to me and signed. "He is hot, and he likes you."

I rolled my eyes at her and signed, "He hates me."

She grinned then, and seeing that was a relief. "No, he does not. He looks at you like he wants you."

I shook my head. "No," I said aloud.

"He is like a guy in this book I read," she signed.

"Definitely not book-boyfriend material," I told her.

"What about book boyfriends?" he asked.

"Nothing," I replied.

"Do you both like to read?"

"I, uh, me not so much, but she loves it."

"Maeme has a big library in her house."

Dovie's eyes went wide, and she clapped her hands together with a giddy grin on her face.

"Seems I won her over. Just need to work on you now," Storm said.

I sighed and leaned back in the seat. "I'll be won over if Dovie is safe."

"She will be. So will you."

I turned my head to look out the window. "What if Maeme doesn't want us in her house?"

"Oh, she'll want you. I might even get my own punch bowl of banana pudding for bringing you back to her doorstep. Dovie will be a bonus."

He sounded so sure. I hated to get Dovie's hopes up, but if this worked out, it would be nice to not always be looking over our shoulder at every moment. Even if it was for a little while.

• TWENTY-THREE •

"Easy enough to guess there was someone important to you that you were hiding."

BRIAR

Opening my eyes, I yawned and started to stretch when I realized Dovie was still asleep and lying on my arm. I blinked, and it took me a moment to realize why we had stopped, but the large, lit-up house reminded me. I sure hoped Storm was right about this Maeme thing. She had been ready to let me stay a night because I had been shot, but she might not be so keen on me and a teenage girl who was on the run moving in for a bit.

Storm opened his Jeep door, then climbed outside and stretched. I nudged Dovie. "We're here."

She moved slowly, sitting up, and then her eyes turned into saucers as she took in the house we were parked outside of. I'd been just as impressed the first time I saw it.

"Nice, huh?" I asked her.

She nodded her head.

"Stay here and let me talk to Storm a minute, okay?" I told her.

She nodded, looking nervous. It had been easier when it was just the two of us. I'd been able to protect her from rejection, and for the most part, I kept the fear to a minimum. Sure, it had taken things like dance parties, buying ridiculous outfits at a thrift store, or making up an elaborate story to entertain her, but it had worked. She was getting older now, and those things didn't do the job they once had.

Opening the door to the Jeep, I stepped out and closed it behind me, not wanting Dovie to hear. She was already worried enough.

"I think I should keep Dovie in the Jeep until you've talked this over with Maeme," I told him, preparing for an argument because this man always wanted things his way and, heaven forbid, I not do as he said.

"Maeme is going to be happy you're both here, I swear," he told me.

I knew he believed that, but I wasn't as certain of Maeme. "Even so, I think I'll stay here with her while you speak to Maeme."

By the grace of God, the man finally nodded and headed for the door. That had almost been too easy.

Turning back to the Jeep, I winked at Dovie, who was watching me. I still wasn't convinced us staying here was a great idea, but then I didn't have any other options at the moment. Being shot at had been alarming. Dovie and I had been in some tough spots before, but near death was not one of them.

The door opened, and Storm didn't go inside. He remained on the front porch, and although I couldn't hear him from here, I could see them. Maeme immediately stepped out onto the porch and looked out at the Jeep as he spoke.

He'd barely had time to say anything when she started down the steps and headed our way. The woman might be small, but the determination in her expression came with a force that commanded attention. Glancing once at Dovie to see she was also watching Maeme approach, I turned my attention back to the woman.

"Let that girl out of the car," she demanded. "No need to keep her locked up inside, only making her anxious."

I nodded, moving to the door and opening it. "Come on out," I told her.

She looked wary, but she slid across the back seat toward me, then climbed down from the Jeep.

"Maeme, this is Dovie. Dovie, this is Maeme."

Maeme took a step toward her and gave her a kind smile before reaching out and taking one of Dovie's hands in hers. "Well now, you are just lovely," she said, patting her hand. "You must be hungry. I've got plenty inside I can warm right up." Maeme hooked her arm around Dovie's. "Perhaps I can fix those taste buds of yours while you're here. If you're real partial to those Pop-Tarts of yours, then I will make you my homemade version. They'll melt in your mouth, and you'll never be the same."

I watched as Maeme walked with her toward the sidewalk.

"We are gonna get on just fine. I've been wondering about you since the day I visited your apartment."

I paused and glanced over at Storm, who seemed confused by her comment as well.

Maeme smiled back at me as if she hadn't just insinuated she knew about Dovie from her visit to our apartment. "Don't go looking so surprised. I knew there was a reason you had to get home that night. You were too adamant about leaving. So, I came and checked things out. Saw the food in your fridge, and I had an inkling then, but it wasn't until I saw the faded pink Converse tennis shoes sitting neatly beside the door that I knew for sure. They were at least two sizes larger than your feet. I knew then that you weren't alone. Easy enough to guess there was someone important to you that you were hiding."

Storm interrupted her, "You knew she was hiding someone and said nothing?"

Maeme cut her eyes to him. "Wasn't anyone's business but hers. Now, stop acting like you've been wronged and go get their things."

"They don't have any here. You walked off before I could finish explaining. They had to leave their car at the exit. Wilder is handling getting it to them here."

Maeme nodded. "Well, we can work around that. Not a problem at all."

We reached the front porch, and Maeme waved for Dovie to go inside, then followed behind her. I started to take another step when Storm's hand wrapped around my arm, stopping me.

"We will be right in," he informed Maeme.

She looked between the two of us, then gave Storm a look that felt like an unspoken warning and he dropped his hold on me. Once I was free of him she turned back to Dovie and started talking about the food options. Did she know Dovie didn't speak? I needed to go with them. Turning back to Storm, I started to tell him that, but he took a step closer to me.

"Don't try and run. Think of Dovie's safety."

Narrowing my eyes, I pointed my finger, shoving my nail into his chest. "I always think about her safety. I don't need you or anyone telling me what to do when it comes to her."

He clenched his teeth as he looked down at my finger. "You've had a kid on the run for four years. That's not a life."

How dare he?! Sure, Dovie hadn't lived a normal life, and, yes, I had kept her on the run, but I'd also busted my ass to give her more than she'd have had with her mom and Roger.

"Every decision I've made since the day I took Dovie from that hellhole has been for her."

His gaze lifted and locked with mine. "Doesn't look that way from where I'm standing."

Anger flared inside me, and if I could effectively punch him in the face, I would. "You have no right to judge me!"

His hand wrapped around my wrist, and he pulled it away, squeezing hard. "You saved her from a monster, but your lifestyle hasn't been fair to her either."

My lifestyle! He was back to the men. Judging me for what he didn't understand. I wasn't doing this. I would not argue with this man here. Dovie was inside, and she needed me. He had saved us today, and I was thankful for that, but I didn't owe him an explanation. Even if I tried, I doubted he'd see it my way. He had never had to live my life.

"Unless Maeme knows sign language, I need to get inside," I said, jerking my arm free of his hold and hurrying inside before he could say anything more to me.

Seeing the disgust in his eyes as he looked my way was difficult. I hated that I cared how he saw me. What he thought about me should be of no significance. But I cared. He'd opened up some emotion inside of me that sex or sexual activities had never done before. He'd made me feel.

However, hearing him say that I had failed Dovie, that she deserved more, it hit a nerve because I feared that very thing every day. Anyone else confirming my fear would be hard, but coming from Storm, it was more painful than a sledgehammer to my chest.

TWENTY-FOUR

"Like you're one to judge someone's sanity."

STORM

Sitting outside in the dark, watching the window where I knew Maeme had put Briar, was borderline obsessive, but it didn't hold a fucking candle to the other insane shit I'd done today. My hand tightened on the flask I was holding. Some switch had flipped, and I'd not even seen it coming. Until today, I wouldn't have believed I could do the messed-up shit I'd done. And all for a woman.

Placing the flask to my mouth, I took another long drink from it. If I'd known she had a kid with her, I wanted to believe I would have chosen another angle. Done it differently. But truth was, I couldn't say I would have. I needed her to fucking need me. Locking her to me, making sure she saw no other way but to trust me. A hard, disgusted laugh came from my chest. I'd manipulated the fuck out of her to get her here.

This might not have been what Wilder had suggested, but he had given me the idea. The crazed feeling in my chest had only gotten more out of hand as I watched her trying to run from me. The idea of her being somewhere I couldn't get to her, see her, touch her, fucking smell her made me feel completely off-balance. Hell, it made me feel feral.

Which was why she was here. In Maeme's house for now. Until I figured out what the hell I was going to do with the fact that she had a teenager with her. One that would be considered a runaway. I had to fix that too. The idea of going to find Netta Ball and helping her have an accidental overdose or perhaps die from a carbon monoxide leak had some merit. Killing her off would make it easier on Briar.

"Fuck," I muttered. Who was I right now? I was trying to kill off a woman so that Briar had one less worry in her life. What next?

I picked up the paperwork Wilder had given me. This was Dovie's new identity. She could start a new life, but she would have to cut her hair and color it. Wear contacts that changed her natural color. That wasn't the kind of life Briar really wanted for her. It would eat away at her. I didn't like the idea of Briar having any more weight on her shoulders.

I couldn't stomach it. Knowing Briar would be worried about something. I wanted to fix every one of her worries. What kind of fucked-up shit was that? I was obsessed with a woman who ran through men like they were dispensable. Sure, I had the money to get her attention, but I didn't want her attention. I wanted her soul. I wanted her clinging to me. Wanting me. Needing me. However, right now, I'd take the money power if I had to in order to get her in my bed. Or just on my cock. All the time.

I tossed back more of the moonshine in my flask. It burned all the way down, but it didn't numb the monster that had come out to play inside me. He was still there, stalking around, growling like a caveman. Demanding I go find Briar and fuck her until I owned her.

"You need a refill?" Thatcher asked.

I hadn't heard him approach. My head had been too locked in on thoughts of Briar. I looked over at him, and he held up the bottle of moonshine that had been sitting on the bar in the lounge room when I went over there to get a drink before coming to watch Briar like a lunatic.

"Yeah," I said, handing him the almost-empty flask. "This shit is strong. Where'd you get it?"

"I know a man who makes it up near Knoxville," he replied. "Had to go make a purchase on a thoroughbred for Dad two days ago and made a stop to get a case."

My gaze swung back to the window that's light was still on. Briar had to be exhausted. Why wasn't she sleeping yet? Was she worried? Planning on leaving me?

"You sitting outside all night like a seasoned stalker?" he asked, handing me back my flask.

"Maybe," I replied, then took another drink.

"Because she's gonna run or because you're obsessed with our little songbird?"

"Mine," I bit out as rage simmered in my chest at him using the word *ours*.

She wasn't ours. She would never be ours. Just mine.

He let out a low whistle through his teeth. "That doesn't sound unstable at all."

He had no idea. This paled in comparison to what I'd done to get her here. Not that I was going to admit that shit. Even to Thatcher, who I felt like would appreciate the effort. He was twisted enough to not see it like the others would.

"Like you're one to judge someone's sanity," I shot back at him.

"I'm not the one sitting outside, alone, drinking while staring at a window either."

Fair point.

"Is it the fucking? Is she just that good?"

My hand fisted as I seethed at hearing him talk about fucking and Briar. "Don't," I warned him.

A sadistic laugh came from him, and he took a drink from the bottle in his hand. "This is gonna be so damn fun to watch."

Before I could react, he turned and walked back into the darkness. Where he belonged.

Shifting my attention back to the window, I saw the light go out, and then a lamp softly illuminated the room. Was she afraid of the dark? Knowing she fought demons from her past tightened my chest, and I wanted to take it all from her. I couldn't, and I knew that, but I was going to do everything in my power to change it for her. To help her forget, move on, realize she didn't need to use me. She had me, and I was going to ruin her for every other man. She'd never want another. She'd belong to me.

    I just had to plan my next steps carefully. Lucky for me, I had all night and a full flask of moonshine to do it. Lashing out at her about the men she'd been through probably needed to stop if I was gonna make her fall in love with me. The jealous fury that rolled through me whenever I thought about it always made me react poorly. I had to get that under control.

• TWENTY-FIVE •

This was all too easy. Too ... pleasant.

BRIAR

A fancy shopping bag was sitting outside my bedroom door this morning, containing panties, a bra, a sundress and even a pair of sandals. I took them out of the bag and was surprised to find the sizes were all correct. Even the bra. Then, I saw the designer labels and balked. I might not be able to afford clothing like this, but I'd dated men who supplied me with nice things.

After an internal struggle, I finally decided to put the things on. I didn't want Maeme to think I was ungrateful. It was just these items seemed new even if they had no tags on them, and the underthings smelled freshly laundered. Whoever they belonged to might not appreciate my borrowing them.

Looking in the mirror, I ran my hands over the luxurious material of the dress. I had always loved nice things, but the cost that had come with them wasn't worth it. The taint behind knowing I had those things because of a man who was buying me had taken any pleasure I might have had wearing them.

Stepping out into the hallway, I noticed the door to the room Dovie had slept in was open. Peeking in the door, I found her bed was made neatly, and there was a similar shopping bag folded up at the foot of the bed. I wondered what Maeme had found for Dovie to wear. Turning, I headed toward the stairs to go find her. She'd been comfortable enough to dress and leave the room alone this morning. That was a good sign. I'd worried over her being okay here until I finally fell asleep last night.

Once I was downstairs, I followed the sound of voices and found myself in a large, bright kitchen with Dovie smiling at something Maeme had said. There was a plate of pancakes in front of her, and the fork was in Dovie's hand.

"How do I sign that?" Maeme asked her.

Dovie placed her fork down on the plate and signed, "Library."

Maeme dried her hands on the red checked apron she was wearing, then repeated the sign. Dovie beamed at her and nodded. My chest squeezed at the sight. Other than me, Dovie hadn't known any kindness. The world she'd lived in for eleven years was ugly. The past four years, she'd been locked away with only me as company.

The thought reminded me of what Storm had said last night. I could have done a better job. He was right. I'd failed her in so many ways.

"Good morning," Maeme greeted me when she noticed me standing in the doorway. "Don't you look pretty as a picture?" She waved at the stool beside Dovie. "Sit down. I'll get you a plate fixed right up."

"Thank you," I told her. "For all of this. You're already giving us somewhere to live. You don't need to dress and feed us too. I don't want to be a burden."

Maeme scowled. "Burden? Shut that up right now. This house is too empty most days. You two have given me some much-needed company. And I cook every morning. It's my love language. The boys stop by when they can, and I always have them a good hot meal ready."

I ran a hand over the sundress I was wearing, then looked at the white linen shorts Dovie was wearing with a sleeveless blue top and Tory Burch flip-flops. She was in designer clothing too.

Maybe not as expensive as mine, but for a teenager, that was stuff dreams were made of.

"The clothing," I said with awe, "it's beautiful."

Maeme smiled, turning quickly from me to pick up a plate. "I'm glad you're pleased with it. I hope everything fit okay."

"Yes! Surprisingly so."

Maeme continued smiling as she put way more food on a plate than I could possibly eat. Walking over to take the seat by Dovie, I studied her closely, making sure she was as good as she appeared to be.

"Do you see my shoes?" she signed.

I laughed and nodded.

"These pancakes are delicious," she signed.

"Better than Pop-Tarts, I take it?"

She nodded her head vigorously.

"Of course they are," Maeme said, placing a plate in front of me. "Good home-cooked food beats that ole processed junk every time."

I didn't disagree, but I felt a twinge of guilt that Dovie had had very little of that in her life too. I'd not cooked for her enough, and our groceries weren't exactly healthy.

Dovie nudged me with her arm, and I turned to look at her. She picked up one of the strawberries on my plate and stuck it in her mouth, grinning. She was trying to lighten my mood. When you lived running with no one but each other, you got to know each other really well. I didn't have to tell Dovie what I was thinking. She'd already figured it out.

"Is there something we can do around here to help? Clean? Yardwork?" I asked Maeme, wanting to pay her back for all this.

Maeme placed a cup of coffee in front of me, prepared the way I liked it. Had she really remembered that small detail from my apartment? It seemed she was incredibly perceptive. This shouldn't surprise me. She'd noticed Dovie's shoes after all.

"I was thinking we'd relax. Let you girls get settled," Maeme said with a smile. "I thought of going to the nursery and picking up some perennials. If one of you has any interest in that, I could use some help in the gardens."

My ears perked up at the idea of getting to plant something that wouldn't be left behind and forgotten. I'd always loved flowers, but after planting them and having to leave them so many times, I had stopped trying. It made me sad to think they'd be forgotten and neglected. Like I had been.

"I love gardening," I told her. "I'm sure Dovie will enjoy being outdoors as long as she has a book in her hands."

Maeme beamed at me. "Then, we have our day all set."

This was all too easy. Too … pleasant. I'd learned a long time ago never to get comfortable.

A day filled with sunshine, gardening, sweet tea, lunch on the back porch, and lemon cookies couldn't have been more out of place for both Dovie and me. Although Dovie hadn't done much in the way of gardening. She had read mostly while sitting on the porch swing. During lunch, Maeme had shown interest in communicating with Dovie. She'd asked Dovie how to sign several things. Seeing Dovie this relaxed and enjoying being around other people gave me joy as much as it did guilt. I'd been unable to give her this life.

While I sat in the bedroom and thought about our day and how all too perfect it had seemed, I worried that I was making a mistake, trusting this. Letting my guard down wasn't a luxury I could afford. Even if Dovie had been given a day unlike any she'd ever had. As much as I wanted all of this for Dovie, I knew it would be fleeting, and we'd have to leave here soon too. What if she got too attached?

My phone dinged, alerting me of a text, and I picked it up to see Storm's name on my screen. I'd not put his number into my phone. So, that meant …

Scowling, I wondered how long it had been here. Since he'd put the tracking on it?

Getting a new phone needed to be at the top of my list once I had my things back, and hopefully, the money I had stuck under my seat in an empty tampon box was still there. If men were raiding my car, they'd overlook a tampon box. Right? God, I hoped so. Why hadn't I kept the money on me? But then where was one supposed to hide a pound of one-hundred-dollar bills?

> Did you have a good day?

I read it twice before responding.

> Why is your number in my phone?

Because seriously, this was just another invasion of my privacy. I didn't want his number.

> I put it there. Now, answer my question, little siren.

Little siren. I couldn't decide if that was an insult or not. Sirens weren't good mythical creatures, and they led men to their death. I was assuming it wasn't meant as a complement.

> It was lovely, thanks to Maeme.

I caught myself watching to see if he was typing and dropped the phone as if it were suddenly on fire. I didn't care if he was texting me or not. Standing up, I walked over to the curtains to close them before changing into the silk pajamas that Maeme had left on the bed for me.

My phone dinged, and I glared at it as if it had offended me for several moments before going back over to pick it up. I should ignore him, but right now, I unfortunately needed his help.

> Sleep well.

That was it? Sleep well? Did he care if I slept at all? I doubted it. The man just liked to keep me confused. I swore he got off on it.
I will sleep just fine, Storm Kingston.
I turned my phone off and placed it on the nightstand before taking off my clothes. The pajamas felt and looked expensive. Did Maeme have nothing but designer hand-me-downs in this place? Although much like the things I had worn today, this didn't appear as if it had ever been worn before. It smelled of lavender when I held the luxurious fabric to my nose.
This life could spoil you fast. I hoped Dovie wasn't getting too attached.

TWENTY-SIX

"Don't turn your phone off again, or I'll come turn it back on myself."

BRIAR

"What can I help you do today?" I asked Maeme as I rinsed the last dish we had used at breakfast.

She'd made the most delicious waffles I'd ever put in my mouth, and I hadn't been able to eat just one. Neither had Dovie. She'd taught Maeme the sign for *delicious* and *waffles*.

"Not one thing. But Storm stopped by this morning early, and he wants to take you both out to see the horses. Maybe even ride. There are jeans and boots for both of you in the sunroom."

He wanted to take us to ride? Even me? No, I was sure if he could, he'd do anything to stay away from me. I had expected to not see him, like yesterday. He was doing this for Dovie. Not me.

Dovie signed, "I don't think I want to see horses up close. I was hoping I could go to the library."

"You sure?" I asked. "They won't hurt you." I wanted to see them. I loved horses.

"I prefer to look at them from a distance," she signed.

I wasn't going to force her to do something because I wanted to. That wasn't fair to her.

• SIZZLING •

I turned back to Maeme, who was watching us with interest. I had to explain Dovie's decision without looking deflated.

"She would rather stay here and check out the library if that's okay. I will find something to keep me busy. If you can think of anything I can do here, please tell me. I want to be helpful."

Maeme waved a hand at me. "Not a thing. But Dovie can stay here with me, and you can go with Storm."

I wanted to laugh out loud. Like that was going to happen. He was not going to want to take me to see the horses.

"Uh, well, I am sure Storm's offer was for Dovie. If she doesn't want to go, I believe he will have other things to do."

Maeme's eyes danced with amusement. "Oh, I think you'll be surprised."

When she took Dovie to the library, I walked out to the back porch and enjoyed the swing out there. I'd been able to see horses in the distance on the other side of a fence yesterday on our way to the nursery to buy the plants. I wished they could be seen from here. That would make this spot perfect.

The breeze smelled of freshly cut grass and honeysuckle. It was clean, and the world seemed like a safe place possibly for the first time in my life. I knew the truth. This wasn't something that lasted. Not for me at least.

But oh, how I wished it were so for Dovie. I'd not seen her smile so much as she had yesterday. Pretending like this was a normal home and this was a good ole Southern family was a mistake I would not make. Yes, Maeme was great, but I knew what went on in this house. I'd been to the basement.

The door to the house opened, and Storm stepped outside. My gaze traveled down his body, taking in the black cowboy hat on his head, snugly fit plaid button-up shirt, faded jeans, and snakeskin cowboy boots on his feet. If he wasn't a walking honky-tonk wet dream, then I didn't know what was. Completely unfair. I tried to act as if his appearance hadn't sent a small shiver through me and gave him a bored expression.

"You're gonna need to change if you want to ride."

I glanced back at the house, wondering if Dovie was still in the library. I hadn't heard a peep from her since Maeme had taken her there. "As nice as your offer was, Dovie wants to stay here with the books. She seemed a little unsure about the horse thing. I think it will take some time before she's willing to even get near one."

Storm leaned against the railing and crossed his arms over his chest. "Yeah, I know. But I'm here for you. Which you would know if you turned your phone on."

I blinked, staring up at him and letting his words sink in to make sure I'd heard him correctly. Why would he take me to see the horses?

"You, uh, want to take me? Even if Dovie isn't interested?"

Storm nodded his head once. "The invitation was for both of you."

My eyes went back to that hat. Ugh, he looked really hot, wearing it. But then he looked really hot wearing anything. Damn him. Regardless of my body's determination to react to him, I wanted to see the horses. I loved horses, and I didn't need a lesson on how to ride one. I'd dated more than one man who had taken me horseback riding.

Uncrossing my legs, I took a moment of pleasure from seeing Storm's eyes drop and lock in on them as I stood up. "All right then. I'll go change into the things Maeme set out for me."

Storm's mouth curled up as if he found that funny. "You do that. I need to make a phone call. I'll meet you out front. Oh, and, Briar? Don't turn your phone off again, or I'll come turn it back on myself."

I bit back the snarky comment on the tip of my tongue. Mostly because I wanted to see those horses, but also because I believed him. He would show up ... in my bedroom, and, well, I wasn't sure I trusted myself with that.

"I didn't expect you to need to contact me," I explained. "But I'll be sure to keep it on in the future."

Walking past him, I could feel the heat from his gaze as he watched me. I added a little more sway to my hips than was necessary, liking the idea that he appreciated the view even if he didn't like me as a person.

"Don't lie to me." His voice held a warning.

I paused and took a deep breath before looking back at him. "I'm not lying," I assured him, although I wasn't positive what it was he was accusing me of lying for.

"Yeah, little siren. You are, and when you do, I always know."

There was that damn name again. I had to mentally coach myself not to grit my teeth. I'd need dental work soon if I kept that up. Storm had a way of making me do it often.

"What is it I lied about exactly?"

He pushed off from the railing and took three long strides toward me. When he was inches away, he tilted his head to the side, and his eyes drifted down to my cleavage. "You turned off your phone because it has a tracker on it," he told me.

And to keep from getting your texts, I added silently.

Storm smirked then. "It's not a fucking app. I can track you with it on or off."

Oh. Well, damn. Where was the tracker then? Inside the phone? I needed to study the thing more. Maybe YouTube could help me with this one too. Because when I left this place, Storm was not going to be tracking me.

• TWENTY-SEVEN •

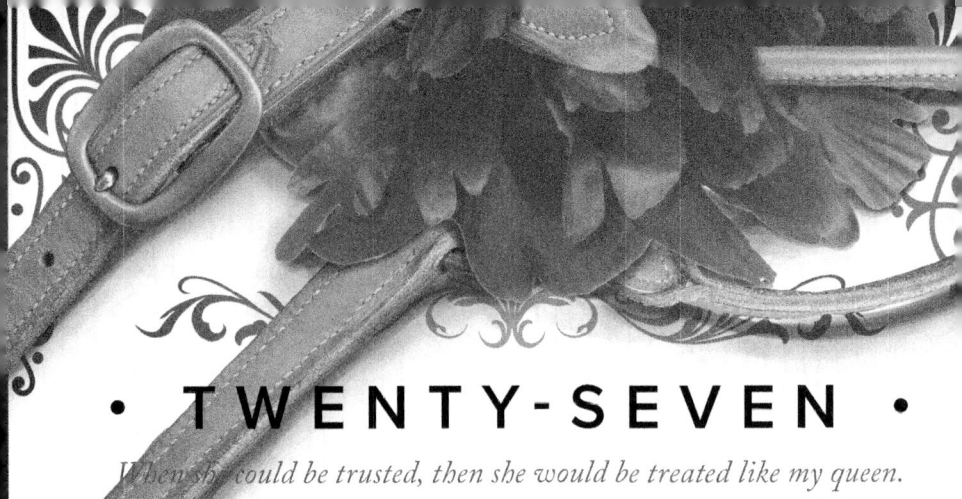

When she could be trusted, then she would be treated like my queen.

STORM

"The car is parked in your garage. I messed it up some, like you'd said, but all the important stuff was left untouched," Marty said as I stood beside my truck, watching the front door of Maeme's house.

Marty was a guy I'd known since high school that I used on occasion to handle things under the table. I'd helped him become a prospect for The Judgment MC, and he owed me for it. I wasn't ready to say he'd paid me back yet, but this last job I'd given him had been successful.

"Good. If you took anything of value—" I warned him.

"I swear I didn't. It's all there. Even the bankroll of cash."

Cash? She'd been driving around with a roll of cash?

Jesus, Briar. That's so fucking reckless.

"How much?" I asked him.

"I have no fucking idea. I wasn't touching it and losing my fingers over it."

If he'd taken any of her cash, he'd lose more than his fingers. I started to say more when the door opened, and Briar stepped out, looking like a goddamn angel. Fuck, that woman could wear a pair of jeans. Maybe I should have gotten her a different top. I'd seen that one and known it would match her eyes, but I hadn't thought about the way it would flash her flat, tanned stomach every time she moved.

If she knew I'd chosen, bought, and paid for the clothes Maeme supplied for her, then I doubted she'd be wearing them. The shift inside me, the one I had given up fighting and accepted how I felt about her, was one she didn't know had taken place. I wasn't exactly sure when it'd happened myself. But there was a switch I hadn't known existed, and Briar Landry had found it and flipped it.

"Camera's installed?" I asked him, lowering my voice.

"Yep."

She was getting closer, and I needed to get off this call.

"Gotta go," I said into the phone before ending the call and slipping my phone into my pocket.

Briar did a little shake of her hips that made my mouth literally water. "I don't know whose clothes Maeme borrowed for me, but I need to send them a thank-you card. These jeans are not meant to wear while riding a horse. They're designer."

And they were worth every fucking penny. I'd buy her a closet full, but not yet. First, I had to make her fall in love with me. How the table had turned on me. I had made this a hell of a lot harder on myself by being a complete dick to her. But in my defense, I hadn't known I was gonna go from being disgusted with her life choices to being completely obsessed with her.

I wasn't over the men and her past. I fucking hated it. I wanted them all dead.

"My sisters are spoiled and have closets full of clothing they've never even worn," I replied. Which wasn't a lie.

Dovie was wearing Nailyah, my baby sister's, clothing. Briar, however, was wearing new things. I hadn't liked the idea of her putting anything used on her body.

"You have sisters?" she asked, pausing.

The surprise on her face reminded me of how much she didn't know about me. Things I wanted her to know. The more I convinced her I wasn't a bastard, the easier it would be to get her to love me.

"Two. Lela is twenty-two, and Nailyah will turn twenty in a few weeks."

"I bet you're the overprotective type of big brother," she replied.

I chuckled. "What? Me? I've only killed two of their boyfriends."

Briar's eyebrows shot up as she looked at me in horror. I couldn't keep a straight face as a laugh escaped me.

"Damn, you're easy," I drawled.

She frowned then and put a hand on her hip. "That was a joke?" she asked as if she wasn't sure or not.

"Yes, it's a joke. Hell, woman, I don't kill guys for dating my sisters. Just if they try and fuck them."

Another horrified expression, and I leaned over to open the passenger door to the Jeep while grinning.

"That was another joke," she said, realizing I'd gotten her again.

"Yep," I replied, holding out a hand for her to take.

She looked down at my hand, then back up at me questioningly.

"It's big step up," I told her.

She glanced at the truck and then down at my hand again before placing hers in mine. Wrapping my hand over her small one had me fighting off the urge to pull her against me and devour those full pink lips. Not yet. I had to play this slow. She was a flight risk, and I had to make sure she didn't want to leave me. Ever. Because the day of sugar daddies was over for her.

Stepping up behind her, I slid my hand over her waist, enjoying the slight tremor in her body from my touch before lifting her into the truck. Having her ass in my face sent the pounding need through me to lean forward and bite it.

"Have you heard anything about my car?" she asked, sitting down and taking that incredible view away from me.

"Yeah, it's making its way here," I lied.

It was already here. In my garage. I wanted to go through it before I handed it over to her. I needed to know exactly how much cash she had and if I needed to make that go away. I'd invest it for her. She needed to be at my complete mercy. If that was all the money she had, then it was going to be easier for me to make her destitute than I'd thought.

A twinge of guilt stirred in my chest, but I shoved it away. I was doing what I had to. A woman like Briar Landry wasn't one who fell in love easily. She was a master at making men want her, and then she walked away. Taking their money with her. I had to be smarter. Cut her off at every angle. Until she wanted no one else but me.

Then and only then, would I worship her the way I wanted to. When she could be trusted, then she would be treated like my queen. Every dream she ever had I would hand over to her. As long as it included her being mine. Because that was nonnegotiable. She was mine now.

• TWENTY-EIGHT •

"When I get naked with you, it never ends well."

BRIAR

I had dated wealthy men. Very wealthy men. But holy shit. I stared in complete awe at the stables while jumping down from the passenger seat. This was insanity. People could live in this, but they had horses in it!

"I was going to help you down," Storm said, snapping my attention back to him.

I pointed at the buildings in front of us. "This is where you keep horses?" I asked.

He nodded, not taking his eyes off me.

I shook my head and let out a laugh. "I've dated millionaires whose houses weren't this impressive."

Storm's eyes darkened as if that comment angered him. "It houses thoroughbreds that make millions. The most sought-after bloodlines in the racing world live in there."

"Wow," I breathed, taking it in again.

There was elaborate white fencing, marking off different arenas and tracks as far as my eyes could see. A track over to the far right had one of those horses he had spoken of running at an incredible speed with a small rider leaned forward on its back.

"Is this where you live?" I asked, turning my attention back to him.

He shook his head. "No. This is the Shephards' property."

But they all worked here. I already knew that much. The horses belonged to the family or Mafia or whatever they were.

"I'm ready to see if the inside is as impressive as the outside," I told him.

"Songbird," Thatcher called as he stepped out of the door closest to us.

Storm moved then, stepping slightly in front of me. What was that about?

"You coming to ride?" he asked as if Storm hadn't just been weird and basically gotten between us.

"Yes, but I wasn't prepared for the grandiosity of what you people call stables."

He smirked. "You didn't expect the best?"

Storm turned toward me and placed a hand on my back. "Let's go."

The door opened again, and an attractive blonde with a short, tight black leather dress came hurrying out with a pair of red stilettos dangling from her finger. It was clear she'd just gotten out of bed and chosen not to check the mirror or run a brush through her hair. Her eyes scanned over me, then lit up at the sight of Storm before moving on to Thatcher, who was lighting up a cigarette.

"You left me," the woman cooed as she sauntered toward Thatcher slowly.

"Time for you to leave," he replied before inhaling the smoke deep.

The woman let out a soft laugh as if he were teasing her. "Already? What about a shower?" she asked him, placing a hand on his arm.

"That face of yours might have weakened me momentarily, but I'm no longer drunk, and you're no longer welcome," he said with a bored tone while his eyes stayed locked on the horse and rider currently rounding the track at a high speed.

I winced as I saw her snatch her hand back. Her shoulders straightened, and she turned her attention to Storm. A slow, sexy smile spread over her lips, and the sympathy I'd felt for her vanished as she ran her tongue over her lips.

"It's been a while, Storm," she said.

"Not long enough," he replied. "Let's go," he said, turning his attention to me.

Storm's hand was firm against my back, and I tried not to think about how much I liked it. Heading toward the door that the other two had come out of, I looked up at Storm. His jaw was clenched, and I wondered if he'd dated her once. Was he jealous she had been with Thatcher? She was beautiful enough to interest him. Even all mussed from bed. It wasn't like I could ask him about it though. It wasn't exactly my business, and he didn't need to think I cared about his sex life. Even if ... part of me seemed to care. A lot.

Turning my attention back to the stables we'd just entered, I was once again struck by complete opulence. I would live in one of these stalls and be happy about it. Holy crap, this was luxurious. One of the horses moved forward, sticking its head out of the stall, and I froze.

"What is it?" Storm asked, his hand flexing on my back.

"What do you feed these horses? That thing is massive."

Storm chuckled and leaned closer to me. "That's a thoroughbred, baby."

Okay, so clearly, I had never ridden a thoroughbred, and I was now questioning my agreeing to ride today. Because I was not getting on that thing. And ... had he just called me *baby*? Was it on accident? Or just a saying he tossed out at women and he'd not meant to when speaking to me?

"Come with me," Storm urged, pressing his hand against my back.

We walked in the direction of the monster he'd called a horse. I stopped several feet away and refused to go any closer. Storm seemed amused, but I was trying to decide if that thing could get out and maul me.

"This is Sword. He's one of our champions," Storm informed me.

"I bet. All the other horses run scared of him. How could he lose?" I asked.

That got a full laugh out of Storm, which distracted me momentarily. I liked that sound. The deep rumble made my chest feel light and my stomach flutter.

Trying to focus on the current issue, I found my voice again. "I am not riding that horse or one like it."

Storm slid his hand further around me until his arm was around my back, and then he turned me to look down the row of stalls. He pointed at a stall much farther down on the opposite side. "Your horse is down that way."

"And it's dainty and old, I hope," I replied.

"She's perfect for you," he told me.

I didn't know if that made me feel relieved or not. He let out two short whistles, and I opened my mouth to ask him what he'd meant by perfect for me when a white mane appeared up ahead as the horse stuck its head out from the stall.

As we got closer, I realized the horse wasn't solid white, but was covered in dark spots. Almost like someone had decided to use it as a canvas for their artwork.

When the horse turned its head in our direction, my hand flew to my chest. "Oh my God," I breathed.

I'd never seen a horse that beautiful in real life or photographs. The eyes were ringed with dark spots, making them stand out more against the white. The comparison to art hadn't been wrong.

"What do you think?" Storm asked.

"She, he—it's stunning and not massive, like Sword. Does that mean it's not a thoroughbred?"

"She's an Appaloosa. Nine years old and very gentle."

My gaze swung to look up at him. "This is the horse I get to ride?" I asked.

He nodded. There was a pleased gleam in his eye. "Yes. This one is yours."

I moved closer to her. "What's her name?" I asked, wanting to reach out and touch her, but not sure if that was allowed or if Storm needed to prepare her first.

"Noor," he replied, then nodded his head in her direction. "Go on, you can pet her. She's an affection hog, and she shines when praised."

Stepping up to her, I placed a hand on her neck and gently ran it down. "You are stunning," I told her.

She turned her head toward me, as if to nuzzle me. I giggled without thinking and leaned in closer to her.

"I'll let you two get acquainted, and I'll go get her tack," Storm told me.

I nodded, not wanting to look away from her as she studied me. The dark brown of her eyes was striking. I wondered what she was thinking. Who did she belong to? Was she a horse they kept here for women they took riding? The idea of her not having a specific owner bothered me. She should belong to someone. Know she was loved. That she was special.

I pressed a kiss to her soft mane. I knew all too well what not belonging felt like. The idea of her living the same life seemed terribly unfair. Even if her accommodations were fit for royalty.

The smile spreading across my face was so big that it was almost painful. I'd not been this happy in … well, I couldn't remember. The warm sunshine, wind in my hair, and the freeing feeling of riding on Noor across the smooth, even pasture made the bad stuff seem unimportant. I knew it was brief, but right now, I wanted to embrace it. I wished Dovie would come riding. She'd love Noor.

A large body of water came into view, and Storm slowed to almost a stop on a large black thoroughbred he'd introduced as Poseidon. Noor immediately fell into step beside him. She was smart and seemed to read what I wanted before I even told her. I figured this was where we turned around.

"You not only get on a horse like a pro, but you also canter with ease," he said, his eyes narrowed.

I shrugged. "You're not the first man to take me riding."

His body tensed at my words as if I had said something insulting. Did he think I was suggesting this was a date? Or that he was trying to woo me like the other men? I hadn't meant it that way.

"Shouldn't be surprised." His tone had an edge to it.

Sighing because he was ruining a perfectly good time for me, I rolled my eyes. "I am not comparing this to what I did with them. You're just getting me out of the house. I don't think of this as a … a … date or anything. You don't have to get all uptight."

I would not be insulted. I knew he wasn't a fan of mine, and he'd offered for Dovie's sake. I wasn't an idiot.

"You think I'm uptight?" he asked.

I shrugged. "Call it like I see it, Kingston."

The tight line of his mouth softened.

He began to dismount, and my attention got stuck on his ass momentarily. I blinked and tore my eyes off his assets.

"Are we stopping?" I asked.

"Yeah," he replied as he moved over to me. "Need a hand getting down?"

I shook my head and began to swing my leg over Noor's backside when I realized my legs felt a little like Jell-O. I'd forgotten how this felt when you didn't ride regularly. Both of Storm's hands grabbed my waist as if he'd anticipated this and lifted me, then set me on the ground with ease.

Glancing up at him, I scrunched my nose, feeling slightly embarrassed. "Thanks. Guess I did need a little help."

He didn't release me immediately, and either my mind was playing tricks on me or his hold on me tightened before he finally let me go.

"Do you swim as well as you ride?" he asked me.

My gaze swung over to the water, then back at him. "Uh, yes, but …"

He grinned at me as he finished taking off his boots, then reached up and began unbuttoning his shirt. My eyes dropped to lock in on his fingers as they worked their way down, as if he were doing a striptease meant just for me.

Forcing myself to blink and get ahold of myself, I cleared my throat. "Are you suggesting we swim in that?"

"Not suggesting."

"Not suggesting?" I asked, confused.

He shook his head and tossed his shirt to the grass beneath our feet. "Doing."

I let out a breathy laugh that I wished hadn't sounded so affected. "Doing," I repeated as his hands went to the zipper of his jeans. "Oh." Was he going in naked?

He cocked an eyebrow. "You gonna take those clothes off, or are you waiting for my help?"

Help. His help. Gulp. Naked with Storm would mean we'd do things we had no business doing, and then he'd get mad that he did it and leave me. I'd feel like a fool again, and it would hurt like a bitch.

No thank you. Not again.

I shook my head. "I think I'll keep my clothes on. When I get naked with you, it never ends well."

Storm stilled with his hands on the waist of his jeans he was shoving down over his hips. The black boxer briefs he'd left on did little to hide the size of his impressive cock. I didn't need to be looking in that direction.

"You screaming my name as you orgasmed several times wasn't a good enough ending for you?" he asked, sounding insulted.

I tilted my head back and closed my eyes as I kept my face pointed toward the sky. "Not what I meant, and you know it."

"Why don't you explain it anyway?" he replied, sounding closer than he had been when I closed my eyes.

I wasn't going to open them and see exactly where he was either. I did not need to keep looking at his bare chest or his … other things.

"Yes, you get me off, but then you leave, angry about it. I prefer you not leave me out here alone, if that's okay with you."

His large hand slid over my waist, and he jerked me forward until he had me plastered against his chest. My eyes flew open as I stared up at him.

"I won't leave you out here alone," he said with a fierce tone that didn't seem to fit the conversation. "Now, get your clothes off before I take them off you."

Sweet Jesus. My body trembled as that demanding scowl of his held my gaze. I was a very stupid girl.

"Okay," I replied just above a whisper.

He ran a finger down my cheek, then traced my jawline. "Good girl."

My mouth opened just barely as he stepped back, letting go of me, and thankfully, I didn't crumple to the ground.

Had he really just called me a good girl? Apparently, I liked praise as much as Noor did because I was ready to do whatever he asked of me.

Reaching for the hem of the crocheted crop top I was wearing, I had to drop my gaze from his as I pulled it over my head. My lace bra did little to cover my breasts with its sheer fabric. I knew he could see how hard my nipples were. I kept my gaze on the ground and went for the buttons on my jeans when his jeans hit the grass at his feet.

Swallowing hard, I paused as he stepped out of them, kicking them over to where his boots and shirt were lying. Closing my eyes, I tried to calm myself down. The panties that I was wearing matched the bra, and once I was wet, I might as well be naked. He'd seen me naked. I didn't need to make this something it wasn't.

"Move a little faster, baby, or I'm gonna have to take over," Storm warned, but he'd called me baby again. Had before not been an accident? Had he meant to call me that?

No! I would not set myself up to get hurt by this man again.

I stopped and lifted my head, finally getting control of my reaction to him.

"This is a bad idea," I said, wishing he didn't look like the Greek god his horse was named after.

Holy hell, he was even better in the sunlight.

Storm closed the distance between us, and I tried to move back, but before I could, his hands were at my waist, holding me still. His hands went to my jeans as he shoved my hands away and unzipped them, then shoved the fabric over my hips.

"Take them off—now," he snarled.

Every fiber of my body wanted to do exactly as he'd ordered me to. I knew how amazing he could make me feel. It was the after that I wanted to avoid.

"No," I choked out. "You'll hate me more when it's over."

The calculating look in his eyes unnerved me as he bent over and slid my jeans the rest of the way down, then took off my boots before removing the denim. I stood there, unable to fight it, but knowing I was making another mistake.

"Don't do this, Storm," I begged, knowing the moment he touched me, I was going to be his to command.

He slid his hands up my bare legs, then grabbed my thighs and pulled then open so he could slide a finger underneath the barely there fabric that covered me.

My knees buckled, and I grabbed at his shoulders to steady myself.

"Storm," I breathed, already at the point where I would give in.

That was all he had to do in order to control me. It was pathetic on my part, but the man was perfection. I was weak.

"We were gonna swim, but now that you've let me smell this pussy, we aren't gonna get that far."

I didn't even try to speak. I just stared at him, wanting whatever he was going to give me. Later. Later, I'd deal with the after. Right now, I was going to pretend this wasn't going to hurt me tomorrow.

Storm remained knelt down in front of me while he slid another finger inside. A whimper left my lips. His wicked grin as he looked up at me was one I wanted to memorize. When he was being mean or looking at me as if he hated the sight of me, I wanted to remember this. Know that I didn't always disgust him.

"Spread your legs more, little siren," he growled.

I didn't even hesitate. The moment I had them open, he moved in, shoving his face between my thighs. The pressure of his tongue as he ran it over the crotch of my panties was intoxicating. I buried my fingers into his hair while I panted. I wanted that tongue on my flesh. I was ready to rip the delicate, expensive panties off. Right now, they were in the way.

Storm reached up, and with two fingers, he moved the offending barrier over, then lapped at my desperate, aching core.

"Fuuuck, that's sweet." His voice was raspy. He was clearly as affected as I was. He might hate it later, but right now, he wasn't hating anything.

I tugged on his hair, wanting to force his magical mouth harder against me.

He tore his mouth off me and glared up at me hungrily. His face was wet with my arousal. Another image I was burning into my mind. His hands went to the sides of my panties, and he jerked them down. I heard a rip before they were gone from my body.

My eyes followed him as he stood back up, and he hovered over me, grabbing my face and closing his mouth over mine. My nails bit into his biceps as I held on to him, savoring the taste of me on his tongue.

"Taste how sweet that pussy is?" he asked against my lips. "Fucking addictive."

His hands reached around my back, and the clasp on my bra was swiftly unhooked before the bra fell down my shoulders.

He pulled back enough to take it and strip it from my body before his hands covered my breasts. His hands were large, but I was still more than a handful. He squeezed hard, and a low sound came from his chest.

"Fuck, I want to see these bounce while you're riding my cock."

Yes. "Please," I begged, breathless.

He tilted his head to the side as he ran his hands down to my butt. For one moment, we stood there, locked in each other's hungry gaze, before he picked me up. I wrapped my legs around him, feeling his erection, and the pierced tip pressed against my clit. I shifted my hips to get closer, and he slapped at my butt hard, stopping me, then walked over to the edge of the water before lowering us to the ground.

The coolness of the water lapped up his legs and against me as he eased into it slightly.

"Go ahead," he said, sliding his now-wet hands over my chest. "Rub that needy little pussy on my dick. I want it covered in your juices if I have to put a condom on it before I fuck you."

My hands went to his shoulders again as our gazes held. As I lifted my hips, the bead at the end of his piercing slid over my clit, and a cry fell from my lips. That was amazing. I felt my eyes start to close when Storm grabbed my chin hard.

"Open! You look at me. Know whose cock is making you feel like this," he ordered.

I blinked, startled, when he rocked his hips with a thrust, and the large, swollen tip sank in just until the head was inside. His eyes glazed over with lust, and a hiss came from his lips. I squeezed the head, and his fingers bit into my ass hard.

"That's it," he groaned, barely moving his hips so that the piercing slid in and out of me just enough to drive me crazy.

"OH GOD!" I cried, fighting the urge to lift my hips and sink down onto him, burying all of him inside me.

"Feel good?" His voice was deep and on edge.

I moaned again as a small gush of my pleasure leaked out over him.

"Jesus," he swore. "That pussy is dripping."

My willpower was almost gone. Common sense, good decisions, being smart—it was all about to mean nothing to me. I wanted Storm Kingston inside of me. I wanted to know what being fucked by him was like. Everything else we'd done had been on another level of nirvana.

I moved a little closer, causing him to sink further inside me.

"Fuuuck," he growled, his hand grabbing a handful of my hair and jerking my head back as his eyes bored into me. "You trying to get my dick?"

I sucked in a breath. "Yes," I panted.

His eyes took on a dark, twisted gleam that should scare me, warn me off. But instead, I shivered with anticipation. Whatever that was inside of him that he kept just below the surface, I wanted to see it unleashed. Feel the power behind it.

He moved so fast that I didn't know what was happening until my back was on the damp grass while Storm's body covered me. His hands grabbed my knees, and he bent my legs back and held them open before he thrust hard inside me. All at once, I was full, stretched, and it hurt from his size, but the roar that he let out vibrated through my body, causing me to gush in my excitement.

The hazel in his eyes was almost gone as his pupils dilated while he stared down at me. "Is that it? You want my dick, baby? This what you want?" he asked in a gentle voice that didn't match his unhinged expression. "Fuck, that pussy is squirting. My good girl," he said, reaching up to slide his thumb between my lips. "That's a big dick you took," he said, staring at my mouth. Then, his eyes lifted to meet mine. "Take some more, hmm?" he said softly, then pulled back and thrust back into me harder. "Fuuuck. That's it. Take my big dick."

A sob came from me as I clawed at his back, desperate for more. He was making me as crazy as he suddenly seemed.

"It hurts," I manage with my mouth full of his thumb. "More."

Slowly, he pulled his thumb from between my lips. "You want to be fucked, baby? Raw? My bare cock is buried inside you deep, and you keep talking with that dirty mouth, I'll unload inside of you. You'll be leaking my cum the rest of the day."

Oh, good God. Yes. I knew this was a bad idea. It was borderline insane, but I wanted it. Everything he said, I wanted it.

I nodded my head.

His eyes narrowed, and his hand gripped my neck, squeezing. Then, he moved, sliding out, then slamming back in. His mouth was slightly open as his wild gaze never left mine. Every time I made a sound, his hand tightened on my throat.

Lifting my knees, I watched with my own clawing desperation for where he was taking me. We were flying there faster as our breathing grew heavier and came faster. Storm's eyes dropped to my chest and seemed transfixed with my breasts as they moved with our bodies.

The moment my body hit the peak, I cried out. His hand left my throat, and then he covered my mouth with his. I jerked beneath him as his tongue mimicked the same act as our bodies. He let out a low, deep rumble before he let my mouth go. His eyes back on mine, he shuddered his release, shooting inside me. He didn't close his eyes, but he looked into mine during his most vulnerable moment. It was more intimate than anything I'd ever done. I felt like I was looking into his soul. Seeing what was hidden from the world. His pleasure sent waves through his body at the height of his climax, and I watched it all unfold through those hazel depths.

We stayed like that as our bodies cooled. I was afraid of the moment he realized what we'd done. What he had let me see. I felt more exposed and rawer than I'd ever felt in my life. There was a new ache inside my chest that made it hard to breathe deeply. It was a level of terrifying I hadn't been ready for.

Storm pulled from me, and I winced, knowing it was done. He would leave me here now. I'd be left with all these new feelings, and I wasn't sure I could recover from this. He'd just ... broken me somehow. Taken my soul while letting me get a glimpse of his.

I closed my eyes, unable to see him get up and leave as he lifted away from me. Then, his fingers slid into my tender opening, and they flew back open to see what he was doing. Storm's attention was between my legs as he continued to ... push his semen back into me.

· SIZZLING ·

When he lifted his eyes to meet mine, a crooked grin touched his face. "Not ready for it to leak out just yet. I want to make sure you're marked completely."

Shock wasn't the word I'd use, but it was the closest one I could think of. "Wh-what?" I asked, staring at him, thinking I might have blacked out and I was dreaming.

"My cum, baby. I want it all inside of you," he repeated as he cupped his hand over my vagina, like he was going to literally cover it so nothing could come out.

"Uh," I said, wondering if I should pinch myself but deciding against it. I did not want to wake myself from this if it was a dream.

"I'm clean," he said. "I was checked last week. I have the paperwork if you want to see it."

Clean? Checked? Oh, yeah, he was currently holding his cum inside me.

"Wait!" I said as realization hit me. "Stop! I need to get up!"

I tried to move, frantic as I realized I'd missed my birth control pill last night. It was in my car.

"There is no way in hell I'm letting you move yet," Storm replied, entirely too calm.

"Storm!" I said his name with urgency. "My birth control is in my car. I didn't take it last night!"

He smirked. He literally smirked. Yep, I was dreaming. I relaxed. This was not real.

"One missed pill won't get you pregnant."

"You don't know that," I pointed out. Sure, it was a very small chance, but still.

Storm leaned over me while two of his fingers pushed up inside me. "You're right. I don't know," he said as he began to pump his fingers in and out of me.

"Storm," I breathed, trying not to get turned on.

"Yeah, baby?" he asked, pressing a kiss on my cheek, then my nose.

He was still calling me baby. What was actually happening?

"You don't want me to get pregnant. ME. Remember? The woman you can't stand?"

He paused and leaned back, staring down at me. "Does this feel like I can't stand you?" he asked as he sank another finger inside me.

I shook my head.

"That's right," he replied as he ran the tip of his nose along the side of my face.

"What changed?" I asked, fighting not to lose my concentration.

His lips brushed against the pulse in my neck. "Everything."

• TWENTY-NINE •

I was shelfing that guilt because I hadn't actually do...

STORM

Pacing back and forth in front of my Jeep outside Maeme's, I fought the urge to go inside and throw Briar over my shoulder, then leave with her. I wanted her in my house. In my bed. Naked all the time.

Finding eighteen thousand dollars in cash tucked under the seat of her car had set me on edge. Sure, I'd taken it and hidden it in my safe. There was no way I was letting her have that kind of freedom to leave me.

I was itchy with the idea. I hadn't been able to stay there and continue going through her things. I needed to take her to the car so she could get what she needed, but I had to make sure there was no more money hidden anywhere.

My inability to stay away from her had me back here though. Although I'd put two cameras in her bedroom so that I could watch her, I still wanted to be near her. Yes, I was crossing all kinds of lines, but I really did not give a fuck.

What I cared about was making sure Briar was mine. Keeping her safe. Giving her everything she ever wanted. But first, I had to stop acting like a psychopath in case she noticed.

Looking back at the road, I swore under my breath. Where the hell was Nailyah? I'd called her an hour ago. She should be here by now. I needed to make sure Dovie had something to do so that Briar would be available to go with me. To my house. For the night. Nailyah was coming to meet Dovie and make hanging out with a seventy-five-year-old woman more interesting. The more intertwined I got Dovie into the family, the easier it would be to hook Briar. Nailyah had better become Dovie's best damn friend.

The red Porsche finally slowed and turned into the drive leading up to Maeme's. About fucking time. I waited as Nailyah climbed out of the driver's seat and glanced at me like I was acting unstable. Probably because I was. I had to check that shit, but it seemed every time I tried to stop, I just got worse.

"You okay?" she asked, walking over to me.

"Yeah," I replied. "Thanks for coming over."

She shrugged. "You didn't exactly ask me. You told me. But you're welcome."

I'd been ready to blackmail her ass if needed, but thankfully, she hadn't been difficult. Yes, I had considered blackmailing my baby sister. I was shelfing that guilt because I hadn't actually done it.

"It's not like you don't owe me," I told her, letting the things I could have blackmailed her with hang in the air.

If our parents knew half the shit I'd gotten her out of, she'd lose that expensive car of hers and one or more of her credit cards.

She rolled her eyes. "Don't be a douche," she said, glancing back at the house. "So, this girl is living at Maeme's?" she asked.

"Yes. She's not deaf, but she is mute."

She nodded. "You explained that already. Lucky for you, I know enough sign language from my extra-credit course in high school that I can talk to her. Now, this is because of her sister? You want her alone?"

"You don't need details. But I do want a night out with her sister. Yes."

I hadn't known how else to explain their relationship. I'd figured *sisters* was the easiest way.

I started toward the house. "Briar said that Dovie can swim if you want to take her over to the house to swim."

"That's good. But I was hoping I could get Maeme to make cupcakes first."

"Fine. Whatever. Just be friendly. Keep her happy."

"I'm always friendly."

I could argue that, but we had reached the door, and I was ready to get inside to Briar. Leaving her earlier had been painful. She'd been watching me as if she was expecting me to turn on her at any minute. Which I deserved. I had to prove myself to her. I knew that, and I was going to pull out all the stops to do it.

Nailyah opened the door, and I followed her inside.

Maeme came walking through the doorway leading into the great room, and her face lit up at the sight of my sister. "I'm so glad you're coming to spend some time here. It's been too long since I had any quality time with you," she said as Nailyah walked over to hug Maeme.

"I know. I've been so busy with my classes. But finals are over now, and I have the summer break ahead of me."

Maeme patted her back. "That's good to hear," she told her, then nodded her head back toward the great room. "Come meet Dovie. I've been teaching her how to crotchet this afternoon."

Nailyah grinned. "I haven't done that in years. Are you showing her how to make the dish cloths we always used to make?"

Maeme nodded. "Sure am." Then, she glanced back at me. "Briar will be down shortly."

Which meant she was still upstairs, alone. I'd checked the camera I had in her room before getting out of my Jeep. She'd been walking around in a pair of the panties I'd bought for her. Turning that view off had been hard, but my sister had been on her way, and me having an erection would have been awkward.

"I'll go grab a beer from the fridge while I wait," I told her.

I waited until the two of them were out of sight before heading to the stairs and walking up them as quietly as possible. The only thing better than watching Briar on my phone was watching her in person. My patience was gone, and I'd been away from her longer than I could handle.

Turning the knob to her door, I'd expected it to be locked, but it wasn't. She should lock her doors. Anyone could walk in and see what was mine. I didn't like that idea.

Briar was standing in front of the floor-length mirror with her long hair over one shoulder as she braided it. Her eyes swung to me as I stepped inside the room, then closed the door with a soft click behind me.

"You need to lock your door," I told her, still feeling unsettled about her being in here, where anyone who tried could come inside.

"Clearly," she replied, looking back at her reflection as her fingers continued fixing her hair.

"I don't like anyone being able to walk in on you."

She smirked. "If I'd locked it, then you would have had to knock. What if I hadn't let you in?"

It was my turn to smirk. "I know where the key is."

She frowned, then looked as if she didn't believe me. "And where would that be?"

I slipped my hand into my pocket and pulled out the only key to this room. Maeme didn't know I'd taken it the night I brought Briar here. If she knew, I'd have been dressed down over it by now. I was going to put it back after making two more copies, but I hadn't taken the time to return it yet.

Holding up the key, I enjoyed the mixed expressions on Briar's face. She wasn't sure how she felt about it, but I could tell she wasn't mad about it either. Maybe she wouldn't be angry about the cameras in her room ... no, she'd be pissed. That was something I couldn't tell her about. Ever.

I dropped the key back into my pocket as I walked over to her. The shorts and sleeveless blouse she was wearing looked much better on her than it had on the mannequin in the upscale boutique I'd bought it at in Buckhead.

"Are you finished?" I asked her as she placed an elastic hair band at the end of her braid.

"Yes."

"Then, let's go."

She turned to face me fully then. "Where are we going exactly?"

"To my house." *So I can fuck you in my bed.*

"Oh," she whispered, looking surprised.

I reached out and took her braid, wrapping it around my hand. This was going to be enjoyable later. I pulled at it. "Where were you expecting me to take you?" I asked, unable to keep from watching her mouth as it moved.

"I didn't know, but … I definitely hadn't expected that you'd take me there."

I tugged on her hair gently. "And why is that?"

She licked her lips nervously. "I … well, it's your house. And we … we are … I don't know what we are. Not anymore."

I used my hold on her braid to pull her to me. "What do you want to be?" I asked her when, internally, I was shouting, *MINE*. I couldn't exactly say that to her though. Not yet.

She let out a soft sigh, then laughed that sweet musical sound I craved. "I don't know, Storm. You scare me. I'm afraid to want you at all."

I didn't like that answer. But I had caused this.

I leaned down and brushed my lips over hers, no longer able to wait to taste them. "I'll fix that," I promised her.

• THIRTY •

I was completely green with envy of the woman he'd one day fall in love with and marry.

BRIAR

When I'd imagined Storm Kingston's home, this was nothing at all like I'd expected. The size of it wasn't surprising. I had known the man was wealthy. They all were. Wealth and power came with being in the Mafia. They did illegal things and got away with it. Money came with those illegal things. I tried not to think too hard about what those things all consisted of.

"What do you think?" he asked me as we stepped inside the front door.

Although the style reminded me of something found in the South, pre–Civil War era, it wasn't old. It was new. You could just tell that this was meant to reflect that era of style, but it wasn't from that time. We'd passed his parents' home on our drive back here, and it was an authentic Greek revival home. It had been dark, and the lights were off there, but from what I'd been able to see, it was a stunning house. I'd love to see the inside of it. Not that I would ever ask.

"It's …" I said as my gaze roamed over every detail. "Not what I was expecting."

He moved closer to my side. "And what were you expecting exactly?"

I shrugged. "A modern-looking bachelor pad sort of thing."

"This is family land. The house was built with my future in mind," he explained. "Since I won't be moving or selling it."

I nodded. That made sense. I could see him having a family here, although the idea of some woman living here as his wife with children running around made my insides twist in uncomfortable ways. I shoved that thought aside. Not something I needed to think about. The envy crawling just under my skin was difficult to get under control though. I was jealous of some woman in his future. I had let him in, and that was a mistake. He was starting to take up residence in parts of my body he didn't belong.

"It's beautiful," I told him.

And the lucky bitch who would live here one day had better deserve it.

Storm's pleased expression made me think he actually gave a crap what I thought. Maybe he did. He was acting differently toward me. The disgust was gone, and it had happened so quickly that I was struggling to believe it or this new version of him. I kept waiting for him to go back into complete asshole mode and potentially shatter me. I wasn't sure how deep these feelings I'd developed for him went, but I feared they were much deeper than anything else I'd ever felt.

"I considered different styles and worked with my dad on a few other blueprints, but I decided with my parents' house being a historical home, I didn't need to build something on the same property that didn't fit the same era."

You couldn't see his parents' house from here, but I understood his meaning. The trees we had passed down the long road that led back here fit with the house. They reminded me of an old Southern homestead.

"Let me show you the back," he said as he took my hand in his.

I glanced down as our fingers intertwined before falling into step beside him. Why did our holding hands this way feel like something

… more? We'd had sex, done very naughty things together, but this was different. It made everything we had shared seem real rather than fleeting. I had to stop my head from going there, or I might never come back from it. What then? I'd be on the run with Dovie while always looking back, wondering where he was. What he was doing. Who he was with. If he had met the woman he'd marry before bringing her into this home to live with him.

Yuck. I hated thinking about it. No! I didn't want to believe she was out there. This was Storm's home, and it would only be him living here. I'd tell myself that and hope it stuck.

Realizing I was missing everything because of my internal battle, I tried to pay more attention to the detail. There wasn't much in the way of personal effects. It could be a show home really. One that people vacationed in, but not one that appeared truly lived in. Much like the places where Dovie and I stayed. No photographs or portraits to signify who lived here. Who he loved enough to see on his walls or sitting about on display.

When we reached a set of glass doors, he opened one, then waved his hand for me to go out first. Stepping out onto the wide back porch, I noticed a swinging bed to the right and a fireplace. I started to say something about it when a sweet smell wafted up to us.

I inhaled deeply, then turned to look back at Storm. "What is that smell?" I asked, breathing it in again.

He walked over and flipped a switch. The backyard was suddenly lit with lights illuminating the trees. There were so many large, beautiful trees. Only a few feet from the house, rows began and seemed to go on forever in the darkness.

"Peaches are starting to get ripe," he said simply.

"Peaches!" I gasped, walking closer to the edge of the porch to look out at them. "Those are all peach trees?"

"Yes," he replied. "I have some that I picked today in the kitchen if you'd like one."

Scratch the jealousy thing. I was completely green with envy of the woman he'd one day fall in love with and marry. The man had peach trees! Was it not enough that he was sexy as hell, had a magical tongue, a big and pierced cock, and a house straight out of a dream?

"You have peach trees," I muttered aloud.

Storm moved up behind me, and I felt the heat from his body, wishing I didn't want to turn around and bury myself in his chest. Cling to him like he was mine. Although nothing would ever be mine. I didn't have that kind of luxury.

His arms slid around me, and I closed my eyes.

"Yeah, I have peach trees," he agreed in a husky whisper before he placed a kiss on the side of my bare neck. "I picked some that were especially juicy so that I could lick their juices off your body tonight."

Why was he doing this? Was it not enough that he'd gotten to me? That he had made me want him? Even after all the hateful things he'd said to me, I craved him. He'd accused me of voodoo, but it was him who was spinning some dark, powerful spell over me.

"Don't," I said, trying to step out of his arms, but they tightened around me and held me there.

"Don't what?" he asked as he trailed his tongue along my earlobe.

Jesus have mercy. Or Satan. Whoever wanted to step in and take control of this situation. I was willing to take help from whoever.

"Storm, what are you doing?" I asked desperately.

He hummed, sending shivers down my body. "Tasting you. Thinking you don't need any fucking peaches to taste delicious. You're already the sweetest thing I've had in my mouth."

I wrapped my hands around his wrists, wishing I had the power to rip them away and run. Save myself. If I was even salvageable anymore. I was perhaps too far gone. Wrecked by this man completely.

"I can't do this," I said, panting as he licked at the curve of my neck.

"What, baby? What is it you can't do?"

I shook my head, trying to clear the lust haze that was settling in and about to take over. He made me so weak.

"You."

A deep chuckle vibrated his chest. "You can absolutely do me. And you're going to several times before we fall asleep in my bed."

I tried to take a deep breath, but it was proving impossible. "You …" I said, then let out a small moan as one of his hands slid underneath my shirt, covering a breast. "You're going to hurt me."

He kneaded the breast he was holding. "Yeah, but you like it when I hurt you. That pussy creams like a good little kitty when I do."

I shook my head, biting down hard on my lip until I tasted blood. "Not my body," I gasped, letting go of my abused lip. "My heart." There. I had said it.

I'd been honest. More honest than I'd ever been in my entire life. I had laid it out for him. He could say his cruel words and send me packing.

He stilled completely. My heart was already cracking. I was that far gone. He'd not been after my heart, yet I was so damn needy that he'd taken it without meaning to. He didn't want my heart, and I knew that. I wasn't naive. Storm Kingston only wanted women to fuck.

"How am I going to do that?" he asked as his hold on me eased.

As if I needed this to get any worse. The man wanted me to spell it out for him. Blurt out that I was falling in love with him. Or some messed-up version of it. I had never been in love, so how was I to know if this was that exactly? It was painful, agonizing, terrifying—all the things I had imagined love to be.

"Briar," he said firmly, and then he grabbed my shoulders and turned me around to face him.

But I couldn't look at him. I kept my eyes down, wishing I had said nothing. Just let it happen and licked my wounds in private. I wasn't one to show weakness, yet with Storm, I had done a list of things I didn't do. My survival instinct, which had kept me going for so long, had seemed to shrivel up and die when he walked into my life. Slowly, he'd suffocated it until it was gone.

He grabbed my chin and forced it up, making me lift my head. "Say it, Briar."

I stood there, looking at his hard, demanding face. He was going to make me do this, and for what? To mock me? Was that what he wanted from this?

A whimper escaped me as another part of my soul seemed to crack. Damn him for this. All of it.

He leaned closer until I could feel his warm breath on my cheeks. "Use your words." The huskiness in his voice sent a tremor through me.

"You know what I meant by it," I said, wanting to look anywhere but at him.

He brought his mouth to my ear as he pressed the hard length of his erection against my stomach. I let that detail sink in as my body shifted closer, wanting more of it.

"Just because I know doesn't mean I don't want to hear it come from those pretty pink lips. Now, tell me, little siren. Is this your way of taking my soul?"

I blinked and took in a long, unsteady breath.

"What?" I asked.

He kissed my cheek, then pulled back until his eyes were locked with mine. "I won't allow anyone to cause you pain. Not again. Never again. As for me," he said, brushing his knuckles over my lips, "I'd rather rip my own heart from my chest than damage yours."

My eyes stung as a lump formed in my throat.

"Mine," he whispered.

Before Storm, if anyone had ever said that I'd allow a man to call me his, I'd have doubled over, laughing hysterically.

But then my life before Storm was in the past. No matter where we went from here, there would always be two parts in my story. It was the second half I was ready for even though it terrified me.

Loving Storm Kingston was the most reckless thing I'd ever done, but it was also the one thing I couldn't control. But even if I could stop myself, I didn't think I would.

• THIRTY-ONE •

I should get some kind of reward though for not killing every bastard who had touched her body.

STORM

Sleeping meant closing my eyes, and with Briar beside me, I wasn't willing to do that. Watching her sleep was just one more thing to add to my growing list of obsessions. All of which revolved around her. Every move she made, I wanted to be there. I wanted to be the one to make her smile. I wanted to protect her from every-fucking-thing that would upset her. I wanted to be the one to feed her. If I could chain her to my side, I would.

There was a good chance I needed to seek professional help. I wasn't going to, of course, but the fact remained that I probably needed it. She loved me. She wanted to be with me. I should feel more stable, yet I couldn't seem to ease the other shit in my head.

What if she ever found out the things I'd done to get her here? Would she understand it? Did she love me enough to forgive me or simply overlook it? The things I had done were fucked up, but I had done it all for her. So I could have her here with me. In love with me. Wanting only me.

It wasn't like I hadn't replaced the tires I'd slashed. I'd put four brand-new tires on that car. If she hadn't fucking tried to run,

I wouldn't have had to hire Marty to shoot at my Jeep. I hadn't wanted to scare her like that, but desperate times and all. It had worked like a charm too. She was here with me. That had been the goal.

When she found out that Netta Ball had taken a bad fall and was no longer on this earth, she'd be relieved. The attorney I had getting Briar custody of Dovie was already pulling the legal strings I needed to make sure that it was a smooth process. I wanted it done before Briar's birthday. It was going to be one of her presents. One of so fucking many. I had twenty-six birthdays to make up for. I intended to be thorough. Noor should have been one of those gifts, but I'd been unable to keep her a secret. The moment I had seen the Appaloosa, I'd wanted her for Briar. She wasn't for sale, but I convinced the owner to let me have her. The fact that I'd bought two other more expensive thoroughbreds from the owner helped that decision. I was sure he was still in deep with his wife over selling off her horse. Not my problem though.

Reaching over, I brushed her hair back off her forehead. She was my beautiful girl. My own fucking siren. No one and nothing would take her from me. If that meant I was a touch more psycho than Thatcher, then so be it. I was going to burn in hell long before I laid eyes on her. Now, it was just going to be worth it. I'd happily go to hell after I got a lifetime with her.

I should get some kind of reward though for not killing every bastard who had touched her body. I was fighting off that urge every damn day. There was a good chance I could snap and do it eventually. I wasn't making any promises.

Her phone lit up with a text, and I reached over to pick it up. No one needed to be texting her this late at night. For that matter, no one but me and Dovie should have this fucking number.

I liked Pepper Abe, but I didn't like this fucking text. The guys were missing her? Oh fuck no was she reading this text. I was all Briar needed. Me. I was here if she needed something. Not Pepper Abe.

I deleted the text and then scrolled through her Contacts, realizing there were very few. The text messages were even fewer. Relief settled over me as my finger hovered over Pepper's name. It would be safer if I just deleted the contact or blocked it. But that felt gross to me. I was already going behind Briar's back, doing shit I knew she wouldn't be okay with. Even though I *had* to do those things.

I'd leave Pepper's name in here for now, but I was having all the texts that came through on this phone sent to mine. I had to monitor my girl. She might love me, but there was that trust thing I was struggling with. I had to make sure she wouldn't decide to run. It would be futile if she did. There was nowhere I wasn't willing to go to get her back.

Placing her phone back on the bedside table, I pressed a kiss to her temple.

"Mine."

• ABOUT ABBI •

Abbi Glines is a #1 New York Times, USA Today, Wall Street Journal, and International bestselling author of the Rosemary Beach, Sea Breeze, Smoke Series, Vincent Boys, Boys South of the Mason Dixon, and The Field Party Series. She is also author to the Sweet Trilogy and the Black Souls Trilogy. She believes in ghosts and has a habit of asking people if their house is haunted before she goes in it. Her house was built in 1820 and she finally has her own haunted house but they're friendly spirits. She drinks afternoon tea because she wants to be British but alas she was born in Alabama although she now lives in New England (which makes her feel a little closer to the British). When asked how many books she has written she has to stop and count on her fingers and even then she still forgets a few. When she's not locked away writing, she is entertaining her first grade daughter, she is reading (if everyone in her house including the ghosts will leave her alone long enough), shopping online (major Amazon Prime addiction), and planning her next Disney World vacation (and now that her oldest daughter Annabelle works at Disney she has an excuse to frequent it often).

You can connect with Abbi online in several different ways. She uses social media to procrastinate.

Facebook: AbbiGlinesAuthor
Twitter: abbiglines
Instagram: abbiglines
Snapchat: abbiglines
TikTok: abbiglines

Printed in Great Britain
by Amazon

42874382R00138